Brendan Connell

CLARK

Brendan Connell was born in Santa Fe, New Mexico, in 1970. His works of fiction include *Unpleasant Tales* (Eibonvale Press, 2013), *The Architect* (PS Publishing, 2012), *Lives of Notorious Cooks* (Chômu Press, 2012), *Miss Homicide Plays the Flute* (Eibonvale Press, 2013), *Jottings from a Far Away Place* (Snuggly Books, 2015), and *Cannibals of West Papua* (Zagava, 2015).

SNUGGLY BOOKS

Brendan Connell

Clark

THIS IS A SNUGGLY BOOK

ISBN: 978-1-943813-22-3

Thanks to Eugene Newmann for facilitating the Spanish translation of the song 'Si llego a ver tu sombra.'

for my father

Clark

1

"It's a slow day."

"Better no work than too much."

"Yes, but it's nice to have a little money to go to the cinema now and then."

"I have all the cinema I need right here on the street."

"You need to dream more. Life is too dirty. If you don't have dreams, then you really are a whore."

REPLAY

The prostitutes of Rome had been notorious for more than two thousand years. Of every age, of every description. Fat and thin, tall and short, young and old. Some had broad mouths and narrow feet. Others broad feet and narrow mouths. Skinned rabbits, pomegranates, pork chops, grapefruit, and lean and tender flesh of calf—some a bargain and some dear, for rich or poor, vagrant or hypocrite, disguised bishop or apparent loafer, unloved husband or virgin bachelor. Beneath the ancient walls, those walls that had seen Pertinax and Caesar pass before them, they stood, in sheer skirts and heels, strident voices issuing from painted mouths, clicking their nails together, forever smoking cigarettes and flicking the butts aggressively into the gutter. They laughed and spat out vulgarities: vulgarities that were at the same time shields and mud, vulgarities that fell to the street, blunt and worthless, and undoubtedly wrapped themselves up one to the next and consoled each other with tears.

Susy was blonde. At least that day she was blonde, though on others her hair was red, black, chestnut—whatever the season required.

She smirked, tapped her foot, walked now right, now left, like a woman waiting for someone or something to do but at the same time was content to do nothing.

"It's a slow day," her friend told her.

"Better no work than too much."

"Yes, but it's nice to have a little money to go to the cinema now and then."

"I have all the cinema I need right here on the street."

"You need to dream more. Life is too dirty. If you don't have dreams, then you really are a *mignotta.*"

"Hey, I'm not pretending to be a duchess. Everyone has their work and you either do it or you don't. I'm not one of those girls who go around telling everyone that they're saving up for a house in the country. Because we know damned well there's no house in the country. Maybe you think some nice young man is going to marry you, but I'm not so stupid."

"Everyone dreams of being loved."

"*Cara mia,* I'm loved every night."

A man drove up in a car, a convertible. A Fiat 850 Spyder. Baby blue in colour.

Sunglasses on a handsome face, a face that might have been bread or wine, a draw for hungry eyes and thirsty hands and a whistle was heard from one woman and another stuck out one of her hips—hips that had earned her more than a few *lire* and were for her like a net is to a fisherman and which years before she had watched broaden out with trepidation but which now she wore brazenly, since shyness she had renounced just as some successful playwright or poet renounces sobriety after a certain number of critics praise or condemn his work and his children have discovered he is homosexual and his dog no longer salutes him when he walks through the door.

REPLAY

A man drove up in baby blue convertible. Susy stuck out her hip; her colleague whistled.

He nodded his head.

A moment later he was speeding down the road. Someone was next to him. He hardly knew who—though he did realise that she was looking at him with less interest than he might have expected, but this neglect on her part, if not making him exactly happy, did at least give him a certain sense of comfort as he spun the wheel to the right and heard the tires squeal and then shifted into fourth to race past a 30 km/h sign at 90.

He took off his sunglasses when they entered his apartment.

She looked around, was impressed. The furniture was new, elegant. Some modern paintings hung from the moss-coloured walls and she stood back a bit and looked at one, not out of admiration so much as out of curiosity or the desire to seem to be admiring what she wasn't expected to understand though she did understand the fundamental point: the painting was like a well-designed shoe which set the wearer in a different class, mentally and physically.

"You've got nice things."

"Through here," he said, leading her down a hallway.

They arrived in a large and well-furnished kitchen.

"There is everything you need here. Noodles, tomatoes, vegetables. Meat in the refrigerator."

"But, my friend, what do you want me to do here?"

"Cook for me."

"Cook for you?"

"Yes."

"You need to pick up a woman off the street to cook for you?"

"You know how to love, don't you?"

"Sure, it's my profession."

"Then cook for me—with love."

"*Sei proprio un porco*," she said, looking at him in amazement.

But, setting down her purse and sighing and wrapping an apron around herself, she did as she had been asked, first chopping up garlic and an onion and sautéing them in olive oil and adding tomatoes and basil and while that simmered filling up a large pot with water and putting it on another burner.

Later he ate. And she, with her elbows on the table, chin resting in the palms of her hands, sat looking at him.

"It's good, is it?"

"*Perfetto. Proprio perfetto.*"

He wiped his plate with a piece of bread, stuck that in his mouth, chewed, washed it down with wine.

"And now?" she asked.

"I'll drive you home or wherever you want to go."

"Forget it, I'll walk."

At the door Clark handed her some bank notes.

"Take it."

"No, you're rich, you need it more than me."

Truly, when she left she was a bit humiliated. For he had neither tied her up nor made her crawl on all fours like a dog nor threatened her with a short knife nor cried on her breasts.

The door shut, the phone rang.

It was Clark's agent, Buonaventura.

"Enzo Bandini[1] wants to talk to you."

"About what?"

"A film, I should think," Buonaventura said sarcastically. "Making films is his system, isn't it? Get over there right away. He's waiting for you. It's urgent!"

Clark looked at himself in the mirror. A clever, questioning face. Pressed his lips together. Ran one hand over his bangs.

We follow him as he makes his way down the stairs to

---

1. Enzo Bandini had got his start writing scripts. He had worked with Aldo Vergano and Giuseppe de Santis and was also one of the huge number of writers who had collaborated with Rossellini on *Europa '51*, though, as is the case with a number of others on that production, the lines he had scripted were never used. In 1952 he directed his first film, *Spiagge e tempeste*, which was extremely popular in Italy and won him wide acclaim in the art-house circuits in Europe and North America. MGM briefly considered using him for a film with Eva Gardner, but in the end decided against it. They had worked with Italian directors before, and it had never been a profitable experience. Inevitably money would be lost, some producer's wife seduced, democracy undermined. Bandini for his part had no desire to trade the freedom he had working independently in Italy for the factory-like conventions of American film-making. "What do I care for the Americans? They don't trust talent. When I make a film, it is like throwing a cat in the air. It always lands on its feet." His scripts were masterpieces, breaking down the visual aspect of every scene to its most minor details, explaining every shot in depth in the calm language of poets and philosophers. With coloured pens and crayons he would draw up beautiful storyboards, which displayed the true eye of an artist. Neatly framed scenes. Complex ideas simplified. Preparing stages on which actors could do as they would, since he considered it artificial to write down too much dialog or chain down flesh with mechanical stage directions that lead the characters away from their true natures. "If you set up a good shot," he once said, "the actor could recite a passage from Ouida and it would still seem profound."

his car and then starts it and lets in the clutch and then, once again, speeding down small streets, around tight corners.

We cut to the façade of a palazzo, in a well-to-do area of Rome.

The actor looked up (admiration?), opened the street door, made his way up the stairs, had to press his back against the wall to avoid some porters who were carrying down a marble statue of a naked woman which had been produced in Isernia nine years before by a literate artist who slept on the carved wooden bed of an African king. The door to Bandini's flat was open. Clark knocked lightly as he entered. The front room was full of people. A blind woman sat on the sofa, shooing away flies that did not exist, and a young man who must have come from some tropical island, from Tonga or Fiji, stood flirting with an older gentleman in a double-breasted suit. There were people constantly coming and going. Phone calls coming in from the most unexpected places: Sweden, Japan, or the Soviet Union. A reporter showed up at the door trying to gain admittance but was led away by a very short gentleman with red hair. Gifts of exotic wines and invitations to far away places arrived by special delivery and sleepy women could be seen in well-decorated corners smoking long cigarettes.

Clark saw Bandini over by a grand piano talking to a very ugly woman with a very beautiful figure. The actor approached, but immediately the director walked off to shake the hand of a man wearing a fez who had just entered.

"My name is Elena Sapiente," the ugly woman said, introducing herself.

"Eric."

"I like your eyes. You look like a man who is going to do something."

"I like you too."

"I'm in fashion."

"And I hope to be."

"You're that . . . ?"

"Yes yes."

All of a sudden Bandini noticed him.

"Ah, it's you."

The director took him aside into a back bedroom. A giant crucifix with a green Jesus hung from one wall. The complete works of Balzac bound in Morocco leather stood majestically on a shelf next to a large carafe of water from the Ganges and a leopard skin lay on the floor. There was an odour of couch grass.

Clark had never worked with Bandini, but knew him, having worked the year before with his brother, Claudio,[1] on a picture called *Il tradimento di d'Artagnan*.

"Do you want to be in one of my films?"

"Maybe."

"I need someone really banal whose presence on screen won't detract from the sets. I thought of you. I've seen some of those lousy pictures you're in. You're just the type I want."

"Thanks. And can I see the script?"

Clark was handed a folder. He opened it and saw a single sheet of paper: a childish erotic drawing done in red crayon.

"Well?"

"Yes, I'll be in your film," the actor said, a look of embarrassment on his face.

---

1. Claudio Bandini was a minor actor specializing in swashbuckler films who would die tragically in a hunting accident in 1976.

2

The film was *Ragazzi d'argento*. The story was about a group of wealthy young people in an unnamed provincial town who spend their time in dissipation. Drinking. Talking. Listening to American jazz records. Leading empty lives. A young woman from a poor background (played by Antonietta Caiazzo) wants to become part of their circle. Clark, in the role of the spoiled and perverse Carlo De Santis, a young man whose passion is driving his sports car at high speeds around the back roads of the area and running farmers into ditches, seduces and then tosses her aside, preferring to marry the repellent but rich Contessa Lia Cherè (played by Tina Treville[1]). In the end, the poor girl is taken in by Clark's best friend, played by Marco Nizzica.[2]

---

1. Born in Milwaukee in 1939. After appearing in a number of small roles in Hollywood, she moved to Rome, where she quickly built herself a reputation in the intellectual films of the late 50's, working with names like Giuseppe Masini, Gillo Pontecorvo and Giuseppe Bennati, being routinely typecast in unappealing roles, as a bad woman, which she had the skill to interpret admirably. In real life, however, she was an attractive woman, though not without her physical faults. Her cheeks had a few acne scars on them. Her eyes had a sleepy appearance. Her face was somewhat too round.
2 Yes, he was once handsome, just as the fish on your plate once swam in the rivers and lakes.

The film was done in Collesecco and Capri, the dialogue in large part improvised.

"What am I supposed to say?" Clark asked.

"Whatever you want," Bandini replied. "Be natural."

The director was much more interested in how the shot was framed than what the actors said.

Clark smiled sadly and began to criticise—stretched out vibrant sarcasm—diving slowly into the depths of banality.

"I don't like him," Caiazzo later complained, referring to the actor from Paraguay. "He is difficult to work with. He is very impolite."

Tina Treville disagreed.

"He's just a little shy."

The film was shown at the Venice festival (*Mostra Internazionale d'Arte Cinematografica di Venezia*). The competition that year included Valerio Zurlini's *Cronica familiare* and Tarkovsky's *My Name is Ivan*. Kubrick, Polanski and Godard were all three presenting films, so the competition was stiff to say the least. For all this, expectations for Bandini's piece were extremely high. Two years before, his *Il Robinson gobbo* had been a huge success and there was some talk that he would be the winner this year.

The lights dimmed and the film began to roll. A few men chuckled in the darkness. A woman was heard talking excitedly in French.

Shhhhhhhhhhhhhhhh!

The opening sequence, a rush of violins and credits over a speeding car, was greeted with huge applause, but the *primo tempo* ended with complete silence.

The intermission: whispers over flutes of prosecco; men rubbing their foreheads, women pursing their lips.

Clark stood by himself, smoking a cigarette near a large potted plant.

Treville approached him.

"No one notices me," she said.

"They notice you. They just don't like the film."

After the viewing, after the second reel had run (audience diminished), all refrained from offering Bandini congratulations. Some avoided him, hastily making their way to the restrooms. Others took shelter around the bar, downing shots of whisky and swallowing glasses of cognac as if to wash a bad taste out of their mouths.

"People's expectations were very high, maybe too high," said critic Mario Fontaine. "We all felt let down. The man who he had chosen for the lead, some South American with a silly smile, we were all particularly unimpressed by. The role he was in was very unsympathetic. Truly no one in the story was likable and it is very difficult to sit for two hours with people one does not like."

Georges Charensol, who was a member of the jury, thought the film was incredibly trite.

"I don't like the face of the lead actor," Hans Schaarwechter[1] said. "It reminds me of a cousin of mine who was arrested for embezzling small sums of cash from the register of the Fischfeinkost Delikatessen in Hamburg where he worked."

The three Italian members were less kind. They referred to Bandini as a traitor.

"He calls himself a socialist, but look at the film he has made. There are no struggling farmers, no pregnant daughters. Only rich boys in suits. He seems to have forgotten about the cause of realism, about the struggles of the human soul."

---

1. Another member of the jury that year.

"It is irresponsible, arrogant film-making."

"He has become morally blind. He has become foreign. No longer does he speak for Italians or for Italy. Maybe he should move to Norway where he might be appreciated."

The film grossed a mere nine million *lire*.[1] The cat had not landed on its feet. Due to the lambasting it had received at the hands of the judges, no major distributor would pick it up. Bandini took it personally from theatre to theatre, but very few would consent to show it and those that did were unable to attract an audience.

Clark had hoped that his role in *Ragazzi d'argento* would get him others in more "serious" pictures, but the only direct result was a part in Aldo Franchi's *Cronache di una villa* and another in a French intellectual film called *Qui êtes-vous, Madame Depreux?*, but both of these pictures were extremely small, inconsequential, and were forgotten before they appeared.

"You've got the talent, man, it's not that you don't have that," Reg Park told him. "Is what you need is a break."

---

1. Less than fourteen thousand U.S. dollars.

3

From a review of *Si puo' essere piu carogna di Tonino?*

[...] Despite the banality of the story, this film by Massimo Predi[1] is not without points of originality. Mixing diverse genres, taking on tones now black, now red, it offers up all the usual stereotypes of the gangster pocket literature by which it is clearly inspired. The merit of the director is to have submerged this adventure in a bloody bath of irony, letting lead Eric Clark (Tonino), who is always equal to himself, indulge in some clearly off-script moments of serrated humour. It would be surprising if he did not receive more such roles. [...]

—Maurizio Porri, *Corriere della Sera,*
November 2nd, 1975[2]

---

1. An unremarkable director who often went under the pseudonym of Max Priest. Short and thin, he wore glasses and showed autarchistic tendencies. His best known film was the tepid *La Polizia al servizio della camorra* (1974).
2. This article was published on the same day that Pier Paolo Pasolini died on a beach in Ostia, being run over several times with his own car. It is likely that he was murdered for political reasons.

4

One of the best actors of his generation, Eric Clark was born José Fernando del Torres in Asunción, Paraguay, son of a dealer in transistor radios, son of a man who spent his days dusting off stock, caressing Zeniths and Philcos, standing in front of his shop on the Calle Palma and smoking cigarettes while veterans of the Chaco War limped by. José's mother was a stout woman who was an expert at cooking puchero and river fish. She was possessed of rich brown eyes, dressed very neatly and sometimes talked to Señor Ocampos, the shoemaker who lived opposite, a tall and balding individual with a violent moustache who was a connoisseur of feet of all sorts.

She loved her son ardently.

"Your grandfather, he was fed to caimans," she told the boy. "You have his face, his smile. May God protect you and give you a good life."

Yes, the country had a history of men being eaten by crocodiles, men walking about with empty hat brims and dogs being shot in the streets, but it was also a place where broadcasting towers were managing to rise up from the hills and plains and the population was slowly being guided toward the future by that invention of Marconi which somehow managed to lard its soap advertisements with adventure, its propaganda with romance. The young boy was very fond of those radio dramas that played like trumpets blown into by eternal winds, and would spend his evenings listening to *Los Tres mosqueteros* and *Cabas and Caballería de imperio*, and was particularly affected by a seemingly endless series called *El Baúl macabre*.[1] Another one that most certainly caught his attention was *Aventuras de Tiburcio Vasquez*[2] which played every Tuesday evening at 8:00 and which to be on time for he would rush through his dinner without chewing.

Meanwhile, an education (Jesuit) was being received at the Colegio Cristo Rey: reading, writing, general knowledge, a little English, and, of course, religion. It would be a lie to say that he was an exemplary student, because exemplary students rarely go on to become interesting men, choosing instead to get lost behind their ties, wandering the endless catacombs of some office building or playing violin for the orchestra of a semi-provincial town where pigeons yawn in the square and the priest despotically raises funds so a piece of the true cross can be purchased from a vendor in Caracas.

The priest of the church the del Torres family attended was little interested in such things, however. He was a maniac with a huge jaw who had pretensions toward literature, who spent what time he could writing primitive liturgical dramas, and formed a little theatre group in which José became enrolled, at the insistence of his mother, whose heart was linked to St. Ginés de Roma.

---

1. Melodramatic organ meets screeches of women as heroes traverse dark underground passageways.

2. Later, when he declared himself to be a reincarnation of this Californiano bandit, he mentioned listening to the radio plays as a child and crying a great deal during the final episode when Vasquez was hung.

The subjects of these plays were bizarre, featuring strange situations in which sinners would be cast into purgatory and stupid servants who never questioned their masters exalted to paradise. The simplistic plots were garlanded with naïve dialogue, with monotonous speeches that occasionally lashed out with clumsy violence—against communists, atheists and the anarchy of nature.

On festival days, such as Corpus Christi and Septuagesima, the priest would put the little troupe on donkeyback and take them to the surrounding villages where they would perform before illiterate Indians, before women with babies clinging to their breasts and men with machetes who gazed at the midget performers with indefinable expressions—expressions which could have been wonder or contempt, fear or hatred. Lines were tripped over, tears dropped, bows made to the sound of three or four women swatting their thighs.

In *La Mantanza de los Santos Inocentes*, José played Herod. In *El Juicio Final*, he was a Bad Soul, a being whose only purpose was to shriek and quiver as Doomsday came and swallowed him up, and in *Descensus Christi ad Infernos*, he was Prince Satan himself and when the dialogue between Hades and the Prince was performed all eyes were open large with wonder. The small child, wearing a false beard and invested in red pyjamas, truly did present a frightening spectacle, flogging the air with his hand as he spilled out the banal lines composed by the priest, who, seeking perfection, remained unsatisfied.[1]

---

1. Whether moral or corrupt, of high or low rank, rich or poor, noble or base, all are preoccupied with their own work. —*The Larger Sutra on Amitayus*

"You should have snarled more violently," he said. "Your snarl was not very convincing." And then to another boy: "Hey, Pepe. ¿Why didn't you open your eyes wider? You're the Archangel Michael. I told you that your eyes need to be open very wide. You looked like you were falling asleep."

"I can play a better archangel then him," José ventured.

"¿You think you can play an archangel, do you?"

"¿And why not? Instead of snarling I just open my eyes wide."

"No. You're a demon. You don't have the face of an archangel. No one would ever believe that you were an archangel or any kind of angel with that cunning look of yours."

No one had ever told him that he looked cunning. In fact, his mother had always said that he was beautiful. She had called him an angel. He was unsure who to believe.

One day his mother pulled him close to her. He felt her tears on his face and her kisses which were wetter than her tears. She said something, but he could not understand it. Later his father was there with a note in his hand and rage on his face. He threw a pearl-coloured Motorola Model 51X11 across the room and cursed.

The shop of the shoemaker was closed, never to open again, and somewhere, far away, in Argentina maybe, that man with his aggressive moustache was enjoying the abundant love of Señora del Torres and squeezing lime over a fish dinner.

Undoubtedly his mother had wept for him. Undoubtedly there had been scenes where she had said that she had to leave to rejoin her son and at night he would dream of her, more beautiful and even more tender than she really was, with a halo surrounding her head and her naked feet resting on a pile of plum-coloured roses.

Joy had escaped, but happiness, bearded and sombre, still limped along, the boy wondering more than ever if he himself was cunning or beautiful, would be loved or not.

Through a haze of static he lived, wedged in between the conservative values of his father and the sounds of José Asunción Flores, between young women who smelled like papaya and men who smoked thin cigarettes while sitting in the shade of their broad-brimmed hats. Under the dictatorship of Higinio Morínigo, people refrained from speaking in loud voices. Cats were shy. Only lovers of fiction read the newspapers and the realists took up gardening and navigated their lives by the stars.

During the unrest of 1947, José heavily sympathized with the rebels and, even though he was only fifteen years old at the time, is said to have taken part in some military activity, despite the fact that his family was distantly related to Lieutenant Colonel Alfredo Stroessner Matiauda, the man responsible for later crushing the life out of the insurgency and letting the streets run red.

Then came days when nobody even opened their doors, when even in the darkness of their living rooms they would not look each other in the eyes and virgins sat dreamily gazing at candles as they melted away.

Though open bloodshed had ceased, revolution was still firmly planted in the consciousness of the young. Boys hallucinated the sound of large drums being beaten. In their minds they composed vibrant songs and, occasionally, in the middle of the night, shouted single-syllable oaths from their windows.

José devoured the works of Karl Marx and Max Stirner. He went to secret meetings. Insurrectionary literature was distributed: pamphlets scattered by night in the plazas and cast from high windows on parade days. Soldiers ran after him and his comrades and bullets sped past their ears.

Plans were drawn up for bombing the office of General Bruguez, but never carried out. In the summer of 1950, José was very nearly arrested, several anarchist pamphlets being discovered about his person. He only escaped jail through the intervention of his father, who called in a favour from their distant relative.

"Listen my son," his father said. "Paraguay is a country without a future. It will always be a place where the only truly lucrative career is that of a military man. I can see your left-leaning sympathies, and these will do nothing for you here but find you an early grave."

"A man cannot change his beliefs."

"A man can change anything. I have sold a lot of radios over the years . . ."

"Yes."

Señor del Torres put his hand on young José's shoulder.

"Look, you remember your cousin Pablo?"

"Yes, why wouldn't I remember him? He walks with a limp and always smells of cocoa."

"The brother of his wife lives in North America, in New York."

"Very well."

"His name is Harold Sizemore. He is an academic, a professor at a very famous university in New York."

"But what does this have to do with me?"

"José, I have some money saved. Enough to get you out of here. Enough to get you an education. A real education.[1] I want you to go to North America, to *Los Ustados Unidos*, because it is only there that you can build a real life. It is only there that you can walk in the open and pet the animals along the roadways."

"But North America is the land of the capitalist."

"That is how it is. If you want to be immune from snake bites, you have to drink snake venom."

"And what will I study?"

"Physics, law, medicine—anything you like. You're not stupid."

"Physics could be interesting."

"Of course a lawyer in the family . . ."

---

1. As it says in the *Avatamsaka Sutra*: Going into right conception on the tip of a hair; coming out of right conception in an atom.

5

And so, at the age of nineteen, he left his homeland. The famous university was Cornell. The New York was Ithaca. José had expected to be amongst skyscrapers, the Statue of Liberty, the Empire State Building. Instead he found himself in a place that seemed more remote than where he had come from. The blood-coloured leaves dried up and dropped from the trees which began to shiver as snow fell from the sky and he looked out the window of his little room wondering what sort of insanity had brought him there to that place, that seemed a prison of white ice, from the sunny warmth of Paraguay.

The streets were almost empty. The people were all pale and inhibited and could be seen in the distance, walking past buildings, disappearing through doorways. When approached, they talked in brash voices—like maniacs, surprised, nervous, guilty. There was a high bridge near the campus over a steep gorge and occasionally a student would jump from it, tender young hearts smashed against rocks and high-powered brains joining their spray with the rush of waterfalls. The young men for the most part had large jaws, chins punctuated by dimples, while the young women seemed feverish and walked with exaggerated speed, as if to escape, the greenish circles around their eyes hovering above neurotic giggles. When they heard his voice, his accent, their eyes would narrow and lips grow thin. They would throw forward their hands, instinctively afraid of the foreigner.

When José had first arrived, it was Pablo's brother-in-law who had come to pick him up at the airport. He was a man with a small moustache and sharp teeth who spoke very fast.

"Welcome to the United States. We have everything here. Restaurants. Cinema. Library. Durable goods. Work. Now that the Korean war is over. Liberty. Transportation. Are you hungry? Burgers. Beans? Ribs. World's best pie. Blueberries are native to North America. Supermarkets if you need anything or you can go bowling. Tennis. Meet people. There are other young Spanish speakers here. Many are influential. These are the friendships you should be cultivating."

And indeed there was a group of South Americans. One was the nephew of Laureano Gómez. Another was the son of the president of San Corrados. There were cousins of famous generals and grandsons of rich diplomats and while their families were off subjugating countries of various size and importance, these young men were womanizing at this Ivy League university, thrusting their noses into helmets of honey-scented blonde hair and in their spare time researching firearms and nuclear fission.

"So, you're from Paraguay?" the nephew of Gómez said.

"Yes, from Asunción."

"I have heard that it is a filthy country."

"Undoubtedly. But still less filthy than your uncle."

"Ah, you are a liberal!"

"Yes, the one that got away."

On weekends he walked through the abandoned town. One day he passed by Nabokov who was gazing at shoes in a shop window. Neither man looked at the other and three days later José joined a theatre group. They put on a production of Eugene O'Neill's *Days Without End*. For several weeks he dated a young lady who was short and had large cheeks, not out of any sense of attraction, but out of loneliness, shyness maybe even—some inherent sense of shame, the son of a husband of an unfaithful wife who seeks out a woman he knows will never be unfaithful to him—not because of loyalty, but rather because he thinks she is too unattractive for any other man to touch her. But, bored by the love letters she would slip under his door at the break of day, which always smelled of orange peels and whose words minced across the page in narrow queues and barked like clowns about sympathy and lips and flowers, tired of her uneven caresses and lopsided laugh, he abandoned her, avoided her, tiptoed away when she came close and at the sound of her voice dived between the pages of some almanac.

The son of the president of San Corrados, leaning on a tall young woman with carrot-coloured hair, passed him by. The cousin of a certain Peruvian diplomat threatened him one night with a heavy Webster's dictionary.

He laughed. Instead of reading about gravitational time dilation, he read about Sacco and Vanzetti and took guitar lessons and those books, stacks and stacks of books, term papers, endless lectures, false intellectuals and intellectual falsehoods, were like the walls of a prison which needed to be chipped away at, dug out of, broken through. In the evening he preferred going to the cinema, letting himself be absorbed in dark shadows and abandoned beaches, in the brutal tactics of hard-boiled cops and the snooty kisses of pale-shouldered opera singers. *Dark City. American Guerrilla in the Philippines. The Brave Bulls.* Raw-fisted heroes and love through quirks of fate because in fact there was a certain karma that came into play and guided him toward the inevitable—not to say that free will was not involved, but to point out that his free will seemed still to live within fairly limited confines or it could simply have been that the movie house had a stronger pull than the dull and monotonous voice of the professor whose fate it was to implant information in those who needed it the least.

6

From the Classifieds in *Sound and Stage* Magazine

Do you *aspire* to make others
LAUGH?
Join Dr. Raymond Queue
at a FREE seminar
July 12th at 8 PM (sharp)
523 6th Ave., 9th floor

Do you have what it takes?
ask
H. Nelson
8 gold metal phrenologist
WO 4-4622

Wanted Actress Fresh
30+
Send big close-up photo
(ear or hand) to:
Mr. Bradley
1051 Riverside Drive,
Ward 5

At 3 PM, this Tuesday
The Actors' Studio
will review potential
STUDENTS
Apply in person.
432 W. 44th St.

A New Way To Amuse
Your Friends!
try *miming*
Learn how at a seminar
offered by
Dr. Raymond Queue
523 6th Avenue, 9th floor

Try Beetham's Acting
Plaster
in the 12 oz tin
it's
the real thing

Professor J.A. Lang
HAIR DOCTOR
Consultations Daily
213 14th St.
(above the tailor)

Calypso & Cha Cha
Nicoleau's Dance Studio
Special rates for strangers
430 5th Ave.

East Indian Students
Film Movement
seeks actors with little
or no experience
to profit by this
BA 3-8334

? in a rut ?
Be modern!
Let our electronic brain
find friends who will like
YOU!
reasonable prices
GRamercy 3-0001

Actors-Actresses
Feet sore from looking?
Let us help you.
Jerry White: ***Actor placement***
(registration fee $7)
61 Christopher St.

Young man with a horn
looking for place to play
If you're hip call me at: AL
4-6113

Hamlet needed for
informal reading
4 Cooper Square GR
7-9650

Paul Romano's
CUP OF JAZZ
presents
Bobby Corwin Trio
this week-end
986 Fulton Ave.

Everyone's Miming!
let Dr. Raymond Queue
show you how
weekly seminars!
523 6th Ave., 9th floor

Do your friends say
you're too
WANTON?
Then let Henry Heflin
be your victim
37 Grove St.
Hours 9 a.m.-10 p.m.

One morning he packed a few clothes, a few books of poetry in a small suitcase, abandoned his studies and took a Greyhound bus to Manhattan. He got off amidst the fumes of stale urine, passed automats, swerved in and out of men in trilby hats, well-dressed junkies, and aged distributors of pornography, saw

a crazy lady living out of a bag
and a man with

snot running down his nose,
made his way down the road. There were mostly-empty pool halls and dark beer halls. There were flophouses and women whose glances were too inviting for honest interaction. On Essex Ave., a man selling ready-made suits off a rack grabbed him by the elbow.

"How much?" José asked pointing to a brown one.

"Twelve bucks."

He bought it and in the bathroom of a bar changed. Washed face. Combed hair.

He went to West 44th St., arrived at the worn white façade of the Actors' Studio. A long line had formed pushing from the lobby outside the door—young men who aspired, Marlon Brando lookalikes and runaway girls from Morgantown and Hoisington.

A rifle-thin blond male was standing in line ahead of him.

"You're looking to be an actor?" he said to José.

"Maybe."

"You have nice hair, but you might not have the build for it."

The young man introduced himself as Bob Antony and stated that he was from Oklahoma.

"If you want we can get a Champale together after try-outs."

"I'm new to the city."

"Well, keep it a secret, otherwise you're going to scare people. You can lie all you want, as long as you don't lie to yourself."

José grinned and thanked the fellow for his advice and looked at the patch of pale turquoise above, at some far away land where a few trillion celestial conchs were echoing the canonization of his life.

After waiting for almost two hours, he was admitted. A leanish man with a moustache and glasses interviewed him. It was Lee Strasberg.

"Well, show me what you can do," he said in a tired voice.

José began reciting some lines he remembered from *Descensus Christi ad Infernos.*

"In English, my friend, in English," Strasberg interrupted.

"I remember my boyhood," José declaimed, assuming a strong Scottish accent. "My father left six of us in Glasgow without a penny, and jungle there as thick as here. I went out with my little billhook and cut a path—we all did. But we suffered. Food I got, but light and air—no.

Well, I've shot up among the tops, into the sunlight; but I haven't forgotten."

"Galsworthy?"

"Right."

"Interesting, but I'm not sure this would be the right environment for you."

Strasberg seemed unimpressed by his talents.

"But I can act," José said.

"Maybe you can, maybe you can't. But I'm just not that convinced."

8

The year was 1954. The cover of *Life* magazine showed Gina Lollobrigida next to a cluster of grapes. *Dragnet* was the most exciting show on television. Gas was 22 cents a gallon and a postage stamp 3 cents. An 8 oz box of Kellogg's cornflakes cost 25 cents. A Hershey Bar was 5. A pair of Keds sneakers were $2.49 and one could buy 4 cakes of Ivory soap for 19 cents. (There was one bar for every 548 inhabitants).

Discouraged, but determined, he rented a one-room apartment on 13th Street and Avenue B for 58 dollars a month. He never told his father and had the letters and money the man sent him forwarded from Ithaca.

He rode the subway, bought drinks at Lenny's Hideaway. Attracted to a waitress at a coffee house, he took her home with him, sat calmly by as her hair introduced itself to his lips. Jazz records were bought and Accapulco gold smoked. In the Village he saw artists, men in triple-pleated pants who looked at the world through bored eyes and patrolled the margins of nothingness. Puerto Rican gang members tried to cut him with knives that twinkled like stars and gay cowboys offered him their services at convenient prices. In a hallway he was approached by a man with lips like a baboon. He acquired a painting by Melville

Kitchin. Sipping Jack Daniels he recited passages from *Finnegans Wake*. A tall, sleek woman was by his side, her neck long, supple, white as a crane's and she had belligerent bejewelled hands. His eyes were met by neon lights, flashing-phosphorescents. A man on a street corner who called himself the Reverend Mose M. Jackson was deriding that city of hoodlums and lesbians. Prostitute laughter and his voice could barely be heard above the roar of traffic and the overt perfume enveloped in carbon monoxide and uprising gas of sewer as he went from agent to casting director to producer, unopened doors, snide secretaries, hasty handshakes and hastier goodbyes.

He participated in a student film in which the crew and cast, aside from himself, were made up exclusively of East Indians intent on learning the secrets of American cinema and taking them back home with them—modern day Xuanzangs, going from India abroad, instead of from abroad to India, to carry back with them the sacred treasures of police procedurals and low-rent thrillers.

The unelected leader of the group was one Ramesh Raj, a young man with an encyclopaedic knowledge of cop shows and B-movies—a fellow who could reel off the entire careers of Jack Webb and George Blair. His goal was mediocrity. He was able to read destiny in the more banal elements of American cinema and television, could see that in the future there would be no use for greatness and anyone with even a faint taint of genius would be reviled, put to death with hemlock or left to waste away in the wilderness of their own talent.

"Jack Webb is such a fine actor," he would say. "If only we had such a man back in India, our industry would soon be a powerhouse such as that of the USA. The problem with the Indian mentality is that we have always aspired too high. It is time we came down to earth and hid away our spiritual philosophy."

He was from a family of great wealth and it was said that he received a shoebox full of U.S. dollars by special courier once a month. He would throw delirious parties in his Park Ave. flat which were notable for the lack of women attending and the men who, standing shoulder to shoulder, would hum in loud, drunken tones the theme song to *Shane* until ecstasy was achieved.

They would shoot footage during the day, mostly in Central Park and the Upper West Side, and in the evening, while drinking beer and smoking cigarettes, look at the rushes.

"This footage here seems very successful," Raj would say.

"It's a bit out of focus."

"Okay, but it is almost like something out of *Dragnet*, is it not?"

Clark was silent. He was trying to determine what he was looking at, whether the image on the screen, a thin face with a huge blurry mouth, was him or another.

9

Middle of November, 1955.

He stalked the streets, felt sad, talked in Spanish to a Puerto Rican gentleman on a corner who, in a gritty voice which seemed as if it had been dragged out of an arroyo, mentioned the virtues of women as the light disappeared from the earth.

"They are virtuous."

"Some of them, yes."

"They are all beauties. Even in the dirtiest prostitute I can see the Virgin Maria."

José nodded his head and walked off. He was hungry but did not eat. There was a bar where he took a beer and then a liquor store where he bought a bottle of Van Winkle rye whisky.

He took a sip of it outside and then walked and looked up at the sky and the field of stars which were undoubtedly there but which he could not see, drowned out as they were by the gaudy lights of the city—the street lamps and blazing neon signs for bars, clubs and then the clunky dull light of all-night diners where men sat hunched over 10-cent cups of coffee and chopped sirloin platters; and José stuck out his jaw, opened his nostrils as cars drove by, inhaling their exhaust, the faint sound of Miles Davis or

34

Art Blakey dribbling from their partially open windows, and far above planets spun like remote parasols which were like clocks like little banners on which picture reflections appeared.

Walking by the Forum Theatre on Broadway at 47th Street, he noticed that a film, *The Treasure of Bengal*, was playing. It starred Sabu and was double-billed with *Khyber Patrol*. He bought himself a ticket and entered. The film had already begun and, feeling about in the almost empty theatre, he took a seat and sipping at the rye watched the images move past him on the screen references real or imagined to Indian cults who would pull dogs off the streets and eat them raw embodying far eastern fanaticism leg behind head mumbling mantra as the bottle of rye became lighter and lighter until it was only a bottle without rye and the last reel of the second feature had run its adventurous course the lights turned on and then there was stumbling, placing one foot before the other and the sound of some distant laughter and indirect shapes along streets and then up flights of stairs and finally managing to put a key in a very small keyhole before finding his bed and a pillow.

Still dark in the early hours of the morning and he opened his eyes, at first everything unclear, objects displaced and unfamiliar and then thoughts slowly making their trajectory forward, grasping at some impossibility; a lean face, sad hazy look and José accepted it, that man standing over him, not so much as a reality, but as a truth which needed to be dealt with and possibly even appreciated and then, sitting up, he rubbed his temples and blinked staring at the other in silence as the other looked back at him.

"I thought you were . . . ?" José said.

"I am."

"But you came here."

"Well, I have something to give you."

"You know that we were all so sad . . ."

"The world's a lot smaller than you think. It's not that easy to understand. I'm going to give you this, but you have to take care of it because it might not seem like much but it's a lot more than most have even if it could hurt you and you have to remember that fragrant waters aren't always clear and that the path goes through mud and weeds."

He held something in his hand.

"What is it?"

"Talent."

"Where did you find it?"

"It's for you."

"But why me?"

He took it and pushed it into José's chest and the latter fell back (shadow puppets + water buffalo + onomato-poeic clown-servants)—until shapes of daylight stretched through his window, the sun pounding its sunken chest and calling the city to life the workers arise and flood the ways hats coats filling the world.

That day José walked around in agitation. He had something inside himself that he needed to express, to let cry out—so many voices, vipers and it was as if there were suddenly vast spaces open before him, a previously unfelt liberty and the characters around him, the people in the street, seemed to be laid bare, the mechanisms that made them who they were—the strange psychosis that each individual carried within them, that dictated the way they walked, the way they flung their arms—the past that weighed on certain men's spines—or the inner liberty that made others, criminals, artist, bankrupts, float as if on a mist of disinfectant, as if they themselves did not stink and in the mirror he looked at himself, smiled—the smile of a banker, then of a card player, a human gorilla, a politician, an athlete, of Dr. Maurice Xavier or Bart Hunter or Comte Igor Kourloff. Then, from inside himself, came frowns of all sorts, facial gestures—expressions of prisoners and kings, of beggar and rich man which suddenly existed for him as independent qualities, elements like gold or iron, hydrogen or nickel;—so many flavours, personalities whose qualities were there almost like a book fallen open, a lone tree against a white sky, the pleading eyes of a hungry dog, a place where no one goes, a revelation of wind or alloy of emotions darting off into the future.

10

1) Mr. Lee Strasberg was accosted by a salesman in a café who tried to sell him an Agifold camera for twelve dollars

2) At an art gallery, Mr. Lee Strasberg met a high-rolling patron with an enormous black moustache who talked in a pronounced Southern accent about the benefits of magnesium

3) Mr. Lee Strasberg, while sitting at a bar on Second Avenue, overheard an obnoxious patron discussing watermelon with a blind man[1]

"Mr. Strasberg? Mr. Lee Strasberg?"

"Yes."

"My name is Brad Wint," he said in the voice of a man used to thinking on his feet. "I'm a collection management officer for the Central Intelligence Agency. I'm going to need to ask you a few questions which I expect you will be more than pleased to answer."

"Well, I . . ."

"Yes, thank you. I'll sit down if you don't mind."

Strasberg looked surprised, worried, began fidgeting

----

1. It is a known fact that the blind are extremely skilled at selecting melons of all sorts.

nervously with the end of his moustache. The agent surveyed the room briefly, lit a cigarette and began:

"What are your political beliefs?"

"Political?"

"Yes, I assume you do adhere to some kind of political philosophy. You read newspapers. You admire some people and dislike others."

"I would not go so far as to call myself a political man."

"You wouldn't? Well, we have had reports that you have attended, um, certain meetings."

"I teach acting."

"Yes, and the plays you put on are . . ."

"Are?"

"Russian."

"So?"

"It is my understanding that you are Russian."

"I am a naturalized citizen. I was born in the Austro-Hungarian Empire."

"So, you are stating that you have never been and never intend on going to what is currently designated as the Soviet Union?"

"I would not go so far as to say that. I am sure you are aware of European history."

"Should I be? Do you consider it patriotic to understand the workings of foreign governments?"

"I have never thought about it."

The agent was silent for a moment. And then: "Let me be direct: Are you an anarchist, Mr. Strasberg?"

"I think your language is rather strong."

"Is it?"

The agent removed a 4 × 6 inch pad of lined paper

from his pocket and began reading in a slow and matter-of-fact manner that was not so much accusing as offering undeniable proofs:

"Nov 28th. 3 p.m. Bird Cage Café. Subject spotted conversing with H. Mumford, known social anarchist. December 13th. 7 p.m.[1] Subject (that's you, Mr. Strasberg) seen exchanging documents with a heavily-moustached gentleman believed to be deranged by homosexual tendencies. December 22nd. Subject seen at the Club Capri on Second Avenue making signals to a group of known anarchists led by Romeo Zelaya, President of the Braille Institute of Mendoza, an organization suspected of funnelling money into elements bent on reorganising the MLE."[2]

"But this is absurd! What you are saying is exaggerated. I do not know anybody. I have not been anywhere!"

The agent continued, calm, precise:

"Mr. H. Mumford is better known as José Fernando del Torres. The heavily-moustached gentleman was in fact José Fernando del Torres, student of acting. The obnoxious patron at the Club Capri was none other than I, José Fernando del Torres, desirous of your guidance."

It was at this point that Clark removed the false moustache and bowed, his head reaching forward, not out of humility, but out of the very opposite characteristic.

"You are an actor?"

"Well, I'm talented as hell, but I'm not sure if I'm an actor yet."

"You bastard."

---

1. Cotton futures rose 50 cents to close at $2.15 a bale.
2. The Libertarian Movement in Exile.

"Yes, but I need your help."

"Training. Plenty of training. It is the only way."

Mr. Lee Strasberg waved his hand in the air emphatically, partially enthusiastic, partially embarrassed, most of all relieved that he was not being investigated by the United States government and his mind uncertain if what he had before him was genius or charlatan, bat or pig.

And so it was that José became part of the Actors' Studio.

11

Del Torres became particularly inclined to the Stanislavski system—psychological, emotional. He dragged inspiration up from the gutters, down from glittering spheres, and for months on end spent some ten hours a day locked in his room, above city streets, reciting his lines, first dryly, then colouring them in, working himself up into a frenzy—forgetting his past while still leaning on his emotional memory, as he redecorated his personality—first with leather and then with silk—with rich carpets and then floors of plain, unpainted wood and it was with the same sensitivity he had seen in the eyes of old veterans and heartbroken women that he went about his exercises.

- Psycho-physical actions
- Blindfolded, feeling hairs
- Walking up stairs backward
- Visualising strong, colour-coded emotions
- Playing the piano with the lid down
- Listening to ants walking
- Running through rush-hour traffic
- Bathing clothed
- Becoming angry at nothing
- Imitating the way trees stood on cold winter days

Because he felt now that acting was about more than just changing himself superficially. The part had to grow from the interior and with that primordial quality he seemed to have acquired he read poetry aloud; observed the way he moved his hands and sat in chairs; had a sudden desire to learn the Cherokee language; began working on a play about a Californio bandit, about Tiburcio Vasquez, the first few pages of which he showed to Strasberg, the latter shaking his head in discomfort, saying he did not think it would be appropriate for the New York stage and then slipping the young man a volume of De l'Isle Adam (published by Charles H. Sergel Company, Chicago, 1901).

"Your chance will come. I haven't forgotten you."

"That's fine," José said in a patient way.

Look Back in Anger was at the 41st Street Theatre, *Listen to the Quiet* at Blackfriars' Guild. There were little theatres all over, some in cinemas that had reverted to drama, others in lofts, or cafés, restrooms or phone booths. Men in tight-fitting black shirts mimed sadness and students inspired by Baudelaire or Pablo Neruda or inaccurate translations of Lao Tzu decried the loneliness of modern civilization. Some sang, other declaimed in the brisk lingo of Harlem or the Upper East Side. Pantomimes in animal masks were performed in public parks and select individuals from the arts community were invited to hear long monologues screamed by topless young women in darkened third-storey apartments.

"Your tongues are tied in ribbons gifts of mescaline god queening daintier avaricious with freedom."

"She's acting out."

"If you would only give me your telephone number we could arrange a time for everything."

And then chance did in fact advance and retreat, duck and swerve from side to side—seen running in the distance or felt pressing close on a snowy night in which one might follow footsteps through the park.

José did some one-acts and appeared in a production of *Pale Horse, Pale Rider* at the Theatre de Lys and *Diary of a Scoundrel* at the Phoenix Theatre on Second Avenue. He was billed under the name Joe Torres and received favourable comments in a number of theatre-related reviews.

"It's too bad I received so little money," he complained to a fellow actor.

"You need to get unionised," the other said and handed him an application.

José read:

Are you now or have you ever been a member of the Communist party?

Karma. The paper torn to bits.[1]

---

1. Don't strain your mind.

12

One evening at the Society Club, he met a woman. Her name was Irene. She was wearing a low-cut dress and they danced the mamba together. Later, she took him home with her to her apartment on East 69th St. They kissed and fell backwards. She had wealthy parents and was five years his senior. Part of the cocktail generation. Three weeks later he married her at the City Hall and he immediately applied for citizenship and for a honeymoon they spent a week in Florida, crawling on white sand, visiting alligator farms which reminded him of his grandfather whose eyes he was supposed to be possessed of.

She touched his hand while they were eating fish.

"Every great man has a great woman behind him," she said.

José nodded his head. He was immune to clichés and squeezed lime over his meal.

When they got back to New York, they bought a DeSoto Firedome, the first car he had ever owned or co-owned though it was his name that was on the title and though it was in fact she who paid for it with a cheque drawn on the First Manhattan Bank for six thousand dollars out of an account that had many thousands more provided by a father with a large white moustache and eyeglasses who made more than a living by driving in every morning from Long Island to Wall Street and providing advice legal and otherwise to those who wished to make money by speculation which might even have been called investment.

José accepted all this. But not with anything that could definitely be defined as enthusiasm.

13

He was somewhat better-looking than average, but still not remarkably handsome and knew how to smile pleasantly and had good table manners—two indispensable skills for a man who wants to go places in this world, though skill itself is of course highly over-rated since it does very little if not combined with something higher, a special insight that might come from some god or spirit, some element of nature or ghost which itself might be called or at least mistaken for an elevated quality, a touch of genius and he stumbled about on stage, railed at the sky, and so it was that one evening, after a performance of *The Courageous One*[1] at the Greenwich Mews Theatre (he was in the role of Shishkin), he found himself at one of those parties in the Village—one of those parties where fat-necked men in sports jackets wipe their sweaty palms against the backsides of wigged society girls and itinerant sculptors discuss the theories of Aguilonius in slow nasally voices.

An Earl Grant record was spinning on the turntable. Cocktails hovered beneath painted lips. Some men wore duckbilled hair and sideburns and talked gravely over highballs. A young lady danced alone in a corner. A painting by

---

1. Bland direction, good acting and moist eyes when the curtains closed.

47

De Kooning relaxed on a wall, spilling backward in time.

"Mr. Torres?"

"Yes."

"My name is Pierre Fontmoreau."

"Ah."

"Pierre Font-mo-reau."

"Nice to meet you," José said, nodding at the man who stood before him, whose nose was slightly uplifted, whose eyes stood watch behind black-rimmed glasses—because these geniuses, these intellectuals who continually extol the virtues of farmers and factory workers as well as non-linear structures, are always wary lest someone notice that their jackets are lined with banknotes inherited from some descendent of Philippe Charles d'Orléans and their thoughts travel along the same flattened paths as accountants and clergymen.

"The name says something?"

"I have heard of you."

"This does not surprise me."

"And why should it? You're famous—with the art crowd."

"Lovers of French."

"Well, if we don't love you, who will? Your films are long. No one speaks much. And no one is ever happy."

"But you're smiling."

"I'm from Paraguay. We smile even when we hang ourselves."

"The French also find suicide amusing," he pronounced.

"So it seems."

"But I saw you this evening."

"And?"

"And I make films. And you smile, yes. But I did not laugh when I saw you smile. I was impressed. Saddened. Depressed. I feel not that I like you, but that there is something in the way I dislike you. As a bird which is bloody, but will not die. I might have a little part for you. Paris. We will film you on the boulevards."

"That's a long way to go for a little part."

The Frenchman shrugged his shoulders.

"Some hours on a plane. Over a little ocean. Nothing to be frightened of. You get there, you drink an aperitif. Stand in front of the camera. Walk a little. Afterwards you can sample water from the Seine or simply blow your brains out. Or I know a woman with a nipple on her leg who you would like. Paris is the only city on earth where women live. It is the only truly feminine city. And even the men are more ladylike than the women here in New York."

It was just then that Irene came walking over and José introduced her.

"Your husband has talent."

"Yes, but keep it quiet." She was a little drunk. "He always gets angry when I tell him."

"It just shows how much he loves you."

"That's what I think."

And Fontmoreau looked at her and nodded and smiled in a way that might have been malicious or amused or just curious while José looked down at his drink seeing:

1) Pay dirt + golden fruit
2) Music unborn
3) Allied troops occupying Lille (framed in jade)
4) A solitary boat moving toward the moon

14

Aéroport de Paris, Orly. Pierre Fontmoreau, director, descends from a plane. He is accompanied by a man. Reporters raise black ball-point pens, wave microphones (RCA Dynamic Pressure Type SK-45B and Telefunken Microport). A tidal wave of flashes (glorious waves of motion on the retina). He introduces the man, who smiles rather uncomfortably:

"This is Clark. Monsieur Eric Clark. He is a very famous actor from America. From the New York. From the Broadway. Who I will be using in my next film."

A barrage of questions, in good French, bad English and wild hand gestures.

José said that he was delighted to be in the country of Prudhomme, mentioned something about the barricades of 1848, and stalked forward.

Later in a car en route to the city:

"My name is Eric Clark, is it?"

"Why not? You can't be called José. No one will take someone called José seriously. Everyone wants Americans with short names that invoke the mythopoeic images of Chicago and Tucson. Even if you are not American they want you to be American. You have to be American, really American, if you want to make it in Europe."

50

"And Joe?"

"Eh, I said Eric and not Joe. I do my best. But Clark is a very beautiful name."

"It seems I am famous too?"

"If I tell the reporters you are famous, you are famous," Fontmoreau said, taking a cigarette out of a silver case and lighting it, inhaling deeply, spreading a mist around him which seemed almost mysterious, unearthly, everything he did having a certain quality of artistic affectation which undoubtedly pleased many, certainly displeased some.

They drove past the Arc de Triomphe, past cafés, streetwalkers, unemployed clerks, overfed policemen, painters who moonlighted as waiters and waiters who were semi-professional gamblers, past children in pink dresses who would grow up to be retired gymnasts and aged roués who as children had dreamt of lives of purity, and pulled up in front of a building on the Rue Oudinot—clean, stately, with windows which reflected the sky, some cloud floating overhead, some paradise of intangible smoothness.

"This is the house of Henri Tardaux," Fontmoreau said.

"Henri Tardaux?"

"Yes, he is a patron of the arts. Your host. You will be staying with him while you are in Paris."

"A patron, not a patroness?"

"This is 1959. You need to be open-minded. I am independent. My actors do not stay in hotel rooms and they only sleep with common women. We will be turning the film tomorrow, so today you need to rest, go for a walk, drink a liqueur, be a human being."

The man he stayed with was a thin individual in his forties who stirred his coffee with pinkie extended and was able to talk for hours about the plague, the writings of Ernest Hello, ancient Greek comedy, and the birth of the universe. He was one of those fellows who would comb out their chest hairs every morning—one of those fellows whose dressers are covered with an arsenal of colognes and who spend half their day lounging about in a smoking jacket and serving themselves splashes of Cambus 31 year old Signatory from crystal decanters while remembering the young blonde they had talked to twenty years earlier, for a mere five minutes, in the Jardin de Plantes.

There were paintings on his walls, by Bacon, by Rothko, by Braque. On the mantle was a Ch'ing dynasty jar decorated with mynahs and red maple leaves. A large African fertility sculpture stood by a doorway.

"Welcome to my home!"

"As long as I'm not disturbing you . . ."

"No, I was enchanted at birth. I am not what I seem but actually a man. The keys. Towels. Slippers. Come and go as you please."

Clark and he would have long aesthetic and philosophical discussions over breakfast, Tardaux waving a piece of buttered bread in the air as he spoke, his high-pitched voice making the porcelain on the table grow smaller and the African sculpture move mysteriously.

"What part are we of the universe anyhow?" he said. "I don't even know the mathematics of that. But the earth is just a fraction the size of the sun, and the sun is a just a speck in the universe, which, according to many cosmologists, is some ten billion light years in radius, though I profoundly believe it to be more—an inconceivably endless orange, hundreds of billions of kilometres across, little pieces of light zipping here and there like in the pictures of Giacomo Balla. And only the tiniest portion remains detectable to our inadequate human apparatus!"

"An orange?"

"Ah, but you are Spanish."

"Paraguayan."

"It is possible, yes, but can you imagine suns bursting like blisters, planets smashed to dust! Yes, all things will once again be reduced to the Planck length, or about 10^{-20} times the size of a proton—that is about a billionth of a billionth of a billionth of a billionth of a centimetre. Why, if this universe will be reduced to such an absurdly fine point, I myself and the entire world will be so absolutely infinitesimal as to defy description! To sum things up, my friend, you shouldn't worry so much—for believe me, our lives are really almost entirely meaningless."

15

While in Cuba rebel troops led by Che Guevara were entering Havana, in Paris filming had begun for *Bas les pattes*, Clark taking on the role of Émile, a young man like many other young men. Filming lasted just over three weeks, Fontmoreau writing the script as the film went along, as he was inspired. He used a shopping cart from Prisunic for tracking shots and made all the actors do callisthenics every morning before shooting began. Clark, who knew very little French, spoke his lines in English and was afterwards dubbed by a student from the Académie de la Grande Chaumière, who needed to subsidize his addiction to drawing nude models.

The actor found Fontmoreau to be incredibly pretentious and the filming of *Bas les pattes* to be one of the least interesting times he had ever had in his life, as the entire crew was subjected to endless philosophical diatribes from the director.

"We seem to fancy ourselves apart from the animal kingdom," he would say, opening his arms wide, as if he wished to hug somebody. "The layering of earth and stone. The eruption of foliage. We humans try to rise above the status quo. We try to rise above the four-footed, the vegetable and mineral. But we are also a natural phenomena.

We are also inanimate stones. We are also crawling reptiles. We are fundamentally primitive. We must show this on film. We must show the current state of mankind on film and wave our arms in the air like masturbating herons."

Yawning, blinking, Clark and the other actors did as they were told.

Though the film had very limited success, it can now easily be viewed as a precursor to the French New Wave, with its uneven editing, lack of harmony and crude usage of actors.

"I suppose some people liked it," Clark later said. "To be truthful though, I never did see the completed picture. Maybe it was very good, but I somehow doubt this. I didn't have much faith in Pierre. For all his intellectual posing, he seemed unsure of himself and I had difficulty understanding whether he was really an artist or just another Frenchman trying to get laid."

Every day he would receive a five-page letter from his wife which, after glancing over perfunctorily, he would throw in the trash. Sometimes he would reply with a postcard, of the Rue de Belleville, of a dog being groomed along the Seine, of a man on stilts. Five or ten words scribbled without thought, truth or love.

It was not that he was trying to forget her so much as that he had difficulty remembering her. He could not have said with certainty what was the colour of her eyes. In his dreams it was not her who came to him but a shadow in the shape of Judy.

A few months after filming had been completed, after visiting countless cafés and drinking a vast rainbow of aperitifs, Clark managed to secure a role in the historical *Les fils du lieutenant Brévannes* as François, the handsome young rake who was handy with a sword. This picture starred Lydia Guérin, who at the time was the lover of Italian director Gino Baj. The latter saw Clark on the set and was apparently impressed.

"You remind me of someone. Someone very great," he said, scratching his chin.

"I am me."

"Yes yes," the director murmured, squinting his eyes.

He asked Clark to come to Italy where, the following week, he was to begin filming *Aladino nella citta' degli uomini formica*, a completely incoherent adventure with lavish sets and an international cast. Naturally Clark accepted on the spot.

That evening, when he went back to the Rue Oudinot, he told Tardaux about the arrangement. The latter was sitting in his pyjamas, smoking a Turkish cigarette and drinking a brandy while on the turntable a record was spinning (Vittorio Borghesi e la sua Orchestra Folk Attrazione).

"You were right to accept the role," the rich man told him. "We French are really far too full of ourselves. We all think we are artists, when in fact we are simply boring. It is only the Italians who have any real sense of adventure cinematographically."

He took a sip of his brandy.

"But Paris is nice," Clark commented, making his way to the bottles and crystal decanters.

"Rome is better. The Italians are a beautiful people. The food is admittedly terrible, but the people are beautiful. Just listen to this music—to the sound of children who don't cry, plum sellers, and young lovers kissing under the arcades of Rennaisance temples! In Italy everyone is very uneducated and only from illiteracy can great art be produced. I understand that in Milan wide belts in suede and leather are now popular, while in Florence they are dropping the lapels. You will be in time for next year's Olympics and can harmonize in a place where marble is cheaper than wood and the white light from the sky makes even old hookers look like virgins."

The next afternoon the actor telephoned his wife. It was early in the morning in New York and she was just waking up, her voice groggy, emerging from an aftermath of cocktails, cigarettes and twenty or forty pages of a cheap novel which lay discarded near a single red slipper.

"I won't be coming home," he said.

"Oh, really?"

"I have a lot of work here. Things are happening for me and one thing leads to another."

"Then I can fly out to join you. I haven't been to Europe in ages. Should I bring sweaters?"

Clark did not reply.

"I can be on a plane the day after tomorrow. José? José, honey? Hello? Hello?"

The phone line went dead. The next day she received the following telegram:

DEAR IRENE. SORRY. DO NOT LIKE TO BE HUNG UP ON. TOO MUCH FOR ME. DIVORCE ASAP. THE DESOTO IS YOURS. LOVE JOSÉ AKA ERIC.

16

Three days later Clark took an overnight train from the Gare de Lyon to Rome. He shared a compartment with a travelling salesman from Denmark and two very reticent men from Naples who were eating long sandwiches. In the morning they clattered through Pisa and then along the Golfo di Follonica. Clark looked out the window, at those large rectangular houses, which are built like nowhere else on earth, at the blue of the sea, which seemed almost holy. Then, later, as the train entered Rome, he caught sight of the ancient aqueducts and ancient walls. He stepped off in the Central Station. Looking about him he saw:

1) An enormous man with three chins
2) A woman with a moustache
3) Some fat children making faces

"Where are all the beautiful people?" he wondered.

A short individual with a remarkably low forehead and jet-black hair was there to meet him.

"I've been asked to take you directly to the set."

He showed the actor out of the station, put him and his suitcase in a Fiat 500.

"Where is the set?" Clark asked as the car sped down the Via Tuscolana, crowded with traffic.

"Cinecittà," the man said with great gravity.

Soon they were there. A half-dozen horses. An elephant. A sheik walked by with a sword. He was followed by females in veils whose eyes flashed and hips swayed.

This was the El Dorado of beautiful women. A thousand cascades of hair. Tina Louise was dressed as Sappho, Rhonda Fleming as Fabiola. There was Princess Phaedra and the Countess Ogda. Jayne Mansfield passed by in the costume of Queen Dianira. Ziva Rodann as the gorgeous Creusa and, though he took it all in calmly, the young man was as dazzled as anyone would be seeing for the first time imagination become manifest flesh, since really there was nothing concrete about it, faces and bodies appearing and disappearing, cameras capturing them and men with tiny moustaches whispering against plywood walls some dance of drum and tambourine.

"Get him a coffee. Did you get him a coffee? He needs to——you need to change," Baj shouted. "We are filming in thirty minutes."

"But I thought you said it would not be until Tuesday?"

"Change of plans."

"But I don't know what to do. I haven't read the script."

"It doesn't matter. Just do what I tell you. Walk when I tell you to walk. Talk when I tell you to talk."

"And what do I say?"

"Who cares? We'll dub it in later. We have to get this picture going!"

Clark was rushed into a dressing room. A fat man, about forty-five years old, with an almost hairless cranium and unguent manners, wrapped a turban around his head and stuck a false beard to his chin.

"And a little eyeliner . . ."

His part was simple enough. All he had to do was roll his eyes about and make gestures. Throw his arms open. Wave his index finger at a young muscular Italian who was playing the part of Aladdin. And then they put Clark on an elephant and he grinned.

"That boy has talent," a noteworthy producer said.

That night he was swept off to a party at a mansion somewhere on the outskirts of the city, a party tenanted by well-dressed Italians, English women who could read palms, an American businessman who became lost in his cocktail just as the floors seemed to be lost beneath countless rugs and at one point a middle-aged woman in a golden dress came in carrying a giant bowl of candy.

"Bonbons!"

"*Che meraviglia!*"

"Is this the buffet?"

"No, I don't believe in psychotherapy."

"That is why women find you attractive."

The next morning Clark rented a room at a hotel of sorts.[1] A bed not quite large enough. Stretching out his arms he could touch both walls. A sink. Bathroom (usually occupied) at the end of a hallway.

Out onto the street—where he could breath.

He looked about him. He was in Rome. The greatest city on earth. Truly the centre of the universe, where Germans mixed with Spaniards and Americans set their stiff lips against the palms of Swedish princesses. Ancient pillars

---

1. He would later rent an apartment on the Piazza Farnese and fill it with bookshelves and modern art.

and tombs which an endless line of cars sped past. Foul air / an armpit that exudes moisture / a man who steals / a woman who urinates in a bush / a comedic umbrella seller on the Piazza di Spagna. And in buildings others eat, copulate, argue, laugh, stab each other with knives, pray before idols, gaze at their wilted socks, cry, sing, commit suicide, chop onions and read Kant while sticking out their chests, or suck in their cheeks in front of mirrors, later to bathe their bodies or roll on the floor while biting off their tongues. Soiled paper napkins blow through the city. Old plastic bottles rest on the tombs of which even the ghosts are dead. Buildings step on buildings, the domes of cathedrals stick up like the nine hundred mamillae of some reclining demon, some bizarre Venus brazenly flaunting her abstract quality of being fecund while her orifices are trodden on by a million admirers, womb filled with Fiat 500s and Vespas which move in flocks and swarms, polluting the air with black eggs and dirty honey.

17

Flavia (Italian)

American actors are always handsome. I would not marry one, but I would let him take me to the movies or for a walk in a public place.

Helga (Norwegian)

The truth is that if you meet an actor they are not what you think they should be. Inevitably they are shorter than you imagine. Sometimes they have bad skin or say stupid things. I met a famous actor one day on a bus. But why was he taking a bus?

Marapina (Venezuelan)

I have heard that they are very immoral. Maybe it is too much to expect, but I think most women would prefer to have a man who is innocent. If I could choose, I would have a man who was innocent, even if he was ugly. Not that I like ugly men. But there are worse things than to have an ugly man who is faithful.

Katia (German)

I like actors with muscles. When you sit for two hours in the cinema, you want to look at something nice, even if it

is not real. Skinny men do not impress me and I will not
see a film in which one plays the lead.

Francesca (Italian)
For me it is the eyes that are important. It is easy to love
an actor with beautiful eyes.

<h1 style="text-align:center">18</h1>

And Clark was soon signing a contract for another film. In Italy it seemed that bluebirds sang for him and grass grew for him and he quickly gained a reputation, not only for competence, but also for ability, a thing much more rare than is generally imagined. He was able to digest any part given to him, to add a certain flare to his appearances on screen and make them, even the briefest, noteworthy. During the next few years one of his staples was supporting roles in peplums—sword and sandal epics marred by primitive special effects—model ships engaging in warfare in bathtubs, matchstick cities burning, and lava erupting from papier-mâché volcanoes. He was also considered desirable in swashbuckler films, those costume adventures full of pirates and arrows, terror and musketshots.

They would often shoot two films at once, one in the morning and one in the afternoon. In the morning he would play a praetorian guard, sword in hand. In the evening, a rich count with a waxed moustache who drank wine from splendid goblets. For him it was just a matter of changing costumes. He drifted easily from one role to another and, unlike other actors, rarely forgot which film he was in, and though they were completely banal, ridiculous, they did serve as a sort of drawing room where he was introduced to practically the entire world of Italian cinema, thereby providing him with an ammunition of contacts that he would later [be] exploit[ed by], for all sorts of famous people could be seen around Cinecittà. German actresses and Spanish acrobats. Important dignitaries would be given tours and rich Saudi Arabians come to marvel at the wonders.

Rome might no longer have been the centre of the world, but it was undoubtedly the centre of Europe, since in no other place in Europe was imagination as strong a force, made manifest in cinema, and attracting artists from every part of the planet who were eagerly swallowed up by the cameras at every edge of the city.

This was in a sense the silver age of Italian cinema (the golden age had already passed). Fellini was at the height of his powers. Steve Reeves was playing Sandokan and Richard Harrison went from gladiator to Perseus to pirate. Samson, Ursus and Hercules films filled the theatres. American and English bodybuilders could be seen strutting about in tight-fitting suits. Clark made friends with Reg Park and Cameron Mitchell. There were hands to be shaken, women to be kissed, stairs to be climbed which led to elegant apartments and terraces on which champagne was drunk and witty things said. On the Via Piemonte he saw Mastroianni eating a salad. Paparazzi lingered around the Colosseum and in the evening bell-shaped shadows would pass by accompanied by the mysterious click of heels and the tinkle of kisses floated through the air like moths.

Movie companies were popping up everywhere. Most, built on extremely precarious financial situations, were as ephemeral as dew on grass, coming and going like a flash of lightning. Many would only make one or two pictures;

and some would never make a picture, consisting of nothing more than a few business cards soaking up rain in the gutter.

For organised crime, the cinema seemed an ideal place to launder their money. Rome was filled with both desperate producers and the most creative accountants on earth, and the lenders would be sure to get their money back whether the film was a success or failure, with interest.

There were communists who dropped out of Cinecittà to make their own more political films; barmen, real-estate investors and railroad workers all wanted to get in on the action. Cineriz was making a film a month, and their competitor Lux Film one every six weeks. A.D. Cinematografica, Arion, and Partenope Cinematografica each came out with one film and crashed, their producers woken up by the dreaded midnight phone call from the south.

"Making movies is a serious business," a noted director once said. "In Italy, more producers have died by gunshot than partridges."

The country was full of movie theatres of every shape and size. In Milan, the Corso Vittorio Emanuele was lined with them, some, with multi-auditoriums, holding as many as a thousand spectators. Others, like the Cinema dei Piccoli in Rome, were tiny, showing films from 9.5 mm projectors on bed sheets to children and dwarves. In Naples there were huge grandiose theatres, like the Augusteo, lined with marble, the ceilings frescoed with images of Roman gods and circus animals, which sometimes had upward of a quarter million spectators a year. Then there were the second-run theatres. They operated in deconsecrated churches, old opera houses, and imposing stone structures where Fascist brotherhoods had once met. Projectors were in high demand, and rural theatres often used old models that would frequently break down, giving their audiences the chance to smoke more cigarettes, talk politics, make jokes, while the projectionist, glasses balanced on the edge of his nose, would slowly try and repair the machine. At certain theatres in the south, dancing girls would come on before the film began. At others the film would be prefaced by a comic or a magician.

You could tell how popular a film was by how much smoke was in the theatre. During the most popular the screen could hardly be seen, while the films with little draw had only a few sad cigarettes burning here and there. The majority of the theatres catered to an entirely male audience—individuals who went there without the slightest hope of being able to expand their social sphere and who sat deep in their chairs and smoked Alfas. When someone got shot they cheered. When a female came on scene, they whistled. Crude jokes were made at high volume.

A few of the more respectable theatres were places for lovers to rendezvous. The ticket seller had a picture of San Genesio in her booth. When the lights dimmed and the film began to run, people would clap politely. In the back there would usually be a man with thinning dyed hair holding the hand of a young woman who had just winked at a fellow with a broad unshaven chin who worked with a wheelbarrow during the day and late at night would some-times read a manual on aeroplane photography.

Clark bought an acoustic guitar and spent his spare time practicing. He sang 'I Walk the Line' and 'Nel blu dipinto di blu.' He knew he could be good at anything and some evenings the moon stood above the city like a spotlight, before African winds brought in foamy clouds and dust blew through the piazzas.

After wrapping up a day's filming of *L'Amore di Benvenuto Cellini*[1] he was approached by a man wearing nothing but sandals and a loincloth girded around with a thick leather belt. His muscular chest was shiny with oil.

"Remember me? Bob. Bob Antony."

"I'm sorry, but . . ."

"From Oklahoma. We met in New York City. Drank a Champale at Goody's Bar off 10th Street."

He smiled and showed a mouthful of brilliant white teeth. Carbamide peroxide.

Clark looked him over: a remake of the man he had met in front of the Actors' Studio: shaped like a T—his long frame now dressed in muscles.

"Maybe yes—but you've changed."

"New York didn't do anything for me, so I went to California and started hanging out with the Muscle Beach crowd and going to the gym. I started taking karate lessons from a Chinaman and working out like crazy. Eating lots of steaks. U.S.D.A. Pure protein. Lifting weights. Hold the potatoes. Muscle tissue, man. They love me here in Italy. Beefcake. The women never say no. I work out for two hours a day at the Akros Centro Sportivo. You should come along some time and join the fun."

"Right."

"No, seriously brother. Your pecs could use some firming. And the Italian broads go crazy for muscles. Just flex and they're naked in no time."

"So, you're acting?" Clark asked, changing the subject.

"I'm not sure if that's what you'd call it. I've been in about fifty films since I've been here, but to call it acting

---

1. [...] A limply directed little adventure starring an unknown Italian actor, overtly dubbed into English. [...] —Derrick White, *Bridgeport Telegram*, May 5th, 1962

would be a stretch. Right now we're doing some kind of historical thing over there in studio F. I'm not sure what it's about, but I do what they tell me and when it's over I get an envelope full of money."

And, in fact, Antony had become a star of sorts, appearing as the lead in a number of strongman films, as Maciste, as Hercules, as Theseus.[1] He would carry giant jars, fight lions and bulls, when put in shackles break them, when put in prison, bend the bars with his naked hands. Pull carriages and barges with his teeth. Leg press elephants and carry horses on his back across raging rivers. His were the films that children and virgins would go and see at the matinees, them usually adorning the lower half of a double bill. Films that, if they managed to ford the Atlantic and make it to America, found brief shelter in the most obscure theatres of Red Hook or the less good neighbourhoods of Philadelphia.

Later that evening Antony took him to a club in which men with very limited vocabulary danced with women with unlimited smiles. Clark drank more J&B than he should have and woke up the next morning next to a head of bright red hair which partially muffled a tulip-like somniloquy which had something to do with eating ravioli and sage, some void bliss dream of sacrificial bedsheets.

He got up, dressed, and stumbled down a flight of stairs and outside. There was a bar on the corner and he drank an espresso. A clock on the wall said it was 10:00.

An hour and a half late for shooting.

He had no idea where his car was and hailed a taxi. Twenty minutes later he was at his dressing-room door.

---

1. He would later star as Hercules in *Ercole sfida Golia*, a film in which Clark would play Xanpactos, a wicked Greek senator who uses his power to try and undermine the son of Zeus.

The director himself still had not arrived and the cast, in full costume, were all at the bar, talking and smoking cigarettes.

A very small man with thinning hair and a shallow moustache approached him.

"Mr. Clerk."

"Clark. Mr. Clark."

"Yes, Mr. Clark. My name is Aldo Buonaventura. I represent the Skout Agenzia dello Spettacolo. I understand that you are without representation."

"No time."

"No time for success?"

"Yes. I seem to be doing fine without it."

The other smiled in a condescending way.

"How much did they pay you for the last film you were in?"

"One and a half million *lire*."

"*Fratello mio*," the agent said, becoming suddenly familiar, unctuous, "only dogs and circus clowns are paid that kind of money."

"So . . . ?"

"You just sign. Read the contract. Take your time. It is part of my system to let clients take their time."

A document was pushed under Clark's nose.

"And what will this get me?"

"What won't it get you—a talented boy like you? You're an artist, not a businessman. Leave business to the specialists and concentrate on what really matters."

The actor was hesitant.

"Come to my office and we'll talk things over," the agent said, tilting his body forward at a forty-five degree angle and then departing.

19

It was during the filming of *Ercole sfida Golia*.[1] Clark, dressed as a Greek senator, went to the snack bar to get a Campari Soda.

While leaning there, drinking his bright red drink and eating peanuts, he noticed, as it would have been difficult not to, a certain woman sitting at a table surrounded by admirers. Though elegantly dressed, she was huge, formidable, with a masculine chin and two small, rather violent eyes. All around were very obsequious to her. One man came running up with a cold drink. Another whispered something in her ear. A few beautiful women glared at her enviously.

Clark asked the barman who she was.

"That's Gina Bradley."

"And?"

"She's the daughter of Jim Bradley, the big American movie producer."

---

1. [...] Opening at fourteen neighbourhood theatres, is the bottom-feeder epic *Hercules vs. Goliath*, a badly dubbed, badly shot picture hacked out of a thousand scripts of a similar nature. Apart from leading man Bob Antony's physique, he has nothing to offer, a fate shared by alleged actress Flora Szath. Some competence peeks out from beneath Eric Clark's pointy black beard, not that anyone cares. [...]
—David Trim, *Philadelphia Gazette*, August 25th, 1963

"So she has some pull?"

"You bet."

Clark shrugged his shoulders and turned back to his drink: a cylinder of neon-red liquid, extract of cochineal, dreamlike—reminding him vaguely of the blood he had seen spilled on those stormy days in 1947. And moving his toes about in his sandals, he wondered how people could adulate money and fat when there was so much poverty and hunger on the earth and maybe even off of it and he swallowed and paid and made his way back to the set, his garments swaying around him, coughing gently as a great orator does before demonstrating his art.

20

It was on the Via Marco Minghetti. Third floor.

The office door read:

BUONAVENTURA

AGENTE DEL SPETACOLO

PCTLPC

Clark opened the door and entered.

"*Per cortesia tenere la porta chiusa,*"[1] a sing-song voice called out.

The agent was sitting in at a very clean desk. The only thing on it a telephone. An unlit cigarette was between his fingers. To one side of the room were a few filing cabinets. One of the windows was cracked. On the walls were a few framed certificates and degrees, which might well have been forgeries, and framed pictures of well known actors—Paul Hubschmid, Karl Malden, Brigitte Bardot. There was a smell of bananas.

Clark sat down in a straight-backed wooden chair.

The agent lit his cigarette and looked at his new client.

"Vikings."

---

1. Please close the door behind you.

"Excuse me?"

"What do you think of them?"

"Vikings?"

"Yes."

"I have nothing against them."

"I should hope not. I have a picture lined up. *Erloff, il vichingo sanguinoso.* Pay: *lire* two million."

He took a drag of his cigarette and blew smoke proudly into the air / a role gotten, but whether from Buonaventura's competence or Clark's desirability was questionable / negotiating an ethereal wilderness / the talent agent later bringing him all sorts of offers—from people wanting him for a whisky advertisement (J&B), to Greek pornographers wanting him for ten minute shorts.

"I can't take these," Clark would object.

"As you wish. It is just part of my system to keep my actors working."

"What other actors do you have?"

"Some good names," the other replied evasively, recalling how he had clambered up, representing trained dogs and overweight ballerinas, aged tenors and pretty Sicilian children whose mothers knew how to flatter a man's heart. "And don't worry. Your time will also come. I was cooking fegato alla Veneziana[1] the other day—just as I like it, with lots of onions—and I looked down and saw that you would be a star."

---

1. Calves' liver Venetian style.

21

The actor made his way up the stairs, to Bandini's flat: A blind woman, a young man from Tonga or Fiji, a very ugly woman with a beautiful figure.

REPLAY

Up the stairs. Bandini's flat.

Clark agreed to be in his film, *Ragazzi d'argento*, about a group of wealthy young people leading empty lives.

It was shown at the Mostra Internazionale d'Arte Cinematografica di Venezia. Lights dimmed. Images on screen with rush of violins and credits over a speeding car at intermission unhappy spectators spilled into the lobby forgetful of their own fragility murky dispersion man smirking unravelling his lips.

Clark stood by himself, smoking a cigarette near a large potted plant.

Treville approached him.

"No one notices me," she said.

"They notice you. They just don't like the film."

————

Men wrapped in gaudy-coloured cloaks. Cardboard towers and flaming arrows. War ships, charging horses, clattering of swords. Bursts of orange. Swathes of green.

In 1962, he was given the role of Pyrrhus, in *Pirro dell'Epiro*. The film was meant to be another entry into the sword and sandal genre, but Clark, seeing in it some indefinite political message, took it so seriously that he raised it above other films of this class. He was dedicated to the role, gave himself to it, became lost in the shouts of the past, in ancient manuals on warfare, in heroic dreams in which he saw himself riding elephants and casting spears. He went about in public with a tunic over his shoulders, head held high, and spent several days gazing at the Greek relics in the Vatican museum in Rome:

Case I, 6. A kylix belonging to the transition period between the black- and red-figured manner—a thing which gave gravity, off of which the actor foraged insight.

Case K, 30. An amphora from the 5th century B.C. with figures of Achilles and Briseis, with self-worth flowing from it.

Case O, 10. An oinochoe with two young men with fighting cocks and this radiated moral value and action (a net of ropes surrounding the whole world).

————

He had clearly had some sort of revelation, drinking from ancient civilization as he had, for instead of playing the role with the stagy bombast so associated with Greek kings, he portrayed Pyrrhus as a strangely shy individual, a megalomaniac addicted to violence, but unable to look even his closest friends in the eyes. A man of vast intellect and generosity whose addiction to war caused his downfall. He counteracted fits of kindness with gross brutality, tempered his courage with anger and fear, just as is the case with almost all real men of power, since its inherent quality is corruption, as the inherent quality of lead is weight.

It was filmed in Yugoslavia and Sicily, being in part done in ancient ruins, in part in natural expanses, and in part on man-made sets.

His presence lent nobility to the cheapness of the latter and excitement to the absurd battle scenes where a few hundred extras were meant to represent armies of hundreds of thousands. He rallied his forces, thrust his arms this way and that, galloped forward on horseback, not as a man pretending to be a general, but as an actual general, having seen well enough as a child in Paraguay despots, men who led armed forces and did not flinch as the most awful deeds were committed before their eyes, at their very command, probably because at a certain point life becomes not valueless but having a value in direct proportion to its utility, uselessness, or the threat it presents.

Amidst the lumbering of elephants, charge of cavalry and the whistling of arrows he stood, head covered with a crested helmet. He had the habit of hooking the air with his finger when he spoke and when silent his hands were continuously clasped behind his back, his chest pushed forward.

The clatter of war. Swords sunk themselves into bellies. Dead were heaped upon dead and he gazed over them massed on all sides. Turning to his adjunct, he gave a strange, rather sad smile.

"They say that without war there would never be periods of peace."

"War is necessary," was the adjunct's comment. "And, anyhow, we have won."

"Yes, we have won. But another victory such as this . . . and we are lost."

The ocean.

22

Thanks to Buonaventura, thanks to the Skout Agency, he did screen tests for a number of important American films, including *Fantastic Voyage* and *Von Ryan's Express*. For the former, Fleischer found him too dynamic,[1] for the latter, Robson found him too sedate. Then there were tests for the roles of King Leonidas in *The 300 Spartans* and Flavius in *Cleopatra*. He was very nearly offered a role in *The Longest Day* and just missed playing Sherif Ali in *Lawrence of Arabia*. But in the end, the important roles in American pictures continued to elude him. The only major American film he would appear in would be John Frankenheimer's *Grand Prix*, and this in an uncredited role that in no way forwarded his career.[2]

---

1. "Grant is a straightforward role. I don't need someone trying to add subtlety to it."
2. Years later, Spielberg ended up offering him the role of Han Solo in *Star Wars*, but he turned it down, choosing instead to appear in *Soft Dogs*. "Maybe it was a bad choice," Clark would say. "I don't know. But the truth is that Joe De Franco offered me more money and the American's script really didn't impress me. A lot of things were going on in my life at the time. The film was proposed as *The Adventures of Luke Starkiller*. I was under the impression that it was a West German production and saw more possibilities in the other role, which my agent advised me was the more high-profile of the two. I had no idea the film would be such a success." From an interview on RAI2,

78

DISSOLVE TO: EXTERIOR. STREET – DAY

He ran into Bob Antony at a news kiosk on the Via del Corso. There were girly magazines next to children's toys. Tobacco and chewing gum. Comic books and religious tracts. Cheap porcelain and right-wing manifestos. Clark held a copy of *Il Riformista*. Antony the *International Herald Tribune*. Both men wore sunglasses.

"I've done a lot of films, but they don't seem to get me anywhere," Clark said.

"Hey, you have a nice car, a nice flat, chicks for the asking. You're in Italy. Good food and wine and it doesn't snow. Life is easy. What more do you want?"

"A little fame would be appreciated."

"You have a little fame."

"Yes, here in Italy. In Turkey and maybe in Germany. But in America and England, nothing," he said without bitterness but with a certain amount of regret, the regret generated not only by egoism but also by pride—the pride of someone with ability trying to fulfil what he saw as an almost spiritual destiny, a duty, to himself but also the disembodied spirits of his past, the ghost of Jim Stark, of Jett Rink.

"Well, if you want to break into the American market you should move to Hollywood."

"You were in Hollywood and moved here."

Bob Antony shrugged his shoulders as if to say, or maybe admit, that he was not so much an actor as some-one who was in films, someone without talent who still managed to get paid simply by being in the right place at the right time—his only real asset in being a somewhat muscular American in the city above all cities in the world

October 3, 1983.

where such a thing was appreciated, because it was doubtful if anyone in Hollywood or Little Rock or Albuquerque would have given him a job as anything more than a soda jerk or short-order cook.

"There's no freedom in the United States," Clark continued. "Their artistic progress is limited by their economic cleverness. I would probably get stuck doing television."

"Then you have to make the right connections here. You have to get in tight with someone with some influence."

"Yes, you could be right." Clark became thoughtful.

23

6:05 p.m. Bar Empire, Via Condotti 25.[1]

It was November. Clark was standing at the bar, drinking a prosecco. A woman came in. Large, fashionably dressed, the fur of some sort of animal resting on her shoulders.

"A rosé," she said, pushing herself up against the counter.

Clark recognised her. It was Gina Bradley, daughter of the famous movie producer. She was saying a few words to the barman. Her Italian was atrocious. She spoke it without any attention to the proper cadence in a thick American accent that made her seem some strange stereotype, embodying stupidity, wealth, gluttony;—a huge banknote stained with drippings. The barman treated her with respect. Professional respect. The well calibrated respect of a man who has served drinks to every kind of person imaginable and would have unblinkingly made a drink for a giraffe or six-armed deity had he been asked.

The actor looked over and she looked at him.

"Um, hello," he said in English.

"Yes?"

---

1. Jeweled purses compete with designer suits and water was once taken to the baths of Agrippa.

81

He smiled self-consciously, gathered courage, moved closer. "I . . . I noticed you were alone and thought you might want some company."

"And why would I need company?"

He smiled weakly, shrugged his shoulders. A woman who was attracted to shy men would have been quite happy. But it was questionable whether Miss Bradley was such a woman. She looked at him coldly, stuffed a finger sandwich in her mouth. He noticed that she smelled a bit, of sweat, though it was not warm.

"I like to watch you eat?" he murmured uncertainly.

"Oh yeah?"

"Do you know who I am?"

"Sure, you're that little Mexican actor . . ."

"From Paraguay."

". . . that little Mexican actor who was in that flop picture. You're not ugly."

"I am from Paraguay," Clark insisted.

"You sound Mexican."

The actor's face remained bland.

"And do you, um, like Latin men?"

"They have a reputation."

"A good one I hope."

"What are you doing?" she asked, fingering a bowl of olives.

"Just talking to you. Can I offer you another drink?"

"Are you going to try and get me drunk?"

"Not at all."

"Too bad. Then I suppose you can buy me dinner if you want."

And he did and fruit for dessert and in the days that followed flowers, boxes of chocolates, felt bears and expensive mushrooms, all without enthusiasm, as a matter of duty, calculation—just as one would put up small stakes in a game of poker before risking larger sums. Because, at a certain point in this world of commerce, one puts less energy into doing what one does, selling or risking ones ability or manufacture, and more into selling or risking one's body or personality, since the latter usually seems easier to hawk.

One evening, after dining at a restaurant where the waiter had recommended the shellfish, they returned to her apartment.

Interior. Night. A divan sits in the middle of a vast and somewhat darkened *sala*. There was a bar and a potted fig tree. There were a few large paintings on the walls by bad eighteenth-century painters. There was a synthetic polar bear rug and some large, porcelain object that might have been a vase or a sculpture.

"Fix yourself a drink," she commanded, pointing toward the bar.

"And can I fix you one?"

"Pour me a vodka. Neat."

Clark did as he had been told and made himself a whisky and water.

They sat on the couch. She drank down her liquor at a swallow. With knees close together, he sipped at his—his manner that of one who wanted to expand, to open his heart, but was hesitant, out of embarrassment, fear—the instinct of self-preservation that was probably wiser than himself—mind always flapping about leading one through ditches and gutters to some wind-exposed place—a cliff, where he stands with headlights bearing down on him, as he trembles on the edge.

He saw her sitting there next to him, observing him coldly, and moved closer. His forehead was beaded with sweat. He felt as if he were in the ring with a bull, could almost hear the shout of spectators urging him on, screaming for blood goring sword thrusts or some military commander urging him forward over the cusp of the trench to dash towards the well-armed enemy with nothing but a broken bayonet. He finished off the drink and set the glass down. He hesitated. A man recalling the lines of a script. And turned toward her.

"You look very beautiful tonight," he ventured.

"You think so?"

"Of course."

"You're a liar."

"No, if I wanted to lie, you would never know it."

"So, you like me?"

"I like you."

"Then prove it. Most men, if they really want something, pull it under the sheets at the first chance. But you've been as timid as a little fish."

Her sharp gaze seemed to be inspecting his soul. He swallowed. And then bent forward, closed his eyes, stretching his lips out as far as he could. A moment later they were pressing against the cold, thin lips of the other, which were unresponsive, seemed indifferent.

"Is that it?" she said.

He laughed uneasily.

"I thought you were from South America."

"I am."

"Not very warm-blooded, are you?"

24

They were married on July 24, 1964, at the Chiesa di Sant'Anselmo all'Aventino. A number of stars, including Anthony Quayle and Gig Young, attended their wedding. Afterwards they had their photo taken at the Piazza del Campidoglio.

"Who is that?" a bystander asked.

"I'm not sure, but he looks like an actor."

"She doesn't."

Then it was on to dinner, a gala affair with nearly one hundred guests. Spit-roasted piglet and gnocchi alla Romana were served. A band was playing and thirty or forty men danced with the bride, covered her cheeks with kisses. There was a lot of noise and people pretending to be having a good time. Bob Antony juggled three apples. Tina Treville drank a little too much and, laughing, went to the restroom where she cried.

Clark, sitting next to Jim Bradley, a dull-looking man whose huge cranium sat firmly lodged in his white collar, tried to engage him in conversation, but the latter only answered with mumbles and jerks of his chin. He did not seem to want to know his son-in-law.

Afterwards the newly married couple went on a ten-day honeymoon on the isle of Rhodes.

She basked in the sun. Bored, Clark wandered about, watched the fishermen, looked at some old stones, sampled the wine and then came back, sitting himself down beside her body, which was beginning to smell like cooked meat.

He pulled his skinny legs up to his chest and looked out at the cerulean water.

"So your father is beginning a film with Kirk Douglas," he began.

"Oh come on baby, let's not talk shop."

"I was only thinking——"

"Hey, you just kiss me on the neck and shut up, frijole. Later we're going to have dinner in bed. I'm getting hungry out here."

For all her connections, she in fact never helped his career in the least. Back in Rome, installed in her now newly decorated apartment (Clark would temporarily sublet his), it was the same as it had been before. When he brought the subject up she either pretended not to hear him or made excuses.

"I hope you didn't marry me for my father," she said.

"Of course not. But that doesn't mean we can't take advantage of the situation."

"But you have plenty of work."

"Yes, but if I could be in a big American picture . . ."

"Then you would have lots of skinny women to sleep with, is that it?"

"Not at all . . ."

"Listen, frijole, if you ever cheat on me, I'll see that you . . ."

She made a stabbing motion with her fingers.

He was silent. He took an Alfa cigarette out of a pack and held it but did not light it. She was looking at him intently.

"So you're in love with me?"

"Yes. Very much."

"I want you to prove it."

"How?"

"Just tell me, frijole, just tell me."

"I love you."

"You what?"

"I love you madly."

"You really aren't a very good actor."

He put the cigarette in his mouth and lit it with a match. "Maybe I just have a hard time playing myself."

And that might very well have been the truth, but another truth was that he had married her, not out of love, but out of ambition—and it was not exactly clear what her motives had been in marrying him, since, if she did love him, her way of showing it was far from standard and she further seemed little impressed with his romantic abilities and sometimes days went by without her offering him her lips and there were times when he felt like she hated him and he would spend long hours at night reading while she slept and slip into bed silently and with a certain amount of fear, trying his best not to wake her up.

25

Actresses ought to be lean, unlike babies who we prefer to be the very opposite. An actress who is not lean is like a house without windows, a sky without a sun, a cherry tree that never blooms. Other things that should be lean are the shanks of a mare, a good cut of meat, and the smile of a rich man. Because all things that are lean are somewhat selfish, and nothing is more selfish than an actress—unless it be an actor, a banker, or a corporate entity.

During the filming of *L'Arciere rosso*,[1] Clark played opposite Flora Szath, a very attractive woman from the Balkans, whose husband was a Southern Italian by the name of Alvaro De Bisogno, a tall, lank individual with an enormous moustache and a receding hairline, the son of a politician of some note. With no visible occupation (he had studied statistics for two years at the University of Messina), Alvaro seemed to follow his wife and moustache through life, passively accepting his minor role. When they walked down the street people stared at her and he held up his head with pride. He would kiss her on the forehead and kept a scrapbook which contained press releases,

---

1. […] A wretched little adventure, only made palatable by the moderate acting ability of lead Eric Clark. […] —Tad Walters, *Liverpool Echo*, November 3rd, 1964

88

newspaper clippings in which she was mentioned, publicity photos.

Clark could not understand how such a man could have won such a woman. Looking at her small, cleft chin, her white, triangular face, he had difficulty remembering his lines, and when during filming he had to touch his lips to her nose and cheek it seemed to him that something was transmitted, some emotion that he very much wanted to take part in and then he spat out his words and finished off the scene.

It was like some distant memory. Something from his past that he could not recognise. An almost familiar warmth of a friend that he had never really known.

Later, while the set was being adjusted, he caught sight of her slipping out a door and he followed her, into the strong sunshine of July. She was against a wall, lighting a cigarette.

"You smoke . . . ?"

"Yes, but don't tell Alvaro. He doesn't approve."

"How could he?"

"Yes."

Clark pulled her toward him. Her dull blue eyes looked up at him. He held her tightly.

"If I can just touch your mouth . . ."

Later that day, after filming, Alvaro approached him. The latter was walking quickly. His face wore a serious expression.

"Alvaro . . ."

"Come on, let's go get a drink."

They went to the bar and ordered two white wines.

"That woman, she is as cold as ice. She doesn't realise how much I love her."

"You've been arguing with her?"

"No, no. I wouldn't go so far as that."

"What did you tell her?"

The Italian made an indefinite gesture.

"Did she do something?"

"No, nothing. Not really. But listen . . ."

"Yes?"

A hunted look came into Alvaro's eyes. His voice dropped. "She is a beautiful woman. I understand that. I am also a lover of beauty. Her personality. . . . So special. So very deep. . . . And. And, I sometimes wonder if she is seeing another man."

"Impossible."

"And why is that?" Alvaro asked, looking Clark directly in the eyes.

"With a husband like you, why would she go looking for another man?"

The Italian pressed his lips together, stood suddenly very erect, and nodded in agreement.

"Yes, maybe you're right. My uncle was a general under Mussolini. I have been told that our family is descended from Roberto il Guiscardo. In my village, the muleteers kiss my hand when I pass. There is no reason why she would stray to another pasture. I have money, looks, and name. My grandmother always praised my intelligence. It would be very foolish of Flora not to be content with such a treasure."

"Precisely," Clark agreed and drained off his drink. He had an appointment with the other man's wife at an unscrupulous inn on the Via Appia Vecchia and did not want to be late.

And that is how it began.

She would have him meet her at shady hotels, places frequented by prostitutes and travelling salesmen. This bizarre romance being consummated beneath sheets of dubious cleanliness and to the itinerant howl of the street-walkers who stood on the pavement below arguing with innate purity.

"There are nicer places," Clark would say.

"I don't mind."

"What are you thinking?"

"Nothing."

"Nothing?"

"Nothing."

"Do you like me?"

"Yes."

"Yes?"

"Yes."

Clark held her hand very tightly and felt very lonely.

The woman was, in fact, like an empty bowl and they barely exchanged words. Sometimes he tried to engage her in conversation, talk to her about his political beliefs, philosophy, recent weather patterns, the loveliness of colour, anything. But she would just gaze at him with a lost expression. Mechanically, she would latch her lips on to his—not with passion, but as if she had been directed to do so by Vittorio de Sica or Nanni Loy.

He looked for something in her that undoubtedly she did not have. He looked for the Moah she had played in *Maciste contro le arpe*, for the Ka-Mi-Tza she had played in *Un samurai sfida cento e cinque geisha*, for the Elisa she had played in *Un fiore all'incanto*, but it was like trying to eat a still life of a fig. One could see the aurora borealis, lakes and horizons in her eyes, but her heart was cold, her soul warped and muted, some cul-de-sac of the infinite, and it was with great sadness that he came to realise that he had not found anything at all, not because she was not pleasant, not because she was not beautiful, but because she lacked that indefinable thing that he needed so badly, what might have been called love, or possibly been called by another name—it was something he could not enunciate, a vague shape that he was unable to put his hands around, that thing which possibly eludes us all and makes men turn toward religion or stab themselves in the heart.

"You seem sad," Flora said.

"No no, why should I be sad?" Clark asked, looking at the woman by his side, trying to detect some sign of love, emotion.

"No reason." She yawned and closed her eyes.

Outside he could hear a car drive rapidly by. Down below a man was talking in a loud voice.

"How could I feel bad about cheating on my wife?" he said with a shrug of his shoulders, answering a question which had never been asked. "The miracle would be if I remained loyal to her. But if I were loyal to her I would be disloyal to myself. Because I need to find something. Something I can almost touch, that I can smell not far away."

He turned toward the actress. She was snoring very lightly, her mouth open / some rose of Bengal—without either thorns or scent.

26

On the set he detected sarcastic smiles. Men would nudge each other or exchange comments and laugh while his back was turned. Women, engaged in whispered conversations, would fall silent when he approached.

"You need to watch that girl," Bob Antony told him.

"What girl?"

"Your wife."

Clark did not reply, but afterwards thought about this. During the past week or so he had noticed her acting strangely—using more make-up than usual and wearing low-cut dresses. She had been more friendly. The night before she had made him soup. He told the director (Egisto Ferro) of the film he was working on that day (*Rocambole ruba ancora*) that he was not feeling well and left early (14:20). The day was one of brilliant sunshine and he drove home slowly, one hand on the wheel, listening to the radio and looking at the world through sunglasses.

Parking in front of the building, he looked up at the apartment and noticed that the shutters were closed.

Up some steps. Through the front door.

He walked into the bedroom, probably already knowing what he would find.

Alvaro was pressed against her huge body. He looked at Clark with sad eyes, the eyes of a man forced to take revenge, even if the cost to him is higher than to the avenged party, honour being all-important.

"You see what happens when you don't know how to treat your woman right, frijole?" Gina said in a sleepy, somewhat bored voice.

"But . . ."

"I know about you."

"And now you know what it feels like to be a *cornuto*," Alvaro whined, making the famous "*gesto delle corna*" with his right hand.

He thrust his head against Gina's breast, grit his teeth, was clearly filled with rage, almost more against himself than Clark, almost more against the woman who he was there with naked than the actor who had caused the problem. Because for revenge, for the sake of honour, he would do anything. Even bite his own head off.

"So, my wife is your . . ."

"Yes, she is my lover!" Alvaro almost screamed.

"Because you know, I am through with *your* wife."

The Italian sat up in bed:

"And? And?"

"And you see, Gina has to be at the airport at about 8:00 tomorrow morning. She is going to America, to visit her father. Her very rich and well-connected father. Isn't that right?" Clark asked, looking at her.

She was now sitting on the edge of the bed with her back toward De Bisogno, putting on her stockings.

"8:30," she replied, looking over her shoulder.

"Well, naturally, I'll be busy," Clark continued. "And she doesn't like to take taxis, so . . ."

"Yes, Italian taxi drivers are very rude. Of course frijole over there isn't exactly a gentleman. He isn't exactly the kind of man who knows how to make a woman smile."

"Right," Clark said with apparent satisfaction.

"But—then—why—I——" Alvaro stammered.

"No, there is no need to apologise. The lease to the apartment is in the top drawer of the desk in the study as well as the bills Gina owes her seamstress, her confectioner, her jeweller and her farrier. She has plenty of money, but she prefers if her man pays for everything. Charmingly old-fashioned. I am sure the two of you can arrange things just fine. Maybe Gina's father can even help your wife with her career. I will leave my keys on the table by the door on the way out so you can have your own set."

And he walked out of the apartment, reflecting how, in the end, getting out of the relationship had been far simpler than getting into it and how, despite his worst fears and Gina's threats, he had managed to come out of the business little damaged—with only the reputation of a cuckold to carry around, a reputation he had been destined to carry around—as the son of a cuckold could expect little less than to one day carry on the tradition started by his father or his father's father before him.

27

- Women in black latex rain coats
- Airplanes taking off and landing
- Gadgets and *bon mots*
- Always dressed in a well-tailored suit
- From casino to jazz bar, ski slope to jungle island
- Seducing every woman / killing almost every man (karate / pistol / micro-bomb / sophisticated poison)
- Exotic locations: Istanbul, Rio de Janero and Java[1]
- Battling nitroglycerine smugglers, uranium smugglers, rocket-fuel thieves, secret document thieves, bikini-clad nymphomaniacs high on heroin and men with round faces who smoke cigarettes lodged in ivory holders knocking off the ashes with their pinkies

During the secret agent craze, he played British Agent 770, the perfect gentleman. A role which was first offered to Michael Cane, who refused. Afterwards, the producers, under direction from the Italo-German Parnass Film group, tried to secure a contract with Neil Connery, the brother of Sean Connery, but he had previous commitments. In the end, after some financial discussions with

---

1. All of these were done with stock footage, the films themselves being rolled in a back-lot 20 km outside of Rome.

the president of the Skout Agenzia dello Spettacolo, Clark was given the contract. And he was of course a far better fit than Neil, the latter being completely incapable of acting. And though the former was not by any means English, it was a simple matter for him to adopt the mannerisms of a suave Englishman and he was naturally athletic so he could move about with agility appropriately combined with the kind of inner solitude of a man who must spy and accepts being spied on, and if the films were not masterpieces it was no fault of his while he inwardly took credit for any success they had—any, since they were for the most part overlooked in Europe, aside from Germany, which seemed to like things most others did not care for as their kitchen has proved for the last few hundred years, but anyhow these films were wildly popular in Turkey[1] where *770 chiama Z-8* was the highest grossing film for the year 1964, bringing in as much as *My Fair Lady* and *Cheyenne Autumn* combined. This led the following year to Clark's only venture into Turkish cinema, in the film *Fenix Istanbul'da bulusalim*,[2] for which he was paid by Turkish standards the astounding sum of sixty-five thousand Turkish *lira*. The film was partially funded by A.G. Film out of Beirut. The music was lifted from the score Georges Van Parys did for *Nathalie, agent secret*. The director was Yilmaz Yurdacul,

---

1. All together, three films were made. Unfortunately, the second of these, *770 sfida 668*, is now almost completely lost, only fourteen minutes of footage remaining, which can be found in recycled form in the Turkish movie *Sataniz Osmanli saraylarinda* (Sataniz in the Ottoman Palaces).

2. Primitive cutting, with scenes changing while characters were in mid-dialogue, and the theme music, appropriated from *Apocallisse sul fiume giallo*, sometimes being sliced away in mid-note / rhythmic maze of blank tangle.

who had become famous for such films as *Moscow karakolu* (Moscow Police Station) and *City canavari* (Monster of the City) and who, in the previous seven years, had been responsible for directing over three hundred films.

In Turkey, Clark was treated as a true star. He was put up at the Acropol Hotel in the centre of town, with a view of the Hagia Sophia, fed famous meatballs and set to drink hundreds of cups of tea. At propitious hours women with hair smelling of oil of carnations and eyes done in green kohl would slip into his room and, embracing him, offer cigarettes loaded with opium from Afyon.

"Filming was actually somewhat difficult," Yurdacul would later recall.[1] "Word had got out that a famous American actor was making a picture and crowds would gather to see him. We ended up having to do most of the shooting in the early hours of the morning, when the streets were relatively empty. His co-star was Mehmet Hazinses,[2] who at that time was extremely popular, particularly in the Black Sea Region. But, just as a Turkish woman cannot have two husbands, a Turkish film cannot have two stars. Unfortunately, Hazinses became rather jealous of Clark and is said to have tried to pay the Istanbul Revenge Brigade to do away with him. I am not sure if that is true or not, but one can certainly detect tension in the scenes they did together."

[commercial break for Dr. Oetker Kazandibi Mix]

---

1. From an interview done on Kayseri Kanal 38, December 3rd, 1985.
2. Hazinses had begun his career as a rural circus acrobat and, upon appearing as the somersaulting superhero Maskeli Atmaka (Masked Hawk), immediately entered the hearts of the Turkish people. He would later become renowned for his recurring role as Kovboy Emiliyano, in a kebab western series of the early 70's.

- Belly dancers
- Starch and sugar
- Sunglasses and moustaches

He had slipped out of his hotel, was wandering along the empty, unlit streets. Then footsteps behind. He turned. A figure in the distance pushed itself into the shadows.

When he got back to his room, he noticed on the coffee table an envelope with his name on it. He opened it. A bullet slid out. A note:

Get out of Istanbul, or the next one's for you.

There was a bottle of Ankara on the dresser and he fixed himself a short drink. The telephone rang.

He hesitated before picking it up.

"Hello?"

"Hello."

"Who is this?"

"Aldo Buonaventura, Skout Agenzia dello Spettacolo. And who is this?"

"It's Eric."

"I've been trying to get a hold of you for hours."

"I went for a walk."

"It's late."

"For you to be calling."

"How do you like Istanbul?"

"It's beautiful."

"Good, because you can stay there."

"Excuse me?"

"Televizyon Film has offered us a twelve-picture contract. The terms are favourable. The Akbas brothers are working on your script right now."

"No."

"What? This is a bad connection."

"NO."

"No? Why no?"

"Because, Mr. Buonaventura, it is a part of my system to stay alive."

[insert theme music to *Mata Hari, Agent H21*]

28

He worked / testing device of demonstration / fattening of the studio / method same kind of dissatisfied youth African north houseboy adorned with peacock feathers dances tight pants his own lack of renown with something resembling courage because it takes at least that to be an artist of any kind let alone an artist who actually creates art.

- He read the works of Ivan Pavlov and Yury Tynyanov, Emma Goldman and Lysander Spooner
- A great worker, he would labour away for twelve hours together without ever complaining
- Took his job seriously, always tried his best[1]
- After shoots he would often close himself off and not talk to anyone
- His left-wing leanings made him more than a few enemies, some actors, such as Lando Buzzanca, even refusing to work with him
- He always insisted on doing his own make-up

Of course he did not know exactly what this meant or

---

1. The three worlds are as impermanent as clouds in an autumn sky. —*Lalitavistara Sutra*

what it would mean ranging from the days he had seen her in her slip looking at the mirror and putting on eyeliner to when he himself would be doing this out of necessity rather than out of simply convention cheek rouge / powder / lip liner.

29

During the shooting of *Una donna primitiva* (a film Clark in no way took part in):

There were scenes shot on the streets of Trastevere and scenes shot in a small, run-down apartment on the Via Annibal Caro. A large, idiot lover and a woman without much of a conscience.

Bob Antony and Tina Treville, sitting on the steps, had begun talking while inside the director argued with the cameraman. The subject of Clark came up.

"Have you seen him recently?" Antony asked.

"I have seen him, but I'm not sure that he has seen me."

"You probably make him nervous."

"Why?"

"You like him."

Tina laughed uneasily.

"Is that a mistake?" she asked.

"Well—if a woman is too easy," Antony explained, "it scares a man off."

"I have never thought of myself as easy. Unattractive maybe. Easy, no."

"You're a good actress."

Tina did not reply. She was unsure what he meant by this. Later that night she wrote a letter to Clark, but did

103

not send it, thinking it was a mistake to ruin a friendship
since they are hard enough to have but not entirely certain
the extent of even a friendship, the object of it being evasive. And there were other men to love and other people
to feel lonely for and there were bees that made honey and
mountains that drooled little rivers.

She was a good actress, but she did not really like being
an actress at all and she sat and thought and even tried not
to think.

Some moment of sincerity running through the rain
dressed in dust and obsolete love has short leathery wings
long neck fly only nudging buy white moustache cheap
and short wilting dressed in dust she tried not to think and
after sighing once went to bed.

30

In one bar an African woman adorned with peacock feathers dances brazenly.[1] In another a fat woman plays the piano and sings in a beautiful voice, occasionally lifting a bottle of German beer to her ductile lips. There are bars inhabited by prostitutes and bars inhabited by rich women whose forearms are encased in long white gloves and whose necks are painted with perfume from Ceylon. There are bars which are all but abandoned, the only clients being flies and stray dogs, the pot-bellied proprietor sitting behind the counter drinking a glass of his cousin's home-made wine and reading *La Gazzetta dello Sport*. And then those bars so crowded that one can hardly breathe, eighteen-year-olds in tight pants nudging up against one another, middle-aged men with wilting moustaches buying young women in white blouses drinks, gay art collectors letting out shrill cries while a mysterious man with thick glasses idles near the phone booth an unlit cigarette shivering in his hand.

And we have another:

Bottles ranged on shelves against a mirrored wall barman working vigorously making coffee pouring drinks washing dishes / skinny pimp leans on the counter / man

---

1. We see her from below / sequin dress / trumpets.

smoking a pipe reads a newspaper and Clark sat, the humiliation or anger or regret or dirty humour of what had happened with Gina still there, lingering, like a bad odour that followed him wherever he went and maybe the only way he could really wash it away was to throw himself into some new role, throw himself away and be recreated as something if not the opposite of what he had been at least with the quality of spirit that enables one to face difficulty and danger with firmness—not the difficulty and danger of being cheated on, because that had been almost a relief, but to face his own lack of renown with something resembling courage.

He took a sip of his wine.

"Did you see it?" (He was speaking about *Qualche dollaro in piu*.)

"Yes, it was good," Bob Antony replied. "Everybody's hot to make westerns now. They say the peplums are done. But it's just a passing thing. In three months this whole western craze will be over with and everyone's going to be back on the set in sandals and toga."

"I don't know."

"I do."

"The western is easier for me to relate to, politically. I feel karmically connected to it. The stories of the forgotten, the nameless. These are the kind of films I want to be in."

"Be in?"

"Star in."

"That's what I thought you meant. But you're too pretty for the lead role in a western."

"You think?"

"Well, you don't really strike me as a cowboy." The bodybuilder grinned knowingly.

"Yes, I understand. You know what cowboys look like then?"

"I lived in California."

"You were on the beach."

"There were cowboys there too. Admittedly a lot of them were queer. But some weren't. And queer or not, one thing is absolutely factual, Eric. They're blond. All real cowboys are blond. At least the good guys. And they look a bit tougher than you do. And the bad guys look a lot tougher. I told you that you should have come with me to the gym. You need to firm up your chest."

"Blond?"

"That's right."

"Maybe some aren't. Times are changing. The Mexican cowboy."

Bob Antony laughed. "Even so . . ."

"Go on."

The other took a swallow of his drink. His eyebrows glided closer together. Migratory workers. Picking fruit and vegetables. Peaches and prunes. Could see them in Palm Desert and Coachella as he sped through in a convertible. Under big hats. Black hair. Moustaches. He lit a cigarette and continued.

"Okay, let me concede that times are changing. Let's say someone even goes for the Mexican-looking cowboy. But why should they choose you? You almost look Italian. You're handsome in all the wrong ways. You're too clean, too delicate. More the sensitive type."

"I can act."

"Maybe that's the problem. People want bodies and you're a damned actor."

The two men were silent and stared at their wine, the one half frowning but carefree, because he was living his unimpressive aspirations, the other seeing more than just blood, smiling sadly, because duty compelled him to be discontent until he reached some place where illusion became reality. Because he felt he should honour his own life, which itself contained many lands one could crawl over on all fours or ramble through on horseback, taking in their beauty, gazing at far away mesas and listening to the hymns of nearby creeks.

Presently Mr. Antony spoke:

"I hear there's an Italian-Spanish production in the works. Pedro Cortés is in town talking with Bottega. They must be looking for a lead."

"I've met Cortés," Clark said. "And Bottega—I've slept with his wife."

"And you can speak Spanish. That's something," in a voice that seemed to be saying just the opposite, tinted with sky-blue pessimism; him feeling uncomfortable around the muscular ambitions of the other.

Clark shrugged his shoulders. At 17:15, just as the old women of the neighbourhood were making their way to mass, he telephoned Buonaventura. The agent lacked enthusiasm.

"Forget about it. These films aren't refined enough for you."

Later, in the evening, Clark took a long walk. He recalled the stories of pistoleros he would hear on the radio as a child, the brothers of the Rio Grande and California, of men who never smiled beneath their moustaches and rested between killings beneath the shade of their hats which were as broad as umbrellas; recalled the story of the great outlaw hero Tiburcio Vásquez. For three days he didn't shave or wash. He got hold of a pair of boots, buckskin chaparejos and a poncho and when Mario Bottega arrived at his own office which was situated above a dealer in sacred objects on the Via Macchina di Saponara and opened the door he saw a figure sitting in his chair; those same boots on desk; a hand-rolled cigarette hanging from a sombre mouth and hat tilted over eyes.

"Hey, amico, I think you're in the wrong place," Bottega said with calm yet evident perplexity.

"No, amigo, I don't believe I am."

There was a five-second pause.

"Is that you Clark?"

"Yes, it is."

"Who told you I was shooting a western?"

"You need a lead."

"There are lots of leads. I can pick up a lead on any street corner, in any discotèca."

"You can give me a screen test."

"I know you're a good actor. It's just that . . ."

"I'll work for free."

Bottega's eyebrows rose. He gave an affable smile.

"Hmm. Well, if you get your feet off my desk . . ."

31

It was May of 1966. Django had come out the previous month and producer Mario Bottega, hungry to capitalize on the name, immediately planned a film with the same in its title. The film was called *Quando arriva Django non puoi contare i morti*.

It was done in Spain, with an almost all-Spanish cast, on an extremely slender budget and a very strict time frame. The director was Pedro Cortés. Almost all the shooting was done on a farm in the middle of the desert. Ivan Vandor[1] was hired to do the score. Clark played the lead as Django and the co-star was Peter Herschell Lawrence. The former was mysterious / excessively violent. The latter nasty / brazen / horse thief cattle thief murderer.

The movie was by no means a huge international success. In fact, the only country it had substantial box-office returns from was Spain, probably due to the fact that Clark was able to dub his own voice for the Spanish language version. But it did prove one thing: Clark looked very at home in westerns.

"I'm getting calls from all over," Buonaventura told him. "A lot of offers for horse operas are coming in."

---

1. A Hungarian composer best known for his work on *Agent 3S3 setzt alles auf eine Karte*. He also wrote a well-known book on the music of Tibetan Buddhism.

"Then accept them."

"That's my system!"

Clark's strategy of doing *Quando arriva Django non puoi contare i morti* for free had paid off. Within a month he had signed contracts for three more westerns, two with Mela Cinematografica and one with Arturo Mendez Producciones Cinematográficas S.A.

The first film with Mela was *Il winchester crudele di Yuma*. It was directed by Mario Brodo[1] under the alias of Rod Bradley and shot in Eastmancolor at a cost of only slightly over thirty million *lire*. The filming was done in forty-eight days in September and October of 1966. They would shoot from eight in the morning until around noon and then after lunch look at the rushes while the Spanish extras were taking their siesta. Then from around four in the afternoon until six or seven they would do more filming. Outdoor scenes and gunfights were shot in the morning, while the early evening was reserved for bar scenes and fistfights. It was distributed in West Germany by Adria Filmverleih and as a second tier release in the United States by Film Ventures International. The second Mela production was *Tre buchi in fronte*, and this was followed by the extremely violent *Una carogna, un gringo e un bounty killer*[2]

---

1. Brodo was legendary for his incredible output, making a film on average every hundred days for the duration of his career.

2.

QUEENS TONIGHT

7:00

TERRIFIC ACTION TRIPLE!

Not recommended for children

"REVENGE OF HERCULES"

Plus

Eric Clark

"A Scum, a Gringo and a Bounty Killer"

Plus

Paul Hubschmidt

"Upperseven Man to Kill"

(*The Gleaner*, Kingston Jamaica)

from Arturo Mendez Producciones Cinematográficas
S.A., which was distributed in the United States in a ver-
sion edited down to eighty-two minutes under the title
Django Rides Again.

———

[…] Continuing the seemingly endless cavalcade of badly
dubbed, badly shot westerns which have made their way
through customs like the bad Chianti and salami that give
us headaches and heartburn whenever we are foolish
enough to ingest them, is *Django Rides Again*, which opened
to a predominately male audience at the 86th Street East
Theater yesterday. […]
    —Derrick Small, *The New York Times*, June 18th, 1968

———

Despite the tepid response these films were receiving
in the United States, they were very popular in Europe
and other places of culture [sic] and Clark went on to film
Un grilletto facile per quelli che vogliono il morto and *T'ammazzo
bastardo.* In the latter film, gypsies were hired to play the
Indians, but these, being from two opposing clans, began
stabbing each other on the set and a considerable chaos
broke loose. Someone's wife was stolen and a man was
seen galloping wildly away on horseback. The police
were called in, and most of the gypsies were replaced by
Algerians.

32

Sixteen ways to die by gunfire:

1. Fall through railing of second storey (clutching belly)
2. Fall through window of second storey (head first)
3. Get shot while drinking from a trough
4. First being shot through the palms of both hands (Christ metaphor) then shot in the belly
5. Being shot through the floorboards of a balcony by pistolero below
6. Being shot through the floorboards of a balcony by pistolero above
7. Being shot while riding on a horse or driving a stagecoach
8. A man being shot while he is powdering his face
9. Getting shot while stumbling out of a burning house (near the end of a film)
10. Being shot in the dark when the light from your cheroot gives you away
11. Being shot during a dust storm
12. Being shot while eating a chicken (for laughs)
13. Being shot by an angry prostitute (for laughs)
14. Being shot with a Smith & Wesson double-action handgun while cheating at cards
15. Being shot through the window of a moving train (near the beginning of a film)
16. Being shot by a man leaping out of a coffin

33

Almería was Arizona. Almería was Mexico. Almería was Texas. Arid hills and dusty trails. Cactus. Canyons. Desert. Craggy places and deformed rocks and men were also landscapes. With faces that seemed carved out of wind and rain. Unshaven, with beads of sweat clustered on sunburnt foreheads. And parched lips. And dusty ponchos and worn boots and beneath sombreros burnt the crooked cigars of men waiting to shoot or be shot, to profit or be left for dead.

A few boards nailed together and you have a town.

A pistol, a hat and a pair of boots and you have a hero, an incarnation, a subjugator of the two sexes.

Some shadow, some dust, the creaking of a signboard, to show the loneliness, sadness, desolation of the American west which had nothing to do with America and everything to do with the innate human fascination with that social theory that holds formal government to be both unnecessary and unjustifiable.

The mythology of galloping horses and pistol fights, of card games and barroom brawls; the song of the goat with words of brutality and whippings and the gods are indeed found behind the smoke of guns and heroes wrapped up in jealousy and revenge, greed and untamed appetites, all this not so much speaking to historical reality as subconscious truth and men could be killed for reward or without punishment and ties to women were simple and animal kisses sealed with whisky and the kind of uncleanliness most men secretly or not so secretly wished for drunken cowboy hard case ambush shotgunned lynched with a thick rope the sound of hooves.

"The westerns of Spain and Italy reflect the primal desire of the modern man, the man of Paris and Berlin, to return to his traditions and nature," said director Mario Brodo.

The theatres of Europe were filled with westerns. A good part of the films in the cinema had the word "*dollari*" in them.[1] First there had been the Ringo craze.[2] Then came the Django epidemic.[3] A long list of heroes began to be paraded before the eyes of men. There was Garringo and Sartana, Djamango and Sabata, Joko and El Rojo. Singers like Peter Tevis and Nico Fidenco[4] became popular. Dreams of the great West filled the minds of European men. Sales of J&B whisky skyrocketed as did sales of snakeskin boots, leather vests and bolo ties. Young Italians could be seen strolling about the Piazza di Spagna in brand-new jeans and cowboy hats and speaking

---

1. From 1964-1969 there were over twenty westerns with the word "*dollari*" in the title.

2. From 1965-1970 there were seventeen Ringo films, including *Ringo vadiler aslani* (Turkey) and the German-produced *Wer kennt Johnny Ringo?* The real Ringo (1850-1882) was notorious for shooting unarmed men; was a lover of books and a good friend of Curly Bill Brocius.

3. Over thirty films were marketed under the "Django" banner, including the notorious *Django liebt es, seine Waffe zeigen* in which Bob Antony participated.

4. Fidenco participated in the music for ten western films.

Roman dialect with Texan drawls. Country western bars sprouted up in Turin, Rome and Milan, while in Germany and Switzerland the people went all out, tending somewhat toward the Native American, wearing turquoise jewellery, Indian moccasins—rolling their own cigarettes while upright feathers sat in their blond hair.

- Vaseline smeared over the face for sweat
- Breaking sugar glass with pistol grip before firing out window
- Barmen are fat and unshaven
- Beans and chicken are eaten, the latter with bare hands, the former with big spoons
- Mexican peons shot by firing squad

[cheap executions / blindfolds in virgin white, plumberry and coral]

34

From *Una carogna, un gringo e un bounty killer*

EXT. MAIN STREET – DAY
A blazing hot day. We hear the creaking of a signboard.

JUAREZ[1]

You pigs. You have seen how I enjoy your women. Or maybe see how they enjoy me. A little gift to take with you on your way to hell. Because you must understand, angel face, it is now time for you to die. You have laughed at my people because we are poor and filthy. But you are not laughing now, are you? That is because, at heart, you are all caitiffs. You do not know how to enjoy life or laugh at death. But in life, you know, sometimes you must die.

---

1. He painted his face with chalk and wine, then smeared it with plains dust character powder, to make it look dirty. He smudged a little ash powder under his eyes and put on a pair of false eyelashes and then auburn eye-liner—thus giving him a strange appearance, at once ghoulish and sincere. He put a giant straw hat on his head and climbed into a pair of grubby white trousers; became Juarez, the famous Mexican bandit, a man whose countenance was a curse.

117

FLETCHER
Damned coward! Damned lousy coward!

JUAREZ
(laughing)
No, amigo! A coward would shoot you between the eyes,
and get it over with quickly. (becoming suddenly savage)
But I am going to give you the slow death and, like the
brave man I am, not turn my eyes away from your suffering. (removing the knife from his belt) Have you ever
died slowly? No? Well, tomorrow I'll tell your widow
about it and me and her will smile together before we lay
down in your bed.

WIPE TO:

EXT. OPEN COUNTRY – BROAD DAYLIGHT
We see a group of buzzards flocking around something. A
Spanish guitar lets off a few romantic riffs.

LUPO
(disgustedly)
They died like dogs. . . . Even worse than dogs.

RAMÓN
(voice flat)
Don't complain, Lupo.

LUPO
. . . like dogs.

JUAREZ

Quiet, Lupo. There are only two men who have a right
to judge me in this world. One of them is dead, and the
other has yet to be born. If you are not nailed to a cross
you have no right to judge me. For what I do I do for our
people. For little Carlos and for Juanita. For the people
of Hermosillo and those of El Valle. Come. Let us go.
Tonight we will drink and wipe the taste of blood from
our mouths with mezcal.
(he laughs shortly)
Damned these gringos for making me spill their dirty
blood. Vamanos!

CUT TO:

EXT. DESERT AND HILLS – DAY
Juarez and his band are on horseback, galloping away.
Music plump with trumpet in foreground /
the bottom of a cat's ear
liberated in life
knots of hearts broken
conscious that the magical performance
is not real

35

During the filming of *50 carogne per una colt,* it was very hot, and at lunch he drank too much sangria. He wandered off into the desert, through a canyon, and then came to a stream. On the other side of the stream there was some sort of plant in blossom. He waded through in his boots, and pulled off some of the flowers, which were large and yellow, and ate them. After vomiting, he turned to make his way back to the set but was disorientated.

An old woman came up and asked if he was lost.

"Yes, mother," he replied. "I ate some yellow flowers and now I'm sick."

"Don't complain so much," she answered. "You're stupid to be eating anything you find out there like a cow. It is not making you any more simple if that is what you're hoping. I don't complain about good or evil, but if it's spring, you better not act like it's winter."

"Are you a witch?"

"Well, I know what you are. Go back to work and don't listen to music from empty holes."

- Worm's-eye view (preferably during a gunfight)
- Bird's-eye view, crane shot, as Django walks through an abandoned desert town

- Through a hole in a sombrero (in a bar)
- Canted shot of horse galloping by
- Rope shot (camera is tied to the end of a rope and made to swing back and forth)[1]
- Selective focus of pistolero with dead man in foreground
- Rack focus, first of cactus, then of rider in the distance
- Ped up from boots of gunfighter to his sweaty, agitated face
- Subjective angle from a man who has just been shot between the eyes; blood seeps over lens

[Almost religious. Like a painting by Caravaggio. Martinez (Clark) on his knees. In his right hand a Black Powder Single Action Colt .45. He holds it limply. His head is slightly thrown back. His face unshaven. Bronzed. Glowing with sweat. His hair is plastered over his forehead. Blood leaks from one side of his mouth. This seems a man crucified. Penitent. Behind him the dry desert landscape. Golden. Sky blue as a Mediterranean ocean. The West a mystical, Biblical place where sins are washed clean with bullets and prophets gallop along to the sound of Edda dell'Orso, because the religious significance of a dying pistolero is that of Moses kept from the promised land, that of Krishna when he told Arjuna that every man is born perfect, but must follow his nature's duty.]

---

1. Also called "hanged man's view."

36

"The women!"

Clark nodded his head.

Bob Antony said he thought he could fall in love with a Spanish woman. "It is like a country of nymphomaniacs. Luckily, on the film I'm doing, we don't usually start shooting until 11:00."

They were leaning against the counter of a bar on the Plaza del Carmen, drinking wine.

"I thought you had no faith in these westerns," Clark said.

"I don't. They're just here for a season, but I might as well take the roles offered to me and have a little fun at the same time. This girl last night called me *guapo*."

"That's Spanish."

"Sure it is. We're in Spain."

"Yes, I feel comfortable here," Clark said. "Sometimes I have little epiphanies, memories."

"Don't smoke too much dope."

Clark took a swallow of his wine. "Do you believe in reincarnation?"

"No. I'm a Christian."

"You can be a Christian and still believe in this."

"I still belong to the Big Creek Church of the Brethren. We believe in Christ's agony and death. I'm not without

122

sin but still hope for life eternal in a better place."

"Another glass?"

"Sure."

"*Más sangre*," he told the man behind the counter who poured the liquid out while Clark considered his own agony, the countless resurrections he had undergone and the joy he felt as the sounds of a troupe of drunken men outside shouting out their own sorrows and suffering reached his ears and then Bob Antony said something about Tina Treville and they stepped outside in a trickle of sentimentality and joined the revellers who shouted things that Antony did not understand but Clark well understood because in Spain the language was his, which made him feel somewhat closer to the setting and it was as if he were in some sort of vortex that connected him not only to old Mexico, to Texas or the deserts of Arizona, but also to some past life and so it could be said that the roles he was playing truly interested him, in the same way a revolution, a woman, a glass of liquor might, and just as he was beginning to forget the strange episode of Gina, of his divorce which had now been finalised with signed papers from the lawyer and a few curt telephone calls from the woman herself, he was becoming a true international star. People on the streets recognised him. The money he was receiving for his parts was increasing. For *I cadaveri si moltiplicano, le taglie aumentano* he composed and sang the title song[1] which was released as the B-side of a 45 single on

---

1. *Seré el primero que mata a un hombre,*
   El primero que pide un ataúd para el gringo
   Si algun día llego a ver su sombra.

   Yo no soy idiota qe se ríe
   O que carece de una bala para tí, gringo . . .
   Si llego a ver tu sombra.

Jolly records. He was interviewed by the magazine *Novella 2000* and was asked to speak at the Festival del Cinema di Salerno.

Two men are riding over the hill. The sun hitting them directly, sending their shadows, long and sprawling, behind them. They come across a man sitting by the side of the road, in the shade of a large rock. A lean face. He was smoking a cheroot and his half-closed eyes expressed something profound and immensely poignant which was at once mystifying and frightening just as are the depths of the night because they leave the world unseen to the observer.

He looked up as they approached.

They were riding by.

"Hey," he said.

They turned.

"What do you want?" one of the riders shouted.

No reply.

"You called me. What do you want?"

"He's crazy," the second man stated. "The sun's gone to his brain."

"Are you ready?"

The two men looked at each other. They laughed.

Yo soy un diablo con el cuchillo
Un hijo de puta con una pistola, para tí, gringo . . .
Si llego a ver tu sombra.

Para tí, gringo . . .
Si llego a ver tu sombra.
Para tí, gringo . . .
Si llego a ver tu sombra.
Para tí, gringo . . .
Si llego a ver tu sombra.

Tu vas a morir.

His gun was out of its holster, some oleaginous motion of great quickness; finger pulled back on the trigger
three times in rapid succession and the two men fell dead
from their horses; collapsed in the desert sun, their souls
jerked from their bodies, seeing down, blood oozing onto
the dry dirt some flash of eternity cut out of the sky.

Prego per te . . . ma prima ti uccido:[1] soundtrack switched
back and forth between fast-paced guitar riffs and deep,
solemn chanting, was offset by strikes of the Jew's harp,
and sets which abounded in candles and bowls of roses.
His lips were painted red and his face caked with orangish
make-up, giving him a surreal tan. Indeed this film could
be seen as the epitome of the Gothic western—with its
leather-clad villains, its liberal use of the whip, women tied
to stakes, faces which seemed to have crept out of some
painting by Goya or Delacroix. There were torture scenes
with leeches and horses, tails waving in the air, galloping
madly along vast tracts of wasteland[2]

weapon outside its holster

oily movement of the great rapidity

the finger threw in the trigger

blood that exudes on the dry dirt some diversity of frogs
and mice glutted with woe[3]

---

1. Produced by Tiegielle 33, this picture was distributed in the USA
by Ellman Film Enterprises under the title *The Revenge of Thomas Lawrence*. In Germany it was released under the title of *Thomas blutige Spur*
and distributed by Constantin Film.

2. Yet another western has ridden in hard from south of the Arno, re-
plete with a great deal of cigar smoking and an undeniable overindul-
gence in bloodshed. The formula is far from sure-fire, but Eric Clark
is adequately unlikable as the revenge-seeking Thomas Lawrence of
the title. —Jim Radler, *South Sun Daily*, March 9th, 1968

3. [...] Action served up with an even measure of clichés, the violent and
fast-shooting *Thomas blutige Spur* will be sure to appeal to the sadistic child
in all of us. [...] —Max Bauer, *Kölner Stadt-Anzeiger*, October 4th, 1968

37

In a sense, one could say that his westerns were his most successful efforts. Each one, in its own way, is a classic. He clearly felt most aligned to the parts he was playing. He was able to channel them with great authenticity. And these films became very popular in Europe, and even more so in Third World countries, in Guatemala and Columbia, Singapore and Ghana.

In South America he was better known than Stephen Boyd, and in Nigeria his film *50 carogne per una colt* grossed more than *Bullitt*. He was the hero of community organizers and revolutionaries, of banana pickers and coffee growers. His company was sought after. He was invited to the wedding of the dictator of San Corrados and asked to judge the National Beauty Contest in Laos.

"I have to concentrate on my work," he told Buonaventura over the telephone.

"But this is free publicity!"

"I'm not a product."

The agent did not answer. He wondered what Clark was if not a product.

The actor said that he did not mind playing Mexican bandits, but that did not mean he would do anything or make a fool of himself or fly around the world just to bring smiles to the faces of a few rich men and women in low-cut dresses.

"A Mexican bandit is a product," Buonaventura said stubbornly. "It's like a bunch of grapes that needs to be picked in its season."

"In my past life I was Tiburcio Vasquez," Clark replied. "This sort of role is easy for me. I just have to be myself. Or not so much myself, but what I once was, because, you see, every moment we are reborn and we live on memories of our dead selves."

And yet this was much more than an affectation and those who were close to him said that he genuinely believed it and would often (most especially when drunk) take on the role of the bandit, even in public, occasionally getting into brawls which were not bloody and one time finding himself arrested and then the next day shyly mumbling out an apology to witnesses, because he was someone who really did not care to let others see his true self, whatever that was, whether it was indeed the reincarnation of that bandit or something far different—as often those who are the loudest over a drink are the quietest afterward and everyone in the end is made up of several seemingly opposing qualities, so it is that violent criminals are often extremely romantic and some great intellectuals, great pacifists are known to have beaten their wives.

Clark put down the telephone. He was staying at the Gran Hotel, as was the rest of the cast of *40 pistole per Jiminez*. Across the plaza, at the Hotel Torreluz, the cast of *Un collo, una corda, un cavallo*, the film Bob Antony was working on, was staying.

He went downstairs, left his key at the desk and went to the bar next door. Some tables were planted outside, under umbrellas which were in turn under the sky which was dominated by a giant shining thing that looked like a starfish, and at one of them Helga Sterne[1] was sitting by herself. A drink full of ice sat in front of her. Drops of sweat shone on her neck like diamonds. Her panting lips wrapped themselves around the rim of the glass and sucked in liquid.

Clark waved and sat down by himself at another table. He was not in the mood to talk. When the waiter came, he ordered a bottle of cava.

"It's hot," he said.

"Yes, lovely weather."

"For a lizard."

"Anything to eat?"

"What do you have?"

"Octopus."

"Fresh?"

"The freshest."

"Bring it."

The actor opened the paper and began reading about how El Cordobes was derided by Miguelin for fighting a rather tame, rather small bull who went by the name of Ventilador and then about the exiled exploits of Argentinian dictator Marcos Perez Jimenez in Madrid and supreme court prosecutor Fernando Herrero Tejedor's battle against abortion and 'other forms of vice' and a

---

1. Jet-set Swiss actress of great beauty. Renowned for her prominent role in the West German sex-film boom of the late 60's, she also starred in a number of Italian films, including *Sei moschettieri contro Lady Chatterly* and the amusing *La gabbia senza uccelli*. Aside from *40 pistole per Jimenez*, she co-starred with Clark in *Farfalla, farfalla, fiore, fiore, ali sanguinose e profumo di morte* and *Overdose*, in the former as a murder victim, in the latter as a heroin addict.

man who mistook his wife for a stranger and proposed love to her on a street corner in Toledo and then someone who was arrested and fined ten thousand pesetas for having spent the night in a broom closet at a fashionable restaurant in Seville.

"Excuse me."

Clark raised his head, immediately recognised the person standing over him. It was Sal Mineo.

He stood up and offered his hand.

"Hello. I'm Eric Clark."

"Where have we met?"

"We were both turned down for parts in *Lawrence of Arabia*, I think."

"An actor, yeah. We've talked before?"

"No, but I have a deep admiration for you."

Mineo smiled and sat down. The waiter brought another glass and Clark poured him some cava.

"I'm shooting something up near Madrid. Strictly for the bread. Needed to get away for the weekend, to see some water. I was just walking by. It looks like there are a lot of entertainers around. I don't know what's going on."

Mineo was staring at him intently and was just beginning to say something more when Bob Antony walked up.

"Is this guy bothering you?" he asked Clark.

"It's Sal Mineo."

"I know who it is." And then turning toward the other actor: "I think you better get going. My friend doesn't fly that way."

"What way?"

"My friend doesn't kiss other guys."

"Bob," Clark began, "leave him alone."

Bob Antony would not listen. It was clear that he had been drinking. He stood erect with his legs wide apart and arms crossed, glaring at Clark's guest.

"There's a bar down the street for kids like you," he told Mineo. "Now beat it."

Mineo turned toward Clark: "We'll be finishing up shooting in Rome, at Cinecittà. I guess we can't talk now. But I see something. I need to speak to you."

"I'm on the Piazza Farnese. Number 12."

"Beat it," Bob Antony growled.

Mineo got up, walked off, giving Clark a sad look over his shoulder as he went and Bob Antony pushed himself down in the abandoned chair, served himself some octopus, drank from Mineo's half-empty glass.

"Look," he said, "if you want to make a friend, take Helga over there. She's so hot she needs ice to cool her down."

Clark looked over. The waiter had just brought her a bucket of ice. She took a piece, rubbed it over her forehead, lay a few chunks between her breasts, filled her mouth.

———

The next day they began shooting at around 10 a.m. The sun had already pushed itself up above the hills, and was boldly sticking forward its chest and spitting out flames. Smoke seemed to rise from the desert and six extras who had been imported from Saceda del Rio (cousins and friends of production supervisor Julio Fajardo) to play banditi each demanded a hundred pesetas additional to brave the weather.

"But it's a magnificent day!" the director said.

"For devils and scorpions."

Helga Sterne complained when they put the black wig on her head.

"It's too hot for this thing."

"You're playing a Mexican woman. The wig stays."

"But I'm boiling. Bring me some ice."

A young Italian by the name of Gino Vivarelli was sent back to the town and about an hour later appeared in a Eucort Sedan completely filled with blocks of ice which he had purchased from Cubi Tropical José Antonio y Antonio Ruiz José on the Calle Mango.

A sort of igloo was quickly constructed and Sterne climbed into this while waiting for her scene, rubbing her back, thighs and face against it and sticking her feet in a pile of crushed ice. The rest of the cast looked on with amazement, possibly envy, as sweat streamed down their faces and filled their boots.

About an hour later the director called to her.

"I can't move," she said.

"What do you mean you can't move?"

"My feet. I can't feel them."

A couple of men helped her up. Her feet and legs were in fact a deep shade of blue. She was shivering wildly and her lips were white.

A half an hour later an ambulance appeared and, after she was put in the back on a stretcher, the vehicle drove off rather more slowly than might be expected.

"What was the diagnosis?" Clark asked.

"The doctor said that she has hypothermia," the director replied, wiping the sweat off his face with a handkerchief.

38

An earthquake in Sicily. 231 dead. 262 injured. The Red Army Faction bombs two department stores in Frankfurt-am-Main. Nine days later, in Berlin, a man shoots student leader Rudi Dutschke in the head, but fails to kill him. Picking an abandoned foetus out of the trash in Naples, scavenger Ugo Plauto lets out a rude jest. Workers strike in Paris as Italy wins the European Championship. Pope Paul VI, speaking out loudly against birth control, watches nonplussed as France detonates its first hydrogen bomb. Italy's Internazionale is beaten by Scotland's Celtic, in the European Cup Final. Mina sings 'Quelli che hanno un cuore on Canzonissima.' In Avola, police fire on striking workers. 2 dead. 5 wounded. British racing driver Graham Hill wins the Monaco Grand Prix. 200,000 Warsaw Pact troops along with 5,000 tanks invade Czechoslovakia. Wenche Myhre sings 'Ein Hoch Der Liebe' and Fausto Cigliano releases 'L'ultimo addio.'

He remembered what he had heard; having received no shortage of praise, looked at himself in the mirror as one might look at a beautiful woman, a rare tapestry, a blue lake. When he passed by theatres displaying posters with his own image, he smiled, glad that people were in there, watching him on screen and was like the moon which probably feels a certain amount of self-satisfaction as its face is reflected in various ponds and pails of water and when someone praised him to his face, which was often enough, he bowed his head with modesty—a false modesty, because he truly did believe that he was better than others, not in a fundamental way, but rather as an artist, and when he saw other actors fumble through their parts without talent or inspiration, he looked on, his face without any expression whatsoever, but thinking that for all the trash he might touch, he at least was not trash, never would be since he had in himself the spirit of Dean, given to him one night in 1955: justly, an inheritance from the other world and then later there were times when a certain amount of fear came into play or maybe even paranoia, the label being in a sense a way to deny the magical reality of certain nightmares.

One evening he answered his door. It was Sal Mineo.

"How are you?"

"Good. The filming is over. Now I'm out of work again."

"It should be easy for you."

"They used to offer me a lot of parts. Now it's hard."

"Do you want to come in?"

"No, I need to walk, man."

They walked to the Piazza Navona and then in the direction of the Pantheon.

"I think I know who you are," Mineo said.

"I'm not who you think I am. It's hard to explain . . ."

"Well, try to. I can feel something. I'm not going crazy, am I? Where's Jimmy?"

Clark felt embarrassed. He put his hand against one of the stone pillars.

"I only have a little piece. It's probably not even the important part. It's hard to use it. Like having a rifle and too many things to shoot at. They say that God's name should never be spoken and that's how I feel about it. You know, I'm probably too small to hold it."

"If you've got it, you've got it for a reason," Mineo said.

39

Toward the end of the year he had a sudden urge to return home. He could not hear a polka without his eyes filling with tears and could not see a photo of a caiman without feeling a deep spiritual hole.

He wanted to see his father, to see again the place he had been born, which still came to him in his dreams—something fascinating, enticing, awful, like a womb or graveyard he had come out of, some primordial place where the ghosts of his ancestors dwelled alongside the ghost of his childhood, which seemed to be there staring at him from out of the past.

When he got off the plane in Asunción he was amazed at the sorry state of the airport. What had seemed large now seemed small. What had appeared splendid now seemed ragged.

Lazy-looking people wandered about and a staticky voice said something over the intercom.

His father was old and welcomed him sadly. The actor hardly recognised this man whose withered face was lost behind a giant white moustache. The two embraced emotionally. He felt the other's moustache brush against his cheek. Señor del Torres said something, but Clark either did not hear or did not understand, because, instead of

135

replying, he just looked blankly ahead of him as if he were looking at who he expected his father to be, the sturdy figure of his memories, rather than who he really was.

"I have prepared your room for you," the old man said.

"But I took a room at the Hotel Royal Standard."

His father looked surprised. "Ah, I see. Yes, you need to be comfortable," he murmured distractedly, avoiding his son's eyes and obviously feeling more than discomfort at meeting this man, this son who was almost a stranger, but also shame to be both poor and old, a seemingly un-forgivable combination.

The day after his arrival he visited his father's shop, on either side of which huge buildings had risen up—pushing against it, seeming ready to crush it between them.

The town had become a city. Big structures competed with noisy traffic. He looked over his father's dusty stock. The man probably had not sold anything in years and it seemed he spent most of his time repairing television sets. Clark had never sent him money. In his mind he had always thought of his father as relatively well off, his childhood memories distorting the truth of the situation.

He mentioned something about him having lots of money if any was needed.

"Money?" Señor del Torres said in an offended voice. "Why should I need money? I own the biggest radio shop in Paraguay!"

"But it's not like I'm a stranger."

"No, no . . ." the old man said uncertainly.

But the truth was that Clark, in an environment where he should have fit in perfectly, in the place he had actually been born, was out of place. When he was introduced to people they fell silent. They were distrustful and did not know whether to treat him as a foreigner or a local. They did not know what they could offer or what they could gain. The sun seemed to look on him with regret and even dogs would not sniff at his shoes.

Stroessner was in power and the river port was full of smuggled goods—boats being launched daily stuffed with cocaine and chalkboards, while others would arrive from the distant Atlantic, loaded with luxury cars, cases of expensive brandy, ivory-handled whips and unimportant paintings by Old Masters. The country was not what it had been but was the result of what it had been—another Latin American nation exploited to the best of the ability of a few individuals who were not necessarily uninspired but who put far more store in surrounding themselves with gilded furnishings and stocking their wine cellars to bursting than providing for the inhabitants, for the Indians who still sat on their haunches outside of rural dwellings that did not have running water and had only sporadic electricity.

The Spanish the people spoke seemed rude to him. He saw something archaic in their expressions and the way they held their heads. Hearing the Indians speak Guarani made him remorseful, because even his ancestors had drifted in from elsewhere and he thought he could hear the distant sounds of suffering that had ushered in his birth.

Stepping out of his hotel, someone in a passing car shouted at him:

"Rich man, go back where you came from!"

Clark smiled inwardly at the irony of the remark. The truth was, he was no longer sure where he came from, where his home was, though he felt quite certain that it was not there, was not in Paraguay.

"In Italy they call me an American. In America they think I'm Italian. Here, in the place where I was born, they call me a stranger."

He felt bored and out of place. He had planned to stay there for a month, but after a few days he changed his ticket. Whatever it was that he had expected to find he had not found and felt the need to once again take on the part of another, throw himself into the mosaic of film.

His ticket and passport lay on the table—in a sense symbols of defeat, symbols not only of a man without a country (his passport was American, his ticket was to Rome, Italy), but of a man without a resting place, whose human relationships seemed both unfulfilling and unfulfilled; parting company with a sense of relief and regret; finding it difficult to reconcile squalid reality with his own uncertain mythology.

Clark was folding his underwear and putting them in his suitcase. There was a knock at the door. Opening it, he saw a man in an untended white suit standing before him, a limp moustache sleeping beneath his prominent nose. His head was without hair. He was holding a hat in his hand and smelled of caña.

"¿Yes?"

"¿Is that you, José?"

"¿Who are you?"

"You wouldn't remember me. You used to play in front of my shop. It was a long time ago and I suppose we both look different."

"Yes, I have changed."

"But you do have her eyes," the man said, looking sadly at the other.

"¿What do you want with me?"

"I am Señor Ramon Ocampos, cobbler by profession."

"The shoemaker!"

"¿May I come in?"

[from this point forward, *los signos de interogación inicial* (¿) have been removed by Lisa Schuman, assistant to the editor]

Clark stood aside. The man entered the room and sat down on the edge of a chair, resting his hat on his knee.

"Your mother and I enjoyed many happy moments together."

The actor shrugged his shoulders.

"Anita was a very special woman," Ocampos continued in a voice inflected by emotion. "A woman who made birds sing and flowers bloom. Her breasts were fountains of light. She was very sophisticated but knew how to hold her tongue. Sometimes I would come home intoxicated. But she never scolded me. She loved animals and children. I remember one day when she took a cat in off the street and gave it coffee and cream."

"Where is she?"

"God alone knows. Like all men I have my faults. I was too jealous. Did I have reason to be? Could I tell the difference between my nightmares and reality? I don't blame her. I did not treat her as well as she deserved. But I have received my just punishment. Loneliness. There is nothing worse than loneliness, which is strongest on the afternoon of a hot day. She was like bread. The only woman I ever loved. It is unfortunate that men can never appreciate the good things at their table."

"She never wrote to me."

"She wrote to you."

"No, you are wrong about that."

Ocampos silently removed a packet of six or seven

letters from his jacket pocket and handed them to Clark—envelopes which smelled of time, lost hours, decayed dreams.

"These are the letters I intercepted. I was jealous and did not want you to share in her love. I did wrong but am paying for it. No woman has voluntarily put her lips to mine for many years. I am like a virgin."

Clark took them and clenched his teeth.

"But where is she now?"

The older man looked down at his feet. Maybe he knew or had suspicions or maybe he did not know, it was difficult to say.

"Did you come here for money? Is that why you're here?"

Ocampos rose to his feet.

"Do not insult me. That you put pecuniary motives to such a difficult visit . . ."

"How much?"

"Three hundred guaraníes would keep me going for a month," he said proudly.

A wallet was taken out with a slightly shaking hand and the hat and the smell of caña disappeared and then Clark was taking a taxi—to the airport; out of the city and past dwellings without fences in front of which children without pants played and thin chickens pecked at the earth as he, the actor, absorbed the words his mother had written twenty-five years earlier, not to him, but to a child who he seemed to have very little in common with—one who looked to the future instead of running from the past and who existed only as a phantom and could not be comforted by the neat and vaguely romantic script that loped across the pages and made their reader nervous, made him feel more estranged.

40

actor = a double

noise = music

film = battle

Back in Rome, Clark saw Bob Antony.

"But didn't you say the Euro-western was just a passing fad?"

"Sure man, but I have re-evaluated the situation. There's still a lot of money to be made. This thing isn't over yet. Instead of everyone running off to Spain, they can come to my studio in Cervinara, just south of here."

"Just south?"

"Well, about sixty kilometres south."

"You've already bought property there then?"

"That's right. I'm going to build the thing. An entire western town, with a saloon, bank, barbershop, everything."

"It sounds interesting," Clark said in a flat voice.

But Antony's dream was somewhat more complicated than he made it sound.

The paperwork was a nightmare. Every day saw him trotting off to City Hall, to fill in another form—some obscure document with uncertain origins and less certain purpose. He dined with the mayor, had coffee with the various members of the city council, had sweets sent to them, deposited bouquets of flowers and bottles of wine

141

at their doorsteps, flirted with their ugly daughters and encouraged their shy sons to do jumping jacks. Hundred-thousand *lire* notes had to be slipped to one sub-official after another—usually folded in copies of the *Corriere della Sera* or stuck in packs of Alfa cigarettes.

"Hey, Mr. Bob," the mayor said to him. "My nephew."

"Your nephew?"

"Yes, maybe he's good."

"Good?"

"Films. My sister—his mother—thinks . . ."

"I see."

"He's not bad looking. On the contrary, he is a very pretty boy. And all your paperwork is in order. I just need to affix my signature and everything is clear. So . . ."

"A small part."

"Small like how? A blackberry or a pineapple?"

"Not a pineapple, but maybe a pear."

"William or Abate Fétel?"

"Fétel, of course."

When finally his building permit was put in his hands, he celebrated by opening twenty-five bottles of prosecco, their corks going off like gunfire and making the petty criminals congregating at the Bar Cherokee panic. He took a shovel and dug. He scattered the earth with sand and planted a few dried-up trees along the main street. He built a water trough, a hitching post, sawed boards and dug holes. He laid fencing and shingled roofs.

When Clark came to look, he showed him around proudly.[1]

"I hope to see a lot of you on the set," he said.

"Who's that over there?" Clark asked, changing the subject.

---

1. Old Shakyamuni Buddha looked at this, regarding the world as void, whereupon J.D. bowed, expressing his approval.

"That's Fabio Gallo, the mayor's nephew. I'm having him dig a well."

"Yes, you might need water. Things are drying up."

So, just as the sun was setting on the western boom, just as the last rays were disappearing behind the Capitoline Hill, Remington Studio opened. Tired, one-legged scripts came hobbling in, found a home there, as did nervous cameramen and a few hungry and talentless dreamers whose only asset was their biceps. The films that were made there consisted of little dialogue, of men galloping around the neighbouring fields to the sound of trumpet and romantic guitar, or riding through sandpits in which truck tracks were clearly discernible. Bypassing Milan and Rome, these were the films that went directly to rural theatres, where they were double-billed with Spanish police flicks and low-budget documentaries and later were sold to distributors in South America and Africa for incredibly small sums.

The most suspect producers came to him, money launderers who wanted to make a film for ten thousand dollars and claim they had spent half a million—production companies that came one day and were gone the next. It became the last stop for has-beens and the first stop for those who never would have a career. Actors like the mysterious Lincoln Tate[1] and the enigmatic Jerry Redwoods[2] took their stands. Westerns whose fabulous titles were belied by their horrible production qualities, films that consisted of barroom brawls, bad dialogue, and horses dancing from one end of town to the other.

---

1. Starred in a little-known western by the name of *Tornado ha sparito, solo remane la puzza del polvere*, produced by Dinamica and unreleased in Italy. It was not released until 1984, when it was put out on Beta video in Finland.
2. Starred in two films for Titan, *Cento cadaveri per il malloppo* and . . . *E le moglie anno diventato vedove*.

41

Some of them are square, some triangular, shaped like pyramids, with large eyes and bellies which search for the ground.

Actors are often round, but sometimes appear as rectangles or cylinders, and these have the ability to imitate poles, transform themselves into pipes, play the part of tree trunks or joists.

In many shapes they come and their voices are the colour of marmalade, old boxes and young skylines and, it seems, they draw their inspiration from insects and snails, from tired birds and dazed walruses, now waving their hands to the right, now flopping forward and mumbling words that collapse into the void like bachelors at past midnight onto their cold pallets.

So, they are sometimes square.

"The difficulty is not to start acting, but to keep acting."

"Acting?" Clark asked, looking Buonaventura directly in the eyes.

The agent averted his gaze. "Acting, working. It is difficult to always be coming up with new contracts for my clients. They keep asking for you at Remington Studio but you always say no."

"I'm not quite ready to end my career."

"I thought Bob Antony was a friend of yours. It should be part of your system to always oblige friends."

"What exactly do you have in mind?"

"A little piece. . . . A week of your time."

Clark was thoughtful for a moment. Then, "No," he said, "I won't do it."

"But it isn't part of your system to be turning down roles."

"If I make another western, it will either be to make people laugh or to make them cry. Either a comedy or *La Vida di Tiburcio Vasquez.*"

42

Clark, like a smart investor, had got out before the crash.

The market had become glutted with spaghetti westerns, paella westerns, crêpe westerns and schnitzel westerns. Always looking for a fast profit, production companies like Titanus and Hispamer deluged the theatres with cheap horse operas, while other production companies from France, Germany, Israel and Turkey[1] threw their hands forward, grabbed with their fingers and scraped with their nails, happy to get a piece of the carcass. In the large cities, in Rome, Torino and Milan, it had become difficult to find theatres to screen many of these and it was only in the deep south, in Calabria and Sicily, that a real market remained—apprentice assassins and muleteers still adequately fascinated by men without names whose law was vengeance and who made love to women with few lines. By 1970 the western craze had fallen into complete decay. The country western bars in Rome had been converted

---

1. Some of the Turkish westerns of the period include *Red Kit* (1970), *Vahsetin eserleri* (1971) and the extremely popular *Kucuk kovboy*, starring Ilker Inanoglu, for which Erler Film had managed to secure the direction of the great Guido Zurli. Another interesting film was *Atini seven kovboy*, which made use of dwarves and bootlegged the music from Edoardo Vianello's *La Tremarella*.

146

into pizzerias. The landfills outside of Napoli were full of cowboy boots and tattered Stetsons. In Northern Italy, a group of school teachers who called themselves the LCP (Lega della Casa Pulita) publicly burnt American western novels, the posters (symbolically) of Italo-western films and toy six-shooters.

"This violence is corrupting our children," they complained.

Very few serious westerns were made and those that were made were generally of a very low standard. Instead the western comedy had taken over, had by the hundreds galloped into town sitting backward in the saddle, driving out their more serious counterparts with honks and whistles, with jabbing punchlines and sight gags that seemed to have been extracted from the silent era.

For the most part these films were neither funny nor inspired. Yet, be that as it may, there was money to be made. It was easy to make an Italian audience laugh. Terrence Hill and Bud Spencer had become almost rich with their Trinity films. George Hilton had appeared as Alleluja and Tresette and the incredibly bland Luc Merenda as Cosi Sia. Italians, addicted to low comedy, filled the theatres and chuckled in unison as jokes which had been dredged up from the cloaca of Rome were trotted before them, the toga replaced with chaps and spurs, Philematium replaced by a barroom whore and the commander of a Theban army transposed to McPherson the lame-brained cattle rancher.

It was classic theatre.

In this category, however, the films of Clark truly did stand out. He jumped into these comic roles with astounding ease and his three western comedies were each one more bizarre than the next.

In his two Malcóncio films, he played a character with great similarities to Harold Lloyd—an accident-prone gunslinger who wears a tiger-skin poncho and rides a mule. The films were completely gag-driven, and Clark is said to have written much of the material himself. In *Maledizione Malcóncio, sei proprio un figlio di . . .*, we see him chasing Nazi cowboys around a cemetery to the sound of Piero Umiliani's *Mah-Nà Mah-Nà* / fights a duel in a closet / wideshots so we see his entire body at work / ho ho tobacco-scented air expulsion.

Though the first film was most certainly funny, the second, *E' una lunga strada fino a Tombstone Malcóncio, rilassati*, was a work of genius. The first film had been directed by Catullo Gualdo,[1] whose talents were rather limited. The second was directed by Luigi del Marco,[2] who seemed to be drawing his inspiration from some unknown well—a place populated by hallucinations, by underwater hot-air balloons and flowers which grew from the sky. Comedy requires music and the soundtrack, full of sirens, church bells, gongs and cat meows, added much to the humour,

---

1. Under the pseudonym of Jules Ascot he made a few westerns in the late 60's, most notably *Quel inferno di Texas*. Later, as Bob Snyder, his work became almost completely confined to low-budget comedies, such as *Papà, papà, papagallo*, which had a small success in the second tier theatres of Puglia and Basilicata, and *Bigamania*, which was intended as a vehicle for Lando Buzzanca, but ended up starring Marco Nizzica after the former backed out on political grounds.

2. After working as second unit director on a number of films, del Marco made his directorial debut with *Mondo Danese*, an extremely trashy documentary about the Danish nightlife. He was an expert with special effects and was able to perform miracles with micro budgets— using plastic and glass, small models and camera tricks to create very impressive results.

the theme song itself being a mixture of fuzz guitar interspersed with classical, with Mozart, Beethoven, and snatches of opera.

Luigi del Marco truly had a flare for the dreamlike. A number of scenes were put in fast motion. The sets were inhabited by giant plastic cactuses, psychedelic sunsets, silhouettes of mesas and representational western images. One of the outlaws rode a llama while another wore an absurdly stylish fur coat. The humour made heavy use of polysemy and oil + gurgle + prancing out of town .45 like windmill around finger / those small, ridiculous things.

By not being great, great things are accomplished.

In the third and last of his western comedies, *Un indiano a Dayton City*, he played Sabu, an Indian fakir who finds himself in the Wild West where he is trying to recover a jewel-encrused lingam that has been stolen by outlaws from the Prince of Bengal's train carriage. In one scene he undergoes a Cherokee initiation (à la *A Man Called Horse*), but unsatisfied with the level of pain demands more. The Indians, impressed, make him head of their tribe. He carries a pistol in his turban and cleans his teeth with a bayonet. For once Clark dubbed his own voice, with great comedic skill.

"The reason the film is funny is because you are taking someone and putting them in a different environment," Clark said. "If you take someone from Iceland and you put them in the middle of the desert, that's funny. That's why it is funny to watch a rich man drink bad wine or see a peasant confronted by caviar. He won't like it. He would not even put it on his sandwich. He understands that just because something is expensive does not mean it is good. But people will still laugh at his stupidity."

Though these films were unquestionably among the most humorous of the western comedies, they never brought in the kind of box-office returns that they should have. Too many of the jokes were based on wordplay in Italian, and were untranslatable. The humour, also, particularly in *E' una lunga strada fino a Tombstone Malcóncio, rilassati,* had a certain surreal sophistication to it that American and UK distributors shied away from. *Un indiano a Dayton City,* which had been extremely well received in the theatres south of Rome, could only find distribution in Spain, Turkey and Greece, though in the latter country it outgrossed Theodoros Angelopoulos' *O thiasos* 44 to 1, to the disgust of the intellectual circles of Athens and Salonica, who were unable to lay down their own bad taste, mistaking boredom for depth and austerity for spirituality.

43

In 1933 the fascist government had issued a decree that all foreign films were to be dubbed into Italian. French and English would not be tolerated. The language of Machiavelli and Dante, the most beautiful language on earth, had to be preserved.

"Everywhere I go I hear the lyrics to 'Let's Fall in Love,'"[1] party secretary Achille Starace complained. "Enough is enough!"

Original-language Laurel and Hardy films were burned in public, and new reels, dubbed by Alberto Sordi and Mauro Zambuto, released.

The people became habituated to hearing the stars of foreign cinema speak Italian. The actor's real voice became of no importance. Everyone would be dubbed into Italian anyhow. German, French and American actors were thrown together. Oftentimes, particularly in the lower-budget affairs, the actors were not even given the script, but just stage directions. That lip synchronization was usually completely nonexistent mattered not. The audience was used to it and were happy, and happiness should never be underrated as neither should a proper night's rest, the quality of milk, or the intelligence of a child.

---

1. Harold Arlen.

151

The doppiatori, the voice actors, became an integral part of Italian cinema and these professionals were often as esteemed as the actors themselves.

Men like Guarliero de Angelis and Paolo Stoppa made their mark in the Roman School, the former dubbing the voices of Cary Grant and Errol Flynn—lending those stars robust and virile voices that made women swoon and men nod their heads in admiration,—the latter taking on the difficult voice of Fred Astaire. Famous patriarchs of the Milanese school were Mario Besesti, whose genius was hailed for the voice he gave to Sydney Greenstreet, and Gaetano Verna, known for the stallion-like cadences he lent to Lee J. Cob and Alan Hale. Some famous women doppiatore were Lola Braccini, famous for her work on Mae West films, and Rosetta Calavetta, who was able to make Kim Novak more popular in Italy than anywhere else in the world.

———

Over the course of his career, Eric Clark used at least half a dozen different doppiatori, but did most of his films with two:

Bruno Bellini, who had begun his career doing radio-drama but moved on to dubbing in the early 1960's, had great rhythmic and labial skill. He had an extensive range and was able to dub ages 12-95. A specialist in dubbing old men and drunks in western films, he lent these parts much-appreciated comic hints, and was known as one of the best stunt-double voice actors, successfully providing the voice for Mario Salvia[1] when the latter lost his voice during the dubbing process of *Beneath the Planet of the Apes* (Brent) as well as for Ricardo de Vangelis when the latter

---

1. Known as the Hercules of voice actors.

was shot in the chest four hours before dubbing was to begin for *The Heartbreak Kid* (Lenny Cantrow). He was able to dub in 68 foreign accents, and was considered the finest in the business at Japanese and Chinese characters. He excelled in histrionic voices and cartoon characters and made several spoofs of popular songs, admirably imitating the voices of the original singers.

The second was Cesare Romolo. Known as the "prince of voice actors," he was an integral part of the C.D.C. (Cooperativa Doppiatori Cinematografici). He began his career after winning a Concorso di doppiaggio bandito put on by Rex studios. Though he was initially confined to dubbing the voices of children and cab drivers, he soon graduated to more serious roles, providing breakthrough performances for Sidney Poitier in *The Defiant Ones* and Ernest Borgnine in *Torpedo Run*. He was known to be able to say "I love you" in 190 different ways. Even when he got on in years, his voice was so fresh and supple that people said he had made a pact with the devil.

The northern Milanese school and the Roman school were constantly at war. The former derided the abilities of the latter.

"In the south they only know how to farm. They have no idea what dubbing is about."

"The only thing they are able to dub in the north is the voice of Germans. They themselves barely speak Italian, so it is no wonder."

The crowning achievement of Romolo's career was when he won the Concorso italiano internazionale doppiatoristico.

Romolo represented the Roman school, Pisu the northern.

Known for the doughy and baritonal quality of his voice, Emilio Pisu was one of the foremost members of the Milanese school, and head of the famous Gruppo Venti Italian dubbing society. He had a reputation of being able to do the impossible when it came to synchronization.

The competition was held in neutral territory, at the University of Bologna. A large crowd had gathered. The judges were all from Sardinia and the Isle of Malta, and considered impartial. Pisu was known for his discipline. He would stand still as a statue, putting all his expression into his voice. Romolo however was a strong believer in hand gestures, in physically expressing the part he was dubbing. Pisu began by delivering some lines of Diane Brewster from *Quantrill's Raiders*. Romolo matched this by doing Ann Doran from *Joy Ride*. There was applause.

They then went on to more difficult things. Middle-Eastern contacts and teenagers at the beach. They imitated violinists and dance instructors, police informants and over-fed bandits, one-armed sailors and Egyptian caravan drivers.

"I will now provide the voice for a Man in the Back Seat of a Car," Romolo said.

Pisu was unimpressed. He proceeded to give the voice for a Tahitian dancer.

After over four hours both men seemed exhausted. They took a ten-minute break and refreshed themselves at the bar.

The end came when Romolo imitated a Chinese monkey begging a woman for peanuts. Pisu was unable to match this and his attempts were met with derision from the crowd.

44

- Bland face
- Roving close-ups
- Choreographed walk
- Detonation of cerebral corks

He was like a man who, looking into a pool of water, sees his own reflection and falls in love. Rain comes and the water clouds, making the reflection disappear and water and tears run down his face because the loved one seems to have run away and then when the rain stops, and the wrinkles leave the surface of the pool, he can see the reflection again, now crying, and so he dives into the pool to kiss it, to comfort it. But maybe he drowns. Or maybe he splashes around or maybe he goes to some other world.

"You think too much of yourself," Bob Antony told him one day.

"So, is it better to be dishonest with oneself?"

"Possibly."

"You must really believe in Christian virtues then. Because that is what they have been telling us for the last two thousand years while taking away our rights and enslaving us. Telling us that we have to be honest and humble and make sure not to look at the stars. The powerful always profit off the weak, but sometimes it is impossible not to speak the truth."

"Eric, we always get along until you start talking like a socialist."

"I'm not a socialist. My ideas are my own."

"Well, if I were you I wouldn't talk too loud about them. You're really a bastard. In the USA you'd be thrown in prison."

"That is undoubtedly why I live in Italy. The coffee is dense, but at least the people aren't."

Leaving Bob Antony's flat, Clark headed in the direction of the Colosseum, along the Via dei Serpenti. He turned right on the Via Leonina. A woman asked him for a cigarette and he shook his head. He turned right again, up a small alley, climbed steps, entered a modest bar without any clients present.

The barman pointed toward the back.

Clark opened a door.

Eight or nine men, some with beards, some without, were sitting around, some on chairs, some on the floor. Smoke. The smell of long walks under the sun.

"If we did it at night."

"Too much security."

"Risk everything."

"Nothing."

"Nihilism."

"Too many words."

"We've been robbed of everything else. They are the only thing that keep us human. We can do it at dawn when their eyes are half closed. The robbers. If we can just stay isolated a little bit longer. We have to forget about commands, obedience, order, hierarchy, aptitude. Our aim is restitution. Enough with everything else. Patience is running out. The bandits wear the badges. Things can't be any clearer."

"When?"

"A joint decision."

"Get him to make some sandwiches."

"Onions?"

"Naturally."

He met with communists, anarchists, discussed revolution, assassinating the prime minister, sending arms to the rebels in Haiti. Opening up shops where everything was given away and not sold. Soup kitches. Kidnapping the wives of powerful businessmen. He truly believed that capitalism was an evil.

"If a man is denied the ability to earn bread by honest means, he must be given the means to take it by force," he said.

The political significance of the characters he had played in his westerns was very real. In Suriname, the famous Revolutionary Armed Forces group seemed to have based their entire campaign on the script of *40 pistole per Jiminez*. In Cuba, Jamaica and Nicaragua, Clark was more popular than Paul Newman or Telly Savalas. Fidel Castro was reportedly a great fan of the film *Zamora*, a film which was actually banned in Bolivia under the dictatorship of René Barrientos.

One of his favourite conversational topics was the emancipation of the working class—a subject which he was not alone in the willingness to discuss, as the Italian movie industry had a vibrant left wing. When, in 1969, the Piazza Fontana bombing occurred, a number of his acquaintances, including actor Nino de Rita, were rounded up by the police.

"See what your anarchist buddies have done now," Bob Antony told him.

"It wasn't anarchists that did this," Clark said. "Violence is a revolutionary instrument, but anarchists never aim to kill ordinary citizens, since the movement is about promoting their welfare. This was the work of the Ordine Nuovo, of the neo-fascists. A typical false-flag tactic."[1]

Be that as it may, the reputation of anarchists and communists suffered. The public was filled with a spirit of rage against the left. Stones were thrown through the Socialist Party office in Rome. In Milan a young anarchist, Micki Bertoli, was beaten near the point of death. A number of producers refused to work with Clark. Certain right-wing controlled distribution channels were cut off. European movie-goers were becoming somewhat less sympathetic with those revolutionary roles he played and journalists, instead of aiming their fire at a government corrupt at almost every level, turned instead against writers, poets and actors.

In 1972, *La polizia fa schifo*[2] came out, in which he played the corrupt police commissario Angelo Malacarne, a man who, while railing against communists and criminals, was himself the embodiment of corruption, planting false evidence in order to have communists arrested, ignoring the

---

1. See U.S. Army Field Manual 30-31B.

2. [...] Made with great ability by director Enrico Fabbri, this picture manages to combine suspenseful adventure with a polemic about capitalism and the lack of opportunity in today's society. Eric Clark shines in the role of Commissario Malacarne, which he is able to load with many socio-psychological implications. Those without delicate sensibilities might be advised to bring a pillow, but thinking movie-goers will be wide-awake. [...] —Carlo Schaifferi, *Umanità Nuova*, March 12th, 1972

crimes of the rich, having protesters beaten and spitting on long-haired young men.

The film was produced and financed by Claudio Volta, a young anarchist, son of a rich industrialist, a man rebelling against his father and fatherland. The cast and crew were made up entirely of left-wingers who were disillusioned with Cinecittà, idealists who wanted nothing better than to tear the system down through art.

Though not particularly brilliant, it did have a small and scandalous success and was, if nothing else, influential. When the tree is shaken, flowers fall.

"Do you really think the police are as corrupt as you have portrayed?" Clark was asked during an interview with *Libero International*.

"No, of course not," was his reply. "They are much worse. If people really knew how dangerous the police were, they wouldn't sleep at night. They perpetrate the crimes they claim to be protecting us from."

"I was eighteen or nineteen when I saw the film," later wrote Massimo Prendi.[1] "It was something totally unexpected. Like a hurricane. We all knew the police were corrupt, but that was the first time I heard it said in such a public format. It filled us with anger and excitement and certainly converted more than one to the cause."

"It was new, modern and we had never seen a film like that," said Silvio Maestro.[2] "To be honest, it is the reason I joined the Italian Anarchist Organisation. It was an alarm. We heard it and spilled out onto the streets armed with bricks."

---

1. Head of Movimento Rosso at the time of this writing.
2. A well-known member of the left. He was arrested on October 5th, 1982, on charges of conspiracy to overthrow the government.

In an article in *Il Giornale*, right-wing journalist Mario Falisci declared that Clark should be thrown out of Italy: "This man, who is somehow presented as an icon of our great nation, is in fact nothing more than a foreigner who cannot even properly pronounce our language and must be dubbed by native speakers. Our borders should be closed to him. He should be sent to live under Castro if he believes that communism is such a wonderful thing. Undoubtedly a few weeks without the great cheeses and wines of our land would have him changing his political beliefs. It is all too easy to rail against capitalism when enjoying its fruits."

Enzo Terni, in the *Corriere Adriatico*, was somewhat less kind: "Actors like Eric Clark are the best argument for the reinstatement of capital punishment. By undermining the democratically elected government, he incites violence and undoubtedly many will feel justified in murdering our brothers and raping our daughters after seeing the filth he has thrust into the cinemas. If I had my way, a guillotine would be set up in the Piazza del Plebiscito, and Clark would be the first to test its springs."

On July 14th, 1972, agents of the Polizia di Stato burst into his apartment and, pushing him aside roughly, proceeded to search it.

"What's this?" Clark complained.

"Quiet. We've had reports that you are hiding firearms here."

They threw his record collection about and sliced open the cushions on his couch but found nothing. One man searched through his refrigerator. Another began to take apart his toilet. Two carabanieri climbed up onto the roof and looked under the tiles while people in the street below stared up at them.

"*Niente.*"

"Look in his car."

And, in the glovebox of Clark's vehicle, a detonator was discovered.

He was taken into custody and brought to the Questura di Roma on the Via de San Vitale. A large map of Rome was on one wall, yellow and red pins sticking out of it. Commissario Dario Furgente (gold medal for civil merit) was seated at his desk.

"What's this?" he asked, holding the mechanism between his fingers.

"I don't know. It's not mine. I found it."

"It's a detonator. If it's not yours, then what are you doing with it? If you found it, why didn't you throw it out the window?"

"I found it on the street, by the Castel Sant'Angelo. I didn't know what it was."

"An unusual thing to find on the street!"

"Maybe not. You yourself said I should have thrown it out the window. So finding something like that must not be so unusual after all."

"A comic actor."

"You were looking for a tragedian?"

"We do not appreciate you, Signor Eric. You want to change the world standing in front of your cameras and lenses. But we have lenses also. You want to build a bomb? Build it. Harm the citizens. I will still sleep at night. My wife's cooking is good and my bed is large. I have two children and neither of them is homosexual. They will grow up strong and fill this nation with more than just ideals. Yes, Signor Eric, dance around in front of your lenses and attend your secret meetings. But we're watching you. And not in the cinema only."

There was nothing illegal about having a detonator, so he was released.

Whether the authorities actually suspected him of some real misdeed or were simply upset over his role in *La polizia fa schifo* remained unclear. It was clear, however, that he was rapidly becoming a hero of the left, despised by the right, by the descendents of Mussolini, the slithering sperm of Hitler, who in the north were in the habit of talking seriously of secession from the rest of Italy, and in Rome were filling tunnels beneath the Ministry of Health with machine guns, bombs and pistols.

45

Yesterday morning at 6:15, while taking her dog for a walk in the Parco degli Scipioni, Chiara Marconi, age 53, discovered the body of an unidentified male age 20-25. He had a deep cut on his throat, probably performed with a knife.

It was 15:30 yesterday afternoon when four masked men burst into Jewellery Soldini on the Via Arenula and killed four people with submachine guns. Valuable goods appear to have been taken. Authorities are currently questioning suspects.

Mario Greco, age 63, was shot in a butcher shop crowded with people. There were no witnesses to the crime.

————

The year was 1974. Gordon Lightfoot was popular as was Charlie Rich. This was the year of *Death Wish* and *Foxy Brown*. The year of cops and criminals. Of car chases and small-scale revolutions. Sales of switch blades were skyrocketing and companies like AGA Campolin and Frank Beltrame were making huge profits. In Palermo that year there were 54 kidnappings. In Torino 62. And in Milan, the capital of the industry, 78. In that city which hugged up against the cold north, in May of that year, Luciano Leggio[1] was arrested but only twelve days later, during a union demonstration on a piazza in Brescia, a bomb went off, killing 8 and wounding 101. Alfa Romeo and FIAT jointly laid off over 100,000 workers. Left-wing revolutionaries and police fought, firearms being discharged on both sides, more wounded and more dead.

Mouths were now hungry for a new kind of escapism, one that exaggerated the problems of their society, emphasising its chaotic nature and making the streets they walked in seem filthier than they actually were, audiences craving only one thing: murder. In all its forms. Whether in hard-boiled cop flicks or gialli, they wanted to see pedestrians shot, the throats of rich wives cut, police gunned down in broad daylight;—machine guns and stocking masks—poisoned martinis and men beaten to death in parking lots.

Clark drove a green Plymouth Barracuda that he had had brought over from the United States. He wore sunglasses, left his shirts partially unbuttoned and put lotion on his chest. When he played a cop, he seemed born a cop, when a criminal, born a criminal. He knew how to puff on a cigar and threaten a man with a gun. He was neither temporary nor eternal and showed greed and lust with the force of a man walking through a stone wall.

"I get scared seeing you on screen," a woman told him.

"I have to use it."

"Use it?"

"Yes, I have to use what's there."

Something was going on inside him, but he always smiled. He put away his western persona to play brutal

---

1. A Mafia boss. Head of the Corleonesi clan.

police commissioners and sadistic hunchbacks; no longer movies with a message, or, if there was a message, it was anarchy—the story of the chaos of the Italian streets—cities ruled by punks and corrupt police, where citizens were robbed and murdered with great regularity—streets which were unsafe, where the only economy that mattered was the ghost economy, the economy of criminals and Camorra and stolen money and money from prostitution and drug trafficking—an Italy which lived by the squirt of the needle, the sale of handguns wrapped in towels in backlots, an endless revolution of women selling their daughters and rich men purchasing their sons back from kidnappers.

In his bad-guy roles he excelled. Head swaying. Lips twitching. Eyes blinking. Foot tapping. Clicking the tongue. Swaying the shoulders. Scrunching the nose. Those little inflections which make a man a man, or a man a buzzard, rat or insect—make a man almost human some backward evolution shuffling baboon.

The audience loved him. He looked inside the characters, discovered what was there, gave rationale to their brutal actions and enriched the dialogue of the scripts, thus turning brutal killers into characters one felt sympathy for. There were no stereotypes for him, for he never let himself be confined by the stupidity of a script. He insisted on instilling some level of authenticity into every role he played.

"Scroungers and killers are as interesting as anyone. There is a lot of subtlety there if you can only tap into it. You have to appreciate the intellectuality of everyone—because real stupidity doesn't exist."

"I don't know about that," Gino Baj replied. He had based his entire career on a certain amount of intellectual simplicity and hoped that his work was indeed genuine.

"Is a man stupid because he puts a knife into someone's side on a street corner?"

"In the light of day?"

"Yes."

"It is not intelligent."

"It is neither stupid nor intelligent. Diogenes, after all, carried a lamp during the day."

They were at the Bar Ripa.

An older gentleman with a large nose and somewhat shabby clothing who had been sitting at a table next to them leaned over.

"I did it once."

"What?"

"What you said. Stabbed a man."

Baj smiled and gave Clark a sceptical look.

"It was on the corner of the Via del Corso and the Via Lata," the man continued. "Back in '46. I used a stiletto."

"Why?"

"Because, for stabbing, they are unparalleled."

"I mean, why did you stab a man?"

"They were lean years. My wife had died during the war. I was filled with terror. At home I had two children to feed, one of whom had been born with a lisp. There was no work for me. I was walking through the park. My mind was very low and my shoes had difficulty in lifting themselves from the ground. I heard a voice and looked up. High in a tree was a woman."

"There was a woman in the tree?"

"Exactly. She was radiant and wore a white gown over which hung a grey mantle. I could tell that it was the Virgin Maria. We talked for a few minutes about indifferent things and then, taking courage, I told her of my situation. She smiled with kindness and told me to go to the corner of the Via della Pigna and the Via Gesù at eleven o'clock the next morning and stab a man who would be lighting a cigarette with a Ronson lighter. The next day I went back to tell her what I had done. A crowd had gathered around. A man was there selling roasted chestnuts. People were weeping. This went on for five days, and then a tall priest with thin lips came and began staring at her directly in the eyes. After about thirty minutes of this, she flew to the ground and then we all realised that it was a cormorant."

Baj and Clark got up from their seats and left the bar. About five minutes later two young women, one with blonde hair, one with black, sat down where they had been sitting and ordered two espressos (*macchiato caldo*) in voices that sounded like pearls being dropped into cups of cream.

The old man leaned over.

"I used to be in love," he said.

"Get lost," said the blonde.

"Let him talk," said the woman with black hair and sharp eyes. "He looks nice enough."

"I never knew the woman I was in love with," continued the man, "so I sent her a poem in which I said that I wanted to climb up to her and forget the world."

"You're a woman chaser."

"No, I just don't forget."

<h1 style="text-align:center">46</h1>

From an interview with Helga Sterne

Well, part of the problem was that he started drinking too much and getting into snow. It might seem strange, but Eric was really an introvert. He was such a shy man. He had trouble dealing with people, opening up to them. The substance abuse was a way of giving himself courage. You would not think it looking at his films, but he was a very vulnerable man. I remember during the filming of *Overdose*.[1] We were all on the set waiting for him and I went into his dressing room to get him. He was sitting in front of the mirror, dressed and with his make-up on. I asked him why he wasn't coming out. His response really surprised me. He told me that he was afraid. Afraid of not meeting expectations. I thought he was joking at first but then realised that he was really very scared. I felt so sorry for him. Finally, he poured himself a J&B and acted. And, as you know, that was one of his best performances and he looks absolutely confident in it.

[Interviewer (wearing glasses) looks down at her feet with possible desire.]

---

1. The original Italian title was *Le Droge di Napoli e le polizie sono tutti morti*.

47

- Anxiety
- Shaky camera
- Uncertainty
- Blurry material in foreground
- Close-up of frightened eyes
- Sound of echoing footsteps
- Shapes moving suddenly by windows
- Gloved hand holding straight-edge razor

[...] Especially in the final scene, in the bakery, the film excels in violence, while the preceding laborious investigation is conducted with measured tension, without anything to make one shudder. It need not be envious of certain successful American thrillers, for what it lacks in polish it more than makes up for in excitement. The well-matched cast is dominated by Eric Clark (Commissario Filippo) and Peter Herschell Lawrence (Vice questore Caputo), but it is the former who draws the viewer's attention toward a climax that if anything is unexpected. [...]

—Marco Tizano, *Il Giorno*,
November 2nd, 1975

[…] Despite the macabre unlikelihood of certain scenes, and the limited plausibility of certain situations, the story is gripping. […]

—Maurizio Porri, *Corriere della Sera*,
October 9th, 1975

[…] The film is like too many others and gives the impression of a bad television show, put together in a hurry, underdeveloped, to be displayed late at night when children and wives are asleep. An absurd Italo-German comic-strip, stagnating with useless sub-plots. Not very convincing, to say the least. Aside from a few pretty blondes who are stripped to the nude and smile, probably because their heads are as empty as the script, this film has nothing to offer, unless of course one wants to see how far a once respected actor like Eric Clark has fallen. To sum it up: this is an acutely minor film. […]

—Enzo Facendo, *Il Resto di Carlino*,
October 12th, 1975

In *Farfalla, farfalla, fiore, fiore, ali sanguinose e profumo di morte* he played a reporter desperately trying to find a murderer who is going around Florence killing young women. Long sequences were filmed with fisheye lens. Rapid cuts lent it a decidedly frenetic effect. The music, done by Giancarlo Chiaramello,[1] was full of the spinet, giving it a baroque feel. In the last scene, Clark is finally confronted by the killer: a wretched old man with a long chin wearing a dress who proceeds to cut his throat as extremely bright blood splashes and scatters over the camera lens.

---

1. Best known for the work he did on the prehistoric comedy *Quando gli uomini armarono la clava e . . . con le donne fecero din-don* (1971).

In *La luna uccise sette volte sul sette*[1] he played a priest in a small but sophisticated village in which a deranged killer is rampant—a sort of Jack the Ripper who, however, was less interested in violating women than in killing their boyfriends, attacking them in the woods after they had made love, a dark shadow bursting through windows in slow motion, chasing his victims down restricted hallways, cutting their searching hands with knives and scissors and then investing their masculine feet with red, high-heeled shoes—a priest who, in the final scene, we discover is more than just one to be confessed to but a man only able to express himself in terms of vascular fluid, one who suffers from infantile jealousy, who has flashbacks of his mother bringing lovers home and perversely kicking off her shoes toward the son's hiding place and Clark drew this character out of the abyss, reflecting possibly some deep sadness in himself, having long before lost his maternal anchor, now some crazy boat adrift, brain and spirit a blend of Californiano bandit and incognizable actor searching to reach another world or ocean of worlds.

"It is not difficult to enter into these kinds of roles," Clark said. "Almost too easy."

"So it seems," Bob Antony commented, noticing the strange shine in his friend's eyes.

"The problem is getting out of them."

And he would sometimes stay in character for a few weeks even after the film was over. He was never very

---

1. One remarkable thing about this film is the amount of zoom used. Feet and hands were zoomed in on. Lips and eyes. Ears and half-open mouths. The camera was restless, voyeuristic, seeming to want to brush up against skin, kiss wounds, rummage about in handbags and sniff behind ears.

confident, and these personalities he took on had a simple enough time overcoming their master, rebelling and putting him in chains while they did what they pleased. He could be seen stalking the streets in the early hours of the morning, following women in high heels, hiding behind pillars, disappearing down alleyways, waking up in the morning with a headache a whisker-invaded face putrid scent and melancholy something crushed which needed to glue itself together show itself to the world again unable to discern between the true and the false the half and the whole jettisoning himself and fishing it out again from some black lake at dawn.

48

In *Milano sotto fuoco*[1] Clark played Vinnie, an ex-con with ambition and without a conscience, who, with an elite selection of lowlifes and purse-snatchers, goes on a crime binge which leaves the streets of Milan filthy with corpses.

In *I due calibro .38 di Tony Romano* he played a two-whore pimp who, after being beaten up and having his women taken from him by the kingpin of Rome (played by Martin Balsam), seeks revenge (combat + pistol + force); the whole ending in: crackle of gunfire = fountains of red.[2]

---

1. From a review of *Milano sotto fuoco*: [...] As bad films go, this one is good, mainly due to the presence of Eric Clark (Vinnie), who manages to turn a script full of ridiculous situations and banal dialogue into an asset. Unfortunately, we see relatively little of Clark in this film as the majority of the celluloid used is taken up with car chases which, though done with utmost proficiency, left this reviewer rather bored and wondering how many Alfa Romeos and Fiat 124s could burn up on the streets of Milan in the space of ninety minutes. Though there is enough tomato sauce to keep you awake, look elsewhere for originality. [...] —Alfredo Massimo, *Il Messaggero*, July 9th, 1974

2. [...] The usual car chases, the usual shoot-outs, the usual blood. The type of film Clark seems to be able to make without blinking. And one watches it on automatic pilot as well. [...] —Morando Porro, *Il Giorno*, August 12th, 1974

173

In *La stessa cosa*,[1] he played a farmhand trying to work his way up in the Mafia by assassinating local farmers and eventually kidnapping and killing a high-level union member who he shoots and then drops down a thirty-metre cavern. Darkness distressed by a rain of crimson light. Chase through Sicily bullet holes + cadavers + cadavers + sunglasses + tyres like scared piglets.

Riassunto della prima Sceneggiatura
Title: *Milano sotto fuoco*

1. *Piazza San Babila. Exterior – day*
It's the first of May. The piazza is half deserted. Sleepy people pass by. Roar of motorcycle. Gunfire. An elderly man stares in silence.

2. *Office of Commissario Gesualdo. Interior – day*
Plain clothes officers. Desk covered with papers. Commissario Gesualdo gesticulates and yells from behind his moustache. A map of Milan is behind him in which red, yellow and green map pins are stuck, representing respectively murder, robbery and kidnapping. The usual yelling conversation and righteous exasperation.

3. *Bar on the Via Bergamini. Interior – night*
Drinks. Music. Woman talking on telephone in the background. Marco and Vinnie are drinking whiskies. They talk in vague terms.[2] Language of the *strada* untranslatable inference.

---

1. […] As it lacks any real emotion, one can only watch it with a vague sense of curiosity. […] M.S. *La Stampa*, November 9th, 1975
2. Mushrooms growing in the damp / entering the roster of immortals through the back door.

4. *Banca del Popolo. Interior — day*

People in line before tellers. A guard who is old and heavy. The doors are thrown open. Masked men with machine guns. Burst of gunfire. One man (Vinnie) leaps onto the counter and spills out threats directing his gun at everyone some screams of terror women pressed against the floor.

5. *Third-class room at the Locanda Atlantide.*

Maria, semi-nude, lies on the bed. Bottle of J&B on nightstand. Vinnie strutts about the room. Maria says that she is tired and Vinnie yells at her, calls her a daughter of a whore and then, after slapping her, kisses her violently in a show of desperate aching love.

RED

"People want to feel that they're living in a dangerous world."

"I still think you could do better," Tina Treville replied. "You have so much ability."

"We could all do better. I can't just wait alone in my apartment for meaningful roles to come along."

"Maybe you wouldn't have to wait alone."

"Well, it isn't that I'm scared . . ."

DISSOLVE TO: INTERIOR. ROOM – NIGHT

He saw the shards of his memories decorated in concentric half-circles of plumalsite, corundum, silky metazeunerite; protogeometric patterns and austere silhouettes mostly immobile. Sorrow/nervous as an electric bell: a girl with a round face like a doll's + headlines + lank blonde hair eyes flecks of sky and further back even before the orange dawn life a flash of lightning fragile as a drop of dew and not having shaved it seemed like ants covered his face and, though it was late, he could not sleep. His brain ran on and stopped. Threw itself into reverse and struggled forward. He drifted into the past, stumbled over the present, fell headlong into stormy ideas and threw his head back in agitated exhaustion.

Without an audience.

He took up a book and read, followed the letters as they marched across the page, file upon file, trying to get meaning out of that strange series of symbols that seemed to have been excavated from a tomb, that seemed to be the remnants of some long-dead civilization, that represented he knew not what, were invented by he knew not who, but had a slightly sandy texture, a somewhat bitter taste, like squid ink—some poor beggar murdered upon a beach— or maybe it was Mineo he was thinking of, who had been stabbed in the heart the year before.

It was somewhat after two when he heard the sound. Coming from outside.

He closed his eyes and listened. Tried to translate the subtle undulation of noise. It reminded him of the sound a long silk dress would make slowly sweeping across a wooden floor. But a dress. At past two in the morning. On that abandoned piazza and if it was her wearing it maybe hiding a mother's breast.

He walked to the window and looked out. The fountain was there below, but there was no one. Not a raindrop. Not a snowflake. Not a toad. Not some beautiful woman dipping herself in the water or bandits stabbing a man in his side.

Then a drink poured. A gin gimlet. And back to the book as if everyone were clapping.

Now the letters seemed more like musical notation. A blurry song which tumbled along. Nodding to one side.

Tossing to the other. Bumping over rocks. Squeezing under a fence.

He lifted up his head. Sound. Definitely there. He went to the window. Did not need to put his face against it to see. That long nose jutting out. A long black nose. Shiny and sharp and appearing almost wet.

It tapped on the glass.

He gazed at it. And gradually. Gradually. He could make out an eye. And the eye was looking at him. And he was looking at it. And only then did he begin to feel afraid and later as he talked his dreams to sleep a million figures seated on clouds of pedestals intone the clear and limpid + stone faces forest / asphalt model + dirty zodiac = quality of weasel perhaps or even more, if only things did not fleet away so fast and ancestors far away.

49

Clark answered his door, let Buonaventura in.

"Doing some light callisthenics with the whisky I see," the agent said, nodding toward a bottle of J&B and a half-full glass.

"I do what I can."

"And I am not one to interfere with an artist's inspiration. I am in fact here with three offers for you," Buonaventura said with pride.

"Okay," Clark replied and took a long swallow of his drink which was as refreshing as someone stuffing a rock in his mouth.

"The first is for a film called *Il Commissario di ferro*, and co-starring Janet Ågren. It seems like it will be a big production. Gunfire. Car chases. A bit of blistering romance."

"I'll pass."

"Pass?"

"Yes. I have my reasons. Let's not talk about it. The other offers?"

"*L'alba dei falsi Dei*. A psychological drama."

Clark frowned. The Italian shrugged his shoulders.

"And the third," the latter said, "is hardly worth considering. Nothing I should actually bother mentioning. A waste of your time and mine."

"What is it?"

"Something with Enzo Bandini. A small amount of money for an even smaller film. Something that will give you neither credibility nor artistic satisfaction."

"I'll do it."

"What?"

"I'll do the film with Bandini," Clark repeated.

"You have a strange system!"

50

Director, behind cigarette (Alfa), dark glasses (Wayfarer).

"Yes, the films I make mean something," he had said a number of years before. "But no one goes to see them."

"*Controcorrente*[1] did pretty well in New York, I hear."

"New York? What the hell do I care about New York? I am an Italian and want to entertain Italians. The real art isn't *realismo* or *neorealismo*. The real art is making films for the common man. That is what is really important. Making films that give the common man pleasure. That is the highest art."

And although others might just talk, Bandini really did follow through with his words. His next film was *Un mitra per Francesco*, a crime drama which he filmed in Milan, Amsterdam and Le Mans and which, while disgusting the art crowd,[2] did have a popular run in secondary theatres in Italy and France.

---

1. The last of Bandini's 'intellectual' films. It starred Gerard Mylo, who, a week after filming had been completed, was found murdered in a hotel room in Nice.

2. […] *A Gun for Francesco*, which opened Saturday night at neighbourhood theatres, is textbook proof of the disgraceful foulness the Italian film industry has fallen into. Someone might enjoy this, but I certainly did not. […] —Adam Lace, *The Bronx Times*, November 9th, 1972

From that point, there was no turning back and he completely turned his back on any pretence of art, striving to make films that would excite brick layers and factory workers. He made films quickly, filled them with violence and peppered them with nudity. The critics at first savaged him, then insulted him, and finally simply ignored him. No one remembered films like *Spiagge e tempeste* and *I Mammiferi*, and, if they did, certainly did not associate the man who made those small masterpieces with Bandini the schlock master nostrils blowing out downgraded pimps third-tier thieves had sold many possessions but not the carafe of water from the Ganges now just playing his part in the human comedy making films too common for the common man.

———

Clark had agreed to do the film without even knowing what it was about. Bandini had helped him establish himself and he was happy to work with him on anything. The set was in Turin and on June 3rd, 1977 he showed up, driving past large factories and ugly apartment buildings to an empty lot not far from the Piazza Statuto.

Bandini was arguing with someone in French. He looked run-down, tired. He greeted Clark with a handshake—the handshake of a man who was beyond hope and functioned not out of desperation or aspiration but simply out of habit, because he did not know what else to do.

"Glad you could make it."

"You make good films, so I came."

"This one won't be good though. I am making the film, but it won't be good."

He said it without bitterness, simply as a matter of fact, maybe even with a bit of stubborn vanity. Clark did not reply and seemed embarrassed, because he had seen the man's last productions and they were in fact pedestrian, the product of a great artist who had lost the capacity to produce great art.

"What do you want?" the director said. "You and me both, we have been guilty. We have not respected our talents. You are fortunate, however, for you still have talent. Unfortunately, it has mostly deserted me. I saw it leap out of me one day while I was drinking a caffè corretto in Florence, at some bar across from the Medici Chapel. It went and fell asleep by the sculptures of Michelangelo. But I still make films and people see them or more often don't see them because they are really films for the people."

At that moment Marco Nizzica approached. He looked sleek, well fed. His moustache was as full as ever. He had not aged much, but had grown ugly. He seemed to have thrived, in a very unpleasant way, like ivy clinging to a dying tree.

He threw his arms around Clark.

"Together again. The three musketeers."

The film was called *Dimentica la legge e fai la tua* and was about a newspaper man (Clark in the role of Dante Turrini) who is busy tracking down and killing a group of bank robbers after his wife is shot and killed during the robbing of the Banca Alpi Marittime Credito Cooperativo on the Via San Paolo (across from the Pam supermarket).

The filming went along without inspiration. Bandini worked from notes scribbled on the back of dry-cleaner bills. Gone were the days of those meticulous scripts that outlined the most minor details. Now the characters clumsily loped from one scene to the next, not always sure where they were or why they were there, casting glances of curiosity at the director who seemed hesitant to interfere with their actions, who was indifferent to bad performances and wooden acting and merely intent on gathering together enough celluloid for a feature film, so he could continue to send money to his estranged wife and ex-lovers and continue to support the children who hated him in Milan and Naples. At night he would play solitaire in his trailer while sipping on a glass of mineral water. When he was told a joke, he smiled desolately. When he was confronted with a problem he shrugged his shoulders like a man who had no control over anything.

He had given up his mode of high living years before. He no longer slept with women and he wore darned sweaters and pants which were too tight at the waist. His invitations to gala dinners had ceased long before and the only interviews he did were for obscure Japanese magazines, for far away film buffs who found satisfaction in chewing on the lives of men whose cheeks had become canyons of tears.

He carried with him a huge sadness—the sadness of a man who not only had never fulfilled his potential, but who had long ago ceased even trying and who would have been the first to question his own talent, as certainly he no longer had either the energy or the inspiration to do more than the most slipshod hack work.

"I should have been a writer or a painter," he told Clark. "Film is so expensive and my budgets have become very small. I am in debt. Sometimes I feel like running away to Africa and photographing rhinoceroses."

"Maybe this one will be a big success," Clark replied, trying to sound encouraging.

"Maybe."

The film was funded by an arms dealer looking for a way to launder his money. Midway through production, however, he pulled out, without offering explanation, and another source of financing had to be found. Bandini, after making dozens of telephone calls, knocking on twice as many doors, finally was able to procure limited resources from the wife of an eyeglass manufacturer in Belluno. Many scenes had to be pre-emptively cut and the final print was a rather meagre seventy-two minutes.

It opened at Tiffany Cine in the Galleria Regina Margherita and seemed to have been forgotten before it even appeared, as evanescent as the sound of wind and water.

51

- His English was always very good, though he never got rid of a slight South American accent. Most people were unaware of this, however, since, in Italian, his films were almost all dubbed by someone else, and in English generally as well.

- He worked with the cream of 70's starlets—Northern European women whose main talent lay in shedding their clothes, whose voices were dubbed by husky Italian matrons or, for the English speaking audiences, overweight California voice-over artists who supported their weed-patch lovers by dubbing foreign films and Venice Beach pornography.

- Every time he looked over his shoulder, he thought he saw it—receding into the distance, turning a corner, hiding itself in a crowd. That black figure with the long beak. That monstrosity that seemed to have crawled out of a nightmare (King of Demons).

- "The thing is," Tina Treville said, "that for all his intellectualism, Eric was essentially a spiritual being. He believed deeply, not only in Jesus and Muhammad, but also, really especially, in the Eastern principles. And he wasn't just a dabbler. He read a tremendous amount. He believed strongly in reincarnation and mentioned on more than one occasion that in a previous life he had been a Californian bandit."

- His film *Le droghe di Napoli e la polizia è tutta morta*, though by no means a masterpiece, became a huge success due to the fact that shortly after its 1976 release there was a devastating earthquake which almost completely destroyed the village of Gemona del Friuli. One of the only things left standing was a wall, photographs of which appeared on the front page of every newspaper in Italy, and on that wall was clearly apparent an advertising poster for *Le droghe di Napoli* showing him with sunglasses, moustache and a pistol against a yellow background invaded by criminals and police.

- Before playing a part, no matter what part, no matter how trivial, he always sought an insight. For him it was not enough to simply look like the character. He wanted to be the character—to know what it was to live inside his skin and understand his objectives. Because he realised that everyone has objectives, whether they be a corrupt police official, a murderer, or a bounty hunter. He read biographies and studied faces in the piazzas—the mannerisms of gigolos and hash dealers, part-time narcissists and undercover melancholiacs. For each character, he felt he had to re-learn an entire system of behaviour—how to walk, sit, hold his hands. He strolled through public places, watched people, tried to steal their souls, channel their behaviour, gazing at old men as they ate their soup and noticing the way young criminals swayed their hips when they walked.

- To say he was unsuccessful would be to calumniate him. To say he was successful would be to calumniate him.

52

The plot of *Cannibali del Borneo* was simple: an American scientist, Don Randal (played by Clark), crash-lands his light, twin-engine plane in Borneo, possessed of only a jack-knife, a flashlight, a plastic raincoat and a few packages of biscuits. After wandering aimlessly through the forest for a couple of days, he is taken captive by natives, a group of head-hunter cannibals, primitives (bamboo through nose + face and body crusted with grey mud) who, after stripping away his clothes and torturing him (strains his neck, looks up at the sky, groans), force him to eat human flesh. At first he is repulsed and spits it out, but later, his mental stability severely shaken, succumbs to temptation, jaw working, eyes huge. After almost a year, a group of whites exploring the area for the introduction of a palm oil plantation, come across him in the jungle, bearded and with long, tangled hair, and take him back to civilization. Though cleaned and shaved, he is unable to re-adapt. In a house outside of Pontianak, he proceeds to capture people, drag them into the jungle and eat them. In the end, members of the cannibal tribe track him down, skewer him with spears and eat him while he is still alive in a dramatic and disturbing scene—huddled around him, cutting away his flesh with knives (primitive enjoyment = modern enjoyment).

Certain scenes were shown without sound which, helping to lend the film a documentary feel, made the horror more acute; other scenes were lifted without apology from previous films, from *L'Ultimo mondo cannibale* and *Il paese del sesso selvaggio*, as well as the mondo films *Africa segreta*, *Nuovo Guinea: l'isola dei cannibali* and *Isole violente* (masks, women pulling maggots out of their dead husbands, animals slaughtered).

Though the picture was almost entirely turned in the Peradeniya Botanical Gardens in Sri Lanka, it was spliced with considerable stock footage from Borneo:[1] of giant pitcher plants swallowing up insects, of men eating live lizards, of swarms of fruit bats, and in one scene a Bornean clouded leopard killing and eating an orangutan. By using this borrowed footage, director Franco Bellati managed to make a movie of constant movement, filled with strange rituals, violence and striking nature. It was an odd blend of travelogue and pulp terror, a somewhat banal script electrified by the bright greens of the forest, by high waterfalls cascading to earth, exotic animals mauling each other, colourful birds flying through the air and topless native women picking lice out of each other's hair and anointing themselves with cattle urine before dancing heatedly to the sound of the tom-tom.

The film opened on the 9th of June, 1979. The newspapers were not especially kind to it,[2] but it immediately caught attention as word got out that the lead actor, Eric Clark, had actually died while filming the last scene and that this was graphically shown to anyone with 2,500 or

---

1. Some of the footage has been identified as coming from Hell's Gate National Park, Kenya.
2. [...] Whatever moral there may be in this story is lost in a jungle of crude violence [...] —Eduardo Ferrara, *Il Gazettino*, June 12th, 1979

3,000 *lire* to enter a theatre. During the week that followed, audiences flocked to see it, crowding together in dark, smoke-filled rooms in order to be shocked, hungry to see real blood, to see a scene of true horror. On June 22nd, 1979, it was banned by order of the censorship board, which had been called together for an emergency session. Theatres showing the film were ordered to either cease, or be shut down and the distributor, Interfilm, was threatened with large fines.

A general inquiry was set up for the whereabouts of Clark. Police agents sniffed about his apartment, film studios and discos. Bob Antony, Tina Treville, and a dozen other actors were rounded up and questioned. But no one had seen him. He had completely disappeared from circulation.

On July 6th, 1979, Bellati was arrested at his apartment on the Via Florida. He was charged with the murder of José Fernando del Torres, whose stage name was Eric Clark. Several members of his crew were also placed under arrest, including assistant director Sergio Giustini and the cameraman, Ottavio Bianchi,[1] a short, moon-faced individual with exquisite sensibilities, all on charges of complicity.

When asked what had happened to Clark, Bellati refused to answer, simply making an evasive gesture with his left hand. The crew gave varying, vague accounts. No one was willing to state with certainty that they had seen Clark after the last scene had been filmed.

---

1. "I am completely against all forms of violence," Bianchi would later say. "I am a pacifist. But with my work I am forced to put personal ideals aside. Not only as a practical matter, but also as a matter of ethics. A man who fits doors for a living must put a door on a palace or a prison—because that is his duty."

"I was not even there," Sergio Giustini claimed. "We had filmed a little pig being killed the day before, and my intimate friend Yuvani had cooked it for me with kochchi chillies and made me drink so much palm tree sap wine that I was totally useless."

The case was rapidly brought to court and immediately caught the attention of the entire country. The newspapers were full of long ethical debates and the men of the bars and piazzas talked endlessly about it—some of the opinion that it was all an anarchist plot to overthrow the government, while others declared that bloodshed was justified for the sake of entertainment.

"The Colosseum over there used to be full of lions eating slaves and men stabbing each other with tridents. What's the difference?"

"If we can't even see the films we want . . ."

"Next thing, they will be denying us also the naked bodies of women and enforcing the speed limit on the *autostrada*."

The court case was sensational. The public prosecutor opened his argument with a long and ponderous lecture which touched on nationalism and the corruption of Catholic values, lamenting the decadence of the Italian film industry and declaring that the country was obligated to protect itself against such evil behaviour.

"I have heard," he concluded, letting down his levity, "that patrons to the theatres were given bags with a knife and fork and recipe book on how to make human with polenta. Undoubtedly we have at this moment many hundreds of young people in Rome craving human flesh as a result of this grotesque spectacle which the director, Signor Bellati, so insolently refers to as a film."

The lawyer for the defence, an athletic-looking young man with a large, sharp nose, claimed that the picture was meant to be educational, and in no way sensational.

"The cannibalism is a symbolic representation of our society today and the lethargy of the parliament, demonstrating the naturally aggressive nature of mankind and questioning the validity of Darwinism."

The prosecutor countered this by holding up the various promotional posters, done in bright reds and yellows, and reading their slogans:

"Nauseating cannibalism! . . . Authentic barbarity! . . . People actually eaten!"

He then proceeded to question Bianchi.

"I just did the filming," the latter said. "The special effects were not my department."

"So, you are saying that it was only special effects?"

The cameraman was evasive. "I did not say that. I only said the special effects were not my department."

Dr. Mario Florio was called to the witness stand. His eyes were distorted by a pair of broad-lensed, black-rimmed glasses. His moustache sat alert above his upper lip which was rather thin and depressed.

"It is my opinion that what we saw on film is, in fact, all too real," he stated. "I find it difficult to believe that the blood haemorrhaging out of the abdomen could be produced so convincingly by artificial means."

Bellati smiled when he heard this. All present were horrified.

REPLAY

Dr. Mario Florio was called to the witness stand.

"It is my opinion that what we saw on film is, in fact,

all too real," he stated, adjusting his glasses. "I find it difficult to believe that the blood haemorrhaging out of the abdomen could be produced so convincingly by artificial means. I have performed over four thousand autopsies and am strongly of the opinion that the meat the primitives were appreciating in the last scene of the film was indeed that of a human—the actor they seem to have terminated with their sharp sticks."

Bellati smiled broadly when he heard this, throwing his head back and rolling his eyes. All present were horrified at his obvious indifference to human suffering, a horror which only increased when stills of the scene in question were shown, passed from the hands of the public prosecutor to the panel of judges and then displayed on a Kodak Ektagraphic projector. The defence shrugged his shoulders. Presiding judge Giancarlo Soldini complained of an indisposition, and excused himself to the restroom, where he proceeded to be sick and afterwards smoked half a cigarette while gazing up at a very small window through which he dared not escape.

The newspapers the next day were full of the case, some of the more right-leaning even expressed the opinion that, aside from other charges being brought against Bellati, he should also be charged with crimes against the public morality as outlined in Title IX of the Italian penal code.

"The guillotine is the only place fit for a man like this," roared *Il Secolo d'Italia*.

"This is one case where we envy the Americans their ability to extinguish such infernal fires," the *Avvenire* bleated.

The country was excited, as if on the eve of a great football match.

On the 9th of August, after court had been in session for about an hour, a man walked suddenly into the room. It was Eric Clark. A murmur of surprise rippled over those present. The actor was unshaven, his eyes bloodshot—indeed he looked like a man who had risen from the dead. He was wearing a green army jacket with a Confederación Nacional del Trabajo pin on it.

The judge looked at him with hostility. The prosecution threw up his arms.

Clark explained the situation.

"I have been held up in a villa outside Saronno," he said. "The shooting was an experience. I had to kill the animals I ate for lunch with my own hands. Lizards . . . turtles. . . . Discovering my savage self. In all honesty, I was afraid for my life, though Bellati certainly never did me any harm. On the last day of shooting he took me aside and suggested that if I disappeared for six months there would be thirty thousand dollars for me. A publicity stunt. I was never hurt though. As far as I know, no one was."

Bellati was exonerated of the original charges and fined two million *lire* for mischief. Unfortunately, the film still remained banned, due to its graphic animal cruelty scenes. He was forced to cut nineteen minutes of footage before the Italian censors would lift it.

Raymond Lord, Professor of Film and Screen Media Practice at the University of Bristol, had this to say:

"Cannibal (*Cannibali del Borneo*) might very well be Clark's worst film, but it is also one of his finest roles. Through the shoddy special effects and gratuitous gore, he manages to embody the most frenetic maniac ever seen on film. He is a nightmare, a fanatic—the embodiment of all things evil, captured on celluloid. He took what essentially was a throwaway role, a role any other actor would have just sleepwalked through, and turned it into this strange primordial interpretation of hunger and bloodthirst. The film, understandably, was and is still banned in thirty-three countries.[1] Which is a shame."

53

- The reason I act is to be someone I'm not.[1]
- One-dimensional characters.
- Though a quiet man, he had a powerful scenic presence.
- He made use of a wide range of clichés: When he played a peon, he spit on the ground, when he played a bandit he scratched himself. As a police lieutenant, he smiled from the corner of his mouth or rubbed his nose.
- A very sensitive artist.

We are at knee level looking into the living room of Clark's apartment as Buonaventura strides around in agitation. *Cannibali del Borneo* had not been his idea. Clark had signed the contract without his presence and without giving him a cut of the earnings.

"So that is your system," he said, "to do things behind my back?"

"You don't own me."

The agent threw his hands in the air, looked toward the ceiling, as if he were being nailed to a cross, making direct

---

1. In general, I think actors are people with very weak personalities, since they always have to pretend to be somebody else.

—Elisa (Calabria)

contact with God—like some Christ betrayed.

"Where do you think you would be without me? Still running around in a skirt and sandals like a Swiss virgin. It has been my consistent system to build you up, get you into the finest films ever shot in the country."

"Which would those be?"

"The finest films in the country," Buonaventura repeated. And then, majestically: "Your career would be in ruins without me."

"It is in ruins with you."

"No fault of my own."

"Maybe."

"Your attitude . . ."

"Then *basta*."

"*Basta?*"

"*Ba-sta!*"

The agent rebelled, began to trot out the many years they had worked together, sentiments, brotherhood, debt, love, petty annoyances, poisoned compliments, sophisticated contrasts, childish affronts, but Clark, unfazed, showed him to the door.

Buonaventura suddenly became aggressive.

"Look, this is it," he said, whipping the air with his finger. "It is part of my system never to forgive. If I leave this place, then I'm done with you—for good!"

REPLAY

The agent rebelled, said that he was done with Clark for good, the latter closing him out / some need to cut things down, strip away the oily layers and see what was under / use it / the actor toured the bars, went from a long series of aperitivos to an even longer series of nightcaps—easing a beer down his throat, swinging a whisky up to his lips—wishing to escape something, though he could not have said if it was himself or another, or if he was simply trying to fulfil some vague need for companionship, now making small talk to an old man with a cane, now passing a few words with a streetwalker—untrained psychiatrists who intimated that his case was a difficult one turgid hours of advice some ripples of washed-out colour a distant trumpet.

A figure approached him. Dressed in black, with a black hat. And Clark was quick to spot that long black nose, that beak.

He turned around and walked quickly away, wondered if it wasn't an SISMI[1] agent following him.

"Eric?"

"Yes."

"You have been drinking," Tina Treville stated.

"Probably."

"Have you been working a lot? I see you have films playing all over. I saw one the other night at the Farnese."

"Did you like it?"

"I liked you. But the film . . ." She was looking at him. At his body, his face—this man who was going to seed, whose flowers had dropped away long before.

"Right. They keep coming after me like that."

---

1. Italian Intelligence and Military Security Service.

54

- Actress 23 looks 12
- Sound of men eating
- Distorted faces
- Gutting fish

A discotèca. Interior – night

Clark leaned against the bar. His hair had begun to thin and he was wearing a hat. He was drinking a J&B and gazing at the dance floor—his eyes pointed in that direction though his mind was elsewhere, wandering over far away plains, gliding through egalitarian villages, riding on horseback over the cracked earth of the past toward some imagined pampas of the future; having at least poetry in his mind or spirit or atman if he could not have it in his actual surroundings where poetry was rapidly losing its foothold, not to be usurped by realism or rationalism so much as the cult of ignorance which twenty-five or thirty years later would be in full bloom.

A song by Viola Valentino[1] was playing and men with half-unbuttoned silk shirts out of which chest hair spilled like threads of black spaghetti were dancing with women

---

1. 'Comprami.'

with very sheer pants and a great desire to show their dexterity.

Marco Nizzica stood next to Clark.

"Get a load of the one in white," he said and then smoothed his moustache.

Clark followed Nizzica's eyes, looked more closely, saw that one woman in particular was attracting the attention of everyone as she did the California hustle (three steps forward, three steps backward, hit right foot against left foot, clap, etc.) and did it well, with that looseness or playfulness that not only made others admire, but also ritualistically attracted like some rite of crop growth or communication with the spirit world. She was dressed in a variety of white silk jumpsuit. A black boa adorned her neck and a head of long blonde hair flowed down her back. The men looked at her hungrily, like a pack of agitated animals, spinning their hips more aggressively, doing what they could legally without taking off their clothes and doing things that might have landed them in jail; while she moved her hands like rain, shoulders like waves.

There was something vaguely familiar about the woman, but he could not quite place it—something he recalled from his yesterdays or past lives or some vibration from long ago that was anything but happy but sat there undefined in the undergrowth of music and bad whisky.

The music changed to 'Born to Be Alive', by Patrick Hernandez; at which she stopped dancing, flung back her hair and approached the bar.

Her cheeks sparkled with glitter. Her complexion was plastic. And he opened his eyes questioningly.

"Hello, Eric."

An icy feeling came over him.

"Is—is that you?" he asked.

"Yes. It's me, Gina."

"Gina?"

"Your ex-wife."

He felt dizzy. A horrible smile twisted his mouth and he felt as if his teeth were creeping out of his gums.

"You look different. You've lost some weight."

"Yes. A cantaloupe diet and two hundred thousand dollars worth of cosmetic surgery can work miracles. Breast reduction and lip enhancement and there you have it."

"And you're living in Rome?"

"No, babe. Los Angeles. I'm just here on business."

"Ah."

"A film, babe."

She put herself up against the bar and ordered a highball.

"You're involved in a film?" Clark asked.

"Yes, so it's nice that I ran into you. I would have found you, though. You might have forgotten me, but I haven't forgotten you. You broke my heart."

"Sorry."

"No, I haven't forgotten you. You always wanted to be famous. A big international guy. The talented Mexican. There could be a place in the thing for you."

"Ah, well . . ."

"If you want to make twenty-five thousand dollars."

Clark looked at her. She seemed very serious. Had she forgiven him?

"So you finally think I'm worthy of being in something important?" he asked.

She responded with a smile—which was really no response at all, since her smile could have meant anything at all, from agreement to desire, from mockery to spite. He felt agitated, attracted; they had another drink together and then she slid back to the dance floor and he stepped outside, wandered past women in knee-high boots and young men who bit their lower lips and then back to his apartment where the walls were now painted a very light blue—and soon he was asleep, dreaming of a strange creature, half slim, half fat—a creature with one huge breast which hung down to her knees and eyes which carried with them the depths of the seas, fields of stars.

The next day a lawyer, a serious-looking individual with glasses and a greying moustache, arrived at his apartment with a slender briefcase out of which a contract was produced.

Clark looked over the document, the long blocks of legal formality which bored him, which his agent should have been looking over if he had had one—but at that moment he had not.

The film was called *Wanda*. The part he was to play was that of Gregor.

"What exactly is this film, though?" Clark asked as he signed his name.

"I don't know anything about it. I just know that, legally, you have to put in thirty days of shooting. Knowing the details of the filming itself, however, is not in the scope of my activities. You are the artist, it is your responsibility to interpret your role according to the direction."

The shooting was done primarily in Tuscany at a strange villa which sat on top of a hill—the scene some false historic period where 70's hair styles complemented 17th century clothing and the actors were seen galloping about on horses or striding through well-maintained gardens to the sound of Baroque music.

When he arrived at the set, he was greeted by Gina, who was flanked by two muscle-bound young men in T-shirts, illiterate fellows with huge jaws and small eyes who could only communicate with great difficulty but were capable of grooming themselves with especial care and were undoubtedly good company under certain exemplary circumstances.

"Your leading lady just arrived thirty minutes ago," she said.

"I still don't know who she is."

"Oh, yes. It's Taja Smith."[1]

Clark shrugged his shoulders, accepted the situation as he would any other, though probably questioning his own wisdom in getting involved in this project with its somewhat enigmatic trappings, the leading lady of which was an African American transsexual who had begun her career as an entertainer in New York. Tall and strikingly beautiful, she had won a sort of clandestine notoriety for appearances in those films which would be sold on 8 mm for private viewing, through ads in the *Village Voice* and the *East Village Other* before coming to Italy, like many others in that period, to make herself a star. Producer Lucio Marconi (1.62 m) quickly fell in love with her and was not in the least put off when he found out that she had been a man.

"You are beautiful. I don't care what you were."

And the Italian male movie-going public felt the same

---

1. In the early 80's she went to Greece where she starred in a number of pictures by director Vangelis Mylonakos. In 1984, while filming on the island of Santorini, she mysteriously disappeared.

since they, as a rule, are fascinated by women who are above average in height, with broad shoulders—women with strength as well as beauty—who tower above them like goddesses; avatars of their matrilinear culture.

Taja quickly found herself the starlet of a number of soft porn productions and from there a few low-budget crime films. She was a box-office draw of sorts; and it would have been hard to deny that she did have a formidable on-screen presence.

———————

Gina looked at her ex-husband enigmatically.

Clark: "But I was under the impression that this was to be a Hollywood film. Your father is financing it, isn't he?"

"Did I ever say that?"

"Not exactly, but . . ."

"So this is my own little production. I helped write the script, frijole. And when it's done, it'll be distributed, don't you worry. I have talent too. Now, you better hurry up and get into your livery. Everyone's waiting."

The film was a hodgepodge of sadism and perversion. The set was lit in part with flashing red and blue bulbs. Clark was made to sit on all fours and be ridden about by dwarves. Stripped to the waist, he was whipped. Kissing Taja's ankles; prostrating himself before her, he physically lent himself to the part, though his mind was elsewhere, roaming about hidden forests of lost ideals and bathing in far-off pools of loneliness like a solitary fish; because 1) he was suffering from some sort of emotional vertigo and did not know where to put his feet and 2) the role he was playing was not without its dark temptation, despite the production level of the film being completely incompetent, because he could play a lout, some mental modification and the homogenous nature even of a centipede came through.

The cameraman, a Spaniard dredged up from the refuse of the Barcelona pornography industry, constantly seemed to be falling asleep, and was undoubtedly high on one drug or another. The director, Günter Antel,[1] a German who prided himself on being able to make forty feature films a year, seldom asked for re-takes, was happy as long as he could wriggle off enough footage to fulfil his contract and pay his delicatessen bill.

"I don't think there ever was an actor with a broader range," Antel later wrote.[2] "Clark could play serious parts and really make the tears roll down your cheeks. But he could make you laugh too. And I mean laugh. In fact, his comic roles were my favourite. Which is not to say these were his best films, because they weren't. Some of them were really quite bad. But his facial expressions, the absurdity of some of the parts he played, certainly put him in line to be one of the great comic actors of all time.

---

1. A Bremen-born film director who had spent his formative years in Finland. He began his career by writing film reviews for left-leaning papers and working on the television show *Kerho 58* before getting a position as assistant director on a film starring Henny Valjus. Though he dabbled in almost every genre, he is most noted for a series of widely popular madcap sex comedies done in the 70's, such as *Doktor Chevron's First Night*, and *Drei Bayern in Tirol*; *Klein Kaktus und Super Panik*, which was followed by *Mädchen, frühreifer Mädchen*. Though his films were lambasted by serious critics, Antel insisted that they were social commentary, were his way of undermining the capitalist infrastructure.

2. See *Abenteuer der deutschen Filmproduktion während den Siebzigern und Achtzigern von einem der Hauptdarsteller*, Günter Antel, Ueberreuter ungekurzte Volksausgabe, 1998.

I think his first comic role was in one of the skits in *I Baby, You Baby, She Baby*, where he played a mentally challenged virgin obsessed with the wife of a neighbourhood butcher. I saw it at the Prinznesbit theatre in Hamburg and thought that it would be wonderful to work with the actor. When I was called down to Italy to direct him in *Wanda*, I was quite excited, even though I knew we would only have a little over a week of shooting time and that there would not be any real comedic tone to the piece because the script was really *scheisse*. It is truly a shame that I never had a chance to work more with him. I tried to get him involved in other of my films, but the only other one I was able to sign him on to was *Kommandantin zum Manöver blasen. Kommandantin* is by no means my best film, but it is one I have fond memories of and is, in any case, a far step above *Wanda*, which I found to be somewhat depressing, despite the presence of the lovely Miss Smith and all the macaroni we ate every night after shooting."

Clark felt uncomfortable standing there in front of his ex-wife, recalling the frosty love he had shared with her as he let his manhood be abused on set. She had been ugly and now she was beautiful. She had been flesh and now she was plastic. Gradually his ability to separate himself mentally from the situation, to take it all as a task to be performed in the line of duty, began to give way—his cringing was becoming real, and his cries unpleasantly truthful.

"Look Gina," he said, "I don't think this role is right for me."

"You signed a contract, frijole, so it is certainly right for you." She smiled. She really did look attractive. "And I have to disagree with you anyhow. You never were a very strong boy. So we can let Taja whip you into shape."

Clark wandered about the set, not sure if he was sad or jealous. He realised that, for all her beauty, Gina still had the heart of a pig. But he was lonely, would have liked to have had someone care for him, take him under their wing.

"Don't let her get you down," Taja said. "She's a bitch."

"Yes, but it is humiliating."

"We're professionals, honey. We do this stuff because we like to give a little joy to the world. We have to be in the world, but not of it, if you dig."

"I dig."

A sample of the dialogue:

Wanda: But aren't you my slave, my possession? Didn't you sign a contract?

Gregor: Yes. So I suppose you can whip me when you want.

Wanda: Which is exactly what I intend to do.

Gregor: And if I call for help?

Wanda: No one will hear you.

Gregor: You will.

Wanda: Ah, so you *do* wish to make me happy!

And he was spat on, made to clean the boots of her lovers, who afterwards tipped him some pittance and in the evening he would be pushed off to go prepare soup, fetch wine from the cellar, lay the table for two. After film-ing he would go to his room, collapse on his bed, have ghastly nightmares of red candles and bloody faces and naked bodies coiling together some decoction rushing through frame after frame to then speed away in his car back to Rome.

"To be honest, *Wanda*[1] was his downfall," Franco Adolfo would later write.[2] "In this film, you could see the character take over the actor. Maybe it was some sort of defence mechanism. A way of maintaining his inner purity. In any case, it is a film that is difficult to watch without feeling a certain sadness, like watching a giant topple to the ground."

1. [...] Yesterday at the Penthouse Theatre, Broadway and 47th Street, we were presented with this bare-breasted rendering of *Venus in Furs*. When I say "we," I mean myself and the sole other spectator, a man who sat in the back row and sneezed a great deal. [...] —Darren White, *New York Amsterdam News*, November 3rd, 1979
2. *Dal Bordello dei leoni, Storia di Film Italiano*, Società Anonima Edizioni Delta, 2009.

55

"Ireland?"

"Yes. At the Everyman Theatre in Cork. We would be performing *The Fancies Chaste and Noble*."

"But why?" Clark asked.

"It would do you good," Tina Treville replied. "It would do you good to be out of the movie business for a period. It is a story of platonic love. You would play Octavio, the Marquis of Siena."

"And you?"

"I have signed on as Flavia, Fabricio's wife."

They were walking along the Via del Governo Vecchio. It was mid-afternoon. They passed by a man selling fruit and vegetables off a wooden cart. Clark had his hands in his pockets. Tina Treville was smoking a cigarette, somewhat nervously.

"No," he said. "I have nothing against the theatre, but . . ." he shrugged his shoulders.

She did not pursue the matter—let it drop away and now Clark was talking about something else, some revolution somewhere, gesturing almost frantically, his eyes wandering over the ground, words about cause and effect tripping out of his mouth, and then he was off in a bar for a drink and she continued on her own, making up some excuse not to join him because her disappointment made it difficult for her to appear cheerful and she continued on, down the Via di Monte Giordano and then started across the Ponte Sant'Angelo.

In the middle, she stopped and peered over at the slow-moving water below.

An old man approached her.

"Signora," he said, bowing slightly and raising his hat, "I feel bold . . ."

He was around eighty years old.

"Yes, I feel bold," he continued. "Do you know that there is a certain pearl, that if you cast at the sky will break it?"

"No."

"Crack it like an egg shell."

"You are a bachelor?"

"Yes ma'am. And you are a very beautiful woman. Your husband is fortunate."

"I am not married."

"I know, I know. Neither is the river, but I love her all the same. It is impossible not to be fond of what you can never have."

He continued on his way and she stared after him and then walked slowly on.

56

The low point in his career was probably *Soft Dogs*. A bizarre cocktail of soft porn and torture, meaningless violence and hackneyed mystery, this obscure piece of optical schizophrenia, directed by David Slonisko Sr. (a pseudonym of Joe De Franco)[1] seems to have been put together for no other reason than to disgust. In it we see animals mutilated on camera for no apparent reason, people having their fingernails pulled out, blood spewing across the scene. The actors use the exaggerated gestures of silent film and their lips never match the horrendous dubbing, which forever is running behind them, jumping ahead, imbuing the horrible proceedings with a vaguely

---

1. Director of over two hundred films, Mr. De Franco is famed for combining the genres of porn and horror, with such underground classics as *Frankenstein contro Jack lo squartatore* and *The Sadistic Baron von Satan*. He was reputed to have shot most of his films in less than a week. Little is known about his private life, but he is said to be married and the father of two sons, one of whom manages a screw and bolt factory outside of Milan. Some of the alternate names that Mr. De Franco has directed under are Sarah Sun Lee, O.J. Borsky, Joan Fellini, Mick Garumba, Mick Garummba, Harry Lloyd, Cindy Renard, Guy Joe, Pierre Palomar, Ronald Rolman, Frank Long, Adolf Griffin, Toni M. Martin, Anne Davis, Chuck Gardner, Lulu B. Cabral, Lulu D. Cabral, Jerri Fine, J.P. Mirbeau, Lowel Bigotini, Alice van Husen, Britt Basilio, and Paul Romay.

comic element—some celluloid bardo in which streams of consciousness vaguely grope for a plot and visions of hell dance across the screen to the sound of bad Euro disco.

It was released in theatres in the U.S. in the summer of '79, being distributed in New York, Los Angeles and San Francisco by Bernie Jacon and in Chicago and Kansas City by Mid-America Releasing. In most theatres it appeared at the bottom half of the bill—at the Dale Theatre in the Bronx beneath *Blooded Treasury Fight*, at the Dependable in Pittsburgh beneath *The Capture of Bigfoot*.

"I cried when I saw it," Tina Treville said.[1] "I was in New York, doing a show at the Marymount Manhattan called *Beyond Therapy*. One evening, while on the Upper West Side, I was passing by a disreputable-looking theatre and saw the film advertised on the marquee. I hadn't seen one of his films for a while, so I bought a ticket and went in. There were very few people, and those that were there looked like drug addicts and prostitutes. The place smelled badly of poverty and old Raisinets. There was some horrible film before it that involved a great deal of violence on the Isle of Cyprus, which I caught the tail end of. Then there was a brief intermission during which a fat man in front of me made obscene gestures with his tongue, and the film began. It is hard to write about. Really. It was a nightmare. What he was doing was not acting, but simply degrading himself. I felt sick. I had lost my equilibrium. At first the people in the theatre chuckled and made sounds. But gradually that ensemble of lowlifes began to get up from their seats and leave. Even they were disgusted by

---

1. From an unpublished memoir currently being held at the Bryn Mawr College Library Special Collections, in Bryn Mawr, Pennsylvania.

it—maybe even bored. Then I was alone. The deranged images swam before my eyes. I remembered how handsome Clark had been, and thought of the great films he had made. But seeing him there on screen like that I knew that his career was over, or at least soon would be."

He no longer controlled his talent, but rather his talent controlled him. In a sense, it was like he had crossed over that minute line that separates art from insanity. When he played a part, it was no longer Clark who was playing another, but rather another who was pushing away Clark—the character pushing the actor down a deep hole, gagging and locking him away, nailing up the shutters and extinguishing the lights. The more he thought about himself being others, the more he forgot himself, was unable to define who he really was and it seemed that his true self had gone on a voyage a long time before to some distant place made up of silence and sand and never returned. He found himself increasingly doing things unscripted. Listening to ethereal voices. Letting things go. During the shooting of *Soft Dogs* he allowed the character to completely get out of control. He improvised the most bizarre scenes, taking what was already full of horror and the macabre and carting it to the edge of the possible on impulse, discarding the script abruptly, throwing forward very real emotions that seemed to have been delved up from some primitive, appallingly familiar plane of existence, with dialogue invented on the spot, adding long sequences that were completely unplanned.

"Hey, it's not that I don't like what you're doing," De Franco said. "But the script . . ."

"People go to these films to be disgusted. They pay to be frightened and disgusted, so I'll give them what they want."

The director nodded his head. He was willing to profit by the opportunity, and the brilliance of another.

"Something really interesting was happening there," he later said, "and I didn't want to spoil it. So I just let the camera run and got it down on film. In the evening, when I looked at the rushes from the day's shooting, I was amazed. It was something quite unique."

"I remember we were filming what was supposed to have been a standard, low-interest crossover scene," actor Branko Goric said. "There was tension between us. We did not like each other. He was some sort of communist and I was not. He began to pour a bottle of wine over my head and then hit me with a shoe. It wasn't in the script, but I went along with it. I felt that he wanted me to bite at his ankles and I did it. It was one of the best moments in the movie."

Clark was walking through an area full of perils.[1]

When there is no warmth, you shiver.

That the picture was ever released is a testament to the open nature of the Italian film industry. Psychologically, it was incredibly disturbing, voyeuristic in the worst possible sense. Technically, it was a disaster, incoherent, with brief flashes of genius that made the overall poor quality all the more disturbing.

---

1. Green wax melting into liquid pine needles, some elixir of immortality rumbling of distant explosions hilarious wounds of gasoline-drenched laughter. Now an empty house.

57

From an interview with Joe De Franco

Many people, particularly in America and England, thought that he overacted and maybe this is why he never really succeeded with an English-speaking audience (apart from colonies, territories: Guam, Tokelau, Liberia). But he wasn't overacting—he was actually depicting quite truthfully the characters and life around him—the people of Rome. Because, living in that great city, we all knew people just like those he showed. The characters were outrageous, yes, with crazy hair, always gesturing and sneering. If you went around the train station, or onto any piazza, there were lots of types just like that. Hustlers, pimps, informants—impulsive men who lived in an azure sadness. And even though he was not a Roman, not even an Italian, he was the first actor to really show these characters to the world, and for that the Italian people will always love him. Because he was really more Italian than any of the Italian actors.

58

Buonaventura came to his door. He was unshaven, looked like he had not bathed or had a proper meal for days.

"Clark."

"Yes, come in."

The agent looked around. There was a bowl of fruit on the table. He picked up an orange and began peeling it rapidly, a sweet aroma filling the room.

"Look, I think I can secure you a role," he said as his fingers worked themselves through the skin of the fruit.

"I thought you were done with me."

"One has to be willing to forgive."

"That is part of your system?"

"Yes."

"There is really nothing to forgive."

"Precisely! We could mutually benefit each other." He put a piece of fruit in his mouth. "I'm a dramatist also you realise. No one appreciates it, but I'm out there on the stage every day. I have to put on a show. Make the tickets sell. Get the audience to clap their hands."

"I don't want to be tied down."

"Who's tying you down? I saw the production you did with Taja Smith. If that is the kind of thing that you want to do in your spare time, why would I stop you? Let's just do a little business. Case by case. Ten percent instead of fifteen, *caro mio!*"

"What do you have?"

Buonaventura grinned.

"I have the whole world! Give me thirty minutes and I'll bring you the world. Just wait here!"

He stuffed the rest of the orange in his mouth and left, wiping his hands on his trousers.

Walking with extreme rapidity, he took the Via di Monseratto to the Vicolo della Scimia, turned left, proceeding to the Via Giulia, and then entered the Hotel St. George. He took the elevator to the 3rd floor and knocked on the door of room 307. A very thin, negligently dressed woman with bored eyes answered.

"Buonaventura to see della Rosa," the agent said, bowing slightly.

The woman shrugged her shoulders and let him in. Riccardo della Rosa, the noted Milanese producer, was reclining in a smoking jacket, reading a copy of *Quattroruote* and drinking small amounts of whisky from a very tall glass. On the table in front of him was half a mozzarella and prosciutto sandwich.

"Comedy comedy comedy!"

"Comedy?"

"You said you were putting together a film."

"Right. No script yet, but we have the title. *Giuseppe Cotone, praticamente detective.*"

"Beautiful!"

"My godson thought of it."

"I have a comedian for you."

"So what?"

"I'm offering my services."

"We're about to sign Marco Nizzica for the lead."

"That doesn't sound like a very good system, *caro mio*. Nizzica is only fit for the pig trough. I have a better idea. Why not use Eric Clark?"

"He wouldn't do it for twelve million *lire*," della Rosa said, shaking the whisky around in his glass and leaning back in his seat. "He could make more money selling pornographic postcards on the Via dei Capocci."

"I'll get him to do it for eleven million *lire* if you give me one million."

"*Sei proprio un stronzo.*"

"So it's a deal?"

"If you can make the deal, it's a deal."

Buonaventura grabbed the half-sandwich and left, hurried down the street stuffing the food in his mouth and thinking of fast-moving things. In ten minutes he was back at Clark's.

"It's a deal," he said enthusiastically.

"What is?"

"I secured the part for you."

"Part of what?"

"The role. Giuseppe Cotone. A really fantastic comedy. I've seen the script. It was written by Fellini's godson."

"And if I don't want it?"

"You want it. This is a big production."

"Pay?"

"You Americans are always thinking of money first."

"I'm from South America."

"South, North, East, West—the New World is all about digging for gold. Anyhow, this is a high-class affair.

To show your interest, I would suggest you take the eleven million. After my twelve percent, that will leave you with 9,680,000, clean."

"I thought you said ten percent?"

"Ten is my reduced agent fee and two is for administrative expenses."

Clark shook his head, but agreed to do it. The money was negligible, but he needed to work, to keep busy.

"By the way," Buonaventura said, scratching his cheek.

"Yes?"

"If you could loan me ten thousand *lire* . . ."

59

"I'll do the scene, but it's not funny."

"Okay, it's not funny, but it's humorous, eh?"

"No, it's not humorous. There's nothing there. No smiles. Nothing."

"He's lying on the bed and he asks his girlfriend to pour him some wine. It's just a scene. You do it and we move on. It's a film, not the *Mona Lisa*."

"Is it a comedy or not?"

"Well, yes, but . . ."

"Then there should be an element of humour in every scene. People need to smile and chuckle. There is nothing more miserable than a comedy without laughter. He should be clipping his toenails for one, and he shouldn't tell her to pour him some wine. He should tell her to bring him the bottle. Not this bottle that looks like something rich men drink but one of those big bottles of Chianti in a basket, and then he takes it and sets it between his legs and looks at his toes while taking a long drink."

"And people will laugh?"

"I'm telling you. It's the little things that are funny."

From the late 70's to the early 80's, he appeared in more films than ever before, but received less money. His name was still a pull to certain audiences, but many of his films would receive extremely limited international distribution. In 1979, he appeared in no less than five roles, three of them of a low comic nature, but only one of these was ever shown in U.S. theatres. He wore wigs and daubed his face heavily with make-up. It seemed that he would rarely turn down a role, no matter how inane, as long as he received money for it—not because he was greedy or desperate, but because the money was representative of professionalism, an excuse for a grown man to do and say things that would normally be considered anything but chic. He played out-of-work policemen, rich homosexuals, roving reporters, low-bred criminals—in many of these, with Momi at his side.

Momi.

Lowing fool slobbery molesting din.

Clark had passed him for years as the latter plied his wares on the Piazza di Spagna, had exchanged some words, listened to the man's jokes, which he seemed to have an endless supply of, dredged up from dark sewers and putrid waterways, and had one evening taken him into a bar and bought him a drink.

"You don't want to buy an umbrella?"

"It hasn't rained for two weeks."

"But if you want to . . ."

"Maybe if you had some grass."

"Grass? I'll get you grass that'll make you go etciù etciù."

Momi was short, overweight, with sagging lips and bloodshot eyes. Son of an Austrian casket maker and a Roman mother, he had spent the greater part of his life as an umbrella salesman, happiest when it rained, lazy and rude under the sun—scanning the horizon for some sudden storm, abject during the hot months of summer and full of good cheer when fall came with its downpours, which filled his throat with cheap wine and his belly with macaroni. Everyone who passed through the piazza knew him, and he knew them. He told jokes about cuckolded husbands, women with moustaches and men with limps. Stretched his lips out like a baboon. Opened his wide eyes wide. Waved his fingers in the air. Held his umbrellas like a bouquet of roses. Thrust one forward like a rapier. Leered at young women and bowed to priests. Strutted back and forth sticking out his belly and buttocks declaiming the quality of his wares and the beauty of all things that flew.

"I can learn from this man," Clark thought, enthralled by his gestures, facial expressions, way of speech.

"You want me to find you a girl?" he asked Clark.

"Are they difficult to find?"

"Like apples, it can be hard to get one without a worm."

Bad mannered, a portmanteau of crude behaviour, he followed Clark about through the streets of Rome. A swath of greasy hair hung about his peeled cranium. His huge mouth was repulsive, a gaping hole in which writhed an oversized tongue giving birth to jokes in bad taste which stumbled along unshaven and shirtless.

At that time Clark was just about to begin filming *La vedova affamata cerca un vero uomo e muore di fame*, under the direction of Catullo Gualdo. He approached Gualdo, insisted that a part be written in for Momi.

"The umbrella seller? But nobody wants to pay money to see an ugly idiot like that."

"Ugly men also should be allowed to work," Clark rejoined.

"But a person should learn to act before going on stage."

"Did you learn to chew before eating? Trust me, he will make people laugh."

"I'm not sure . . ."

"I am. I know my audience."

Gualdo shrugged his shoulders, gave in, resigned himself to giving up a small part of a film that he did not care all that much about himself; and an ugly man was allowed to work. And, due to Momi's use of dialetto romanesco, his rotacismo,[1] due to his natural comedic timing, he actually did gain a certain appreciation among the Italian audience—an audience who, while smoking cigarette after cigarette in front of the screen, talking in loud, raucous voices, were far from immune to the charms of low humour, which they had probably been seeing for a few thousand years, since the time of Plautus, and had a taste for its not-so-subtle employment of innuendo, clumsiness, stuttering, stock jokes and slaps timed to the sound of the battacio.

"I—I'm a star," Momi stuttered.

"Now everyone is going to get rained on."

"To hell with them. It's time I had some action."

"Stay calm."

"I feel agitated. Like an elephant. I need to stretch out my trunk."

"Don't stretch it near me."

"I'll stretch it from here to the Parco Ninfeo di Nerone. I'm the Mickey Rooney of Rome."

"Ugly but sweet."

"Like honey!"

The fellow was full of vice; always knew where he could score Clark some blow, dragged prostitutes to his house and shoved bottles of cheap but strong wine beneath his

1. The habit of replacing the 'l' sound with that of 'r'.

face. They would have strange orgies together—orgies in which the man's grotesque humour would shine forth—in which whores would roll on the ground in laughter and Clark would sideline his intellect in order to savour more fully these base Roman events which awoke the neighbours and left him, the next morning, suffering from headaches which would not go away no matter where he placed his hand—depressed—staggering to the window in his bathrobe and looking out at the piazza—at children playing, old men gesticulating to each other, women walking quickly along in high heels—as if he were looking not at human beings, but at phantoms, because normal life seemed foreign to him, abstract, and he was already making his way past the wine he would drink for breakfast to that he would drink for dessert.

Then, later, there would be a knock on the door.

"It's Momi."

"I'm not here."

"*Vaffanculo!* I have a young lady with me who I met at the Campo de' Fiori."

Clark opened the door. The young lady was about thirty. A bit overweight. Nearsighted. But not unattractive.

"I'm standing between two legends," she said enthusiastically.

"*Two*," Clark echoed. "He's the only legend here. A real talent."

It was true that Momi certainly had no great acting ability, but at the same time it must be said that he was never shy in front of the camera and was able to be his natural self. His special ability was being hit, playing the fool, the butt of all jokes. The man who got slapped forty times in a film. Or fell into a fountain. Or woke up in a washing machine. Or found a cat in his spaghetti but ate it all the same. Some delirium of illogical deep-flows.

A tear rolled out of Momi's eye. He blew his nose. His lips stretched themselves out, curled themselves up, reached for his ears, dove down the sides of his chin.

"I'm an idiot," he said.

"No."

"No?"

"No, you're an imbecile."

Momi neighed like a horse.

"He's cute," the not quite young lady from Campo de' Fiori said.

"*Come uno stronzo*,"[1] Clark added.

The nineteen films that Momi starred in himself were some of the most rubbishy in Italian cinematographic history; making it little wonder that many of them are extremely hard to come by.[2] Probably the worst and most bizarre of them was *Sono John Travolta, Imperatore di Roma*, in which he played John Travolta as the Emperor Nero—a truly strange hodgepodge of explicit violence, sex-comedy, stock footage of Roman ruins and absurdly inaccurate costumes (the centurions wore fur coats). That this man ever became a star truly is an attestation to the state of decadence the Italian film scene had fallen into in the 80's, where the entire industry seemed to have descended into a drug-induced madness, squirming naked in filth and flowers, ready to giggle with ludicrous grins at any gesture of folly, some mixture of rotten mice and stubborn scents.

---

1. Non-direct translation: Like an asshole.

2. One, *Il Peperoncino di Domenica* (Sunday Hotsauce), was released on video in Finland in the early 90's, dubbed into English, with Finnish subtitles. The original reels of this film, however, have been completely lost.

60

These two men appeared in a series of nine films together in the early 80's—productions of uncertain quality which, though widely popular in Italy, artistically left Clark very little room to exploit his great skill. The plots were generally not very different one from the next. The characters they played, the lines they used, the gags, seemed like re-heated tripe—a dish which, never good, was served up again and again to undiscerning audiences—corrupted bricklayers and stoned teen-agers habituated to chuckling at anything and everything as they groped their unwashed hair.

Though the banality of the films was breathtaking, they still did have moments of inspiration, which seemed to come from Clark's instincts rather than anything the scripts or directors provided.

One of the more engaging and unusual, *Una trappola per topi*, which was something of a *La Cage aux folles* take-off, was concerned with two gay policemen in Sardinia who were assigned to bust a heroin-smuggling ring. In order to infiltrate it, Clark and Momi (as Enrico Ricciolini and Benito Forlotti) disguised themselves as a straight couple (Momi playing the wife). The whole ended with Clark selling Momi to a homosexual Arabian sheikh (owner of vast opium fields) as part of his harem in exchange for a jewel shaped like an ostrich egg. Eva Robin's [sic] played a small part and there were cameos by noteworthy personalities and much use was made of an esoteric disco soundtrack. This film, bizarrely enough, ran in a theatre in Rome for an entire year, becoming a cult favourite amongst the city's transvestites, and was also extremely popular in the theatres of Madrid where a slightly cut version was circulating under the title *Muchacha Muchacho*.[1]

Says Franco Adolfo of this period:

"People say he did those films just for the money, but I don't believe it is true. I think he felt a certain pride in being in them, just as certain rich men go slumming. He believed that anything he touched would be great. That he was a sort of Midas among actors. And in a certain sense he was correct. But it takes a real connoisseur to appreciate the films he did with Momi. Because it is not simply that the films were unintelligent, it is that the jokes were incredibly hackneyed and the production values abominable. One watches them only for those few rays of light that shine through the darkness, those few absurd moments when Clark overcomes his environment and says or does something so inspired as to make them immortal—as indeed many moments from these films were, lines even being quoted on occasion in Italian parliament. But the world is not Italy. And Momi was no Juliet for Clark's Romeo."[2]

Momi was a bad influence. He knew half the drug sellers in Rome and would routinely bring them by Clark's apartment, where their small, cool eyes would dart about hungrily. And if he knew half the drug dealers, he knew

---

1. The Spanish distributor, Ízaro Films, spliced Momi's head on Helga Liné's body for the movie poster, though she was in fact nowhere in the film.
2. *Dal Bordello dei leoni, Storia del Film Italiano*, Societa' Anonima Edizioni Delta, 2009.

all the prostitutes and would pimp them out to his friend, recommending the lank caresses of this one or the flaccid kisses of another—women in faux leopard skin and stiletto heels whose sexuality was made touching by their sorrows and who left his pillows stained with rouge and smelling of old soup.

Friendship hypothetical commodity an eel muffled in newspaper left on the ground to rot.

In that man's presence, Clark forgot his political ideals, squandering his money on tawdry thrills, laughing nervously, letting Momi lead him into disreputable buildings and introduce him to men with extremely thin moustaches and quick fingers, to women who would rifle through his trouser pockets as he slept and sneering youngsters who were expert in the use of the syringe.

"I feel that something is lacking," Clark one day said to his friend.

"Lacking? *Che cazzo ti manca?*"

"Even with these women and fine drugs, I feel unfulfilled."

"That's it. Of course you are unfulfilled, *caro mio.* Otherwise you wouldn't have *due palle piene cosí,*" Momi said with an expressive gesture of his hands. "But it's better than selling umbrellas on the Piazza di Spagna."

"I never sold umbrellas."

"Where is your brotherhood brother? I did and remember it clearly. No whores would sleep with me. If I told them a good enough joke one would kiss me on the head like I was their grandfather. No one would even smoke grass with me because they said my lips were too wet."

"You do slobber a lot. *Ptialismo.* Sometimes if a person eats too much citrus . . ."

"I couldn't afford to have a good time."

"And now?"

"And now, *caro* . . ." Momi said giving his friend a significant look.

"And the films?"

"You're the Michelangelo of Italian cinema."

"And you?"

"I'm the banana."

There was an audience for these films in Italy, but elsewhere, no. Attempts were made to market them in the United States, but they failed terribly. The jokes were untranslatable and the scriptwriters used for the English versions tended to render the humorous Italian into banal, childish English. And, to make matters worse, those responsible for the English-language distribution decided that, in the overdubbing process, they would not use Clark, as they felt his South American accent would be unappealing to their audiences. So to dub Clark they chose British voice-over artist Jack Hogg, who attempted to lend him what he must have thought was an American accent—a New York/Southern drawl that often slipped into cockney. And so it was that films like *Due ladri umili* and *Sono polizzzzzzzziotto* were reduced to flyby runs in Brooklyn neighbourhood adult theatres before the reels were cast into the East River by projectionists with long kinky hair and tight jeans.

Their most absurd film was undoubtedly *Le calde notti di Faustina minore*.

The filming was done on the set of Tinto Brass's *Caligola*, recycling the lavish cardboard backdrops and plaster-of-Paris temples to give the thing some vague measure of credence.

Clark, in the role of Avidio, wore a historical costume. Momi played an unemployed slave named Felix. A long

series of crude jokes spliced with the requisite nudity en-
sued. Clark looked distracted. Cesare Romolo dubbed his
voice with that of a Roman hawker of fruit. Momi shone.
No one could deliver a dirty joke as convincingly. He had,
after all, spent years doing it on the Piazza di Spagna, exchanging remarks with nightwalkers and off-duty waiters.
He was finally in his element, and seemed like the reincarnation of one of those sewer-fools or clever slaves one
reads about in the works of Menander and Philemon.

"Her skin was soft and smooth."

"That was her armpit you were touching."

"But it smelled good."

"*Mortacci tua.*"

"That's what she said."

"So she spoke to you?"

"Until the cock began to crow."

Clark in some way undoubtedly enjoyed these highly
proletariat exploits. But to continue with these roles he
had to drink around four litres of wine a day. To forget
about his aspirations. Dull down his mind. Because acting had become for him a job like any other. Like peeling
shrimp or bolting together pieces in a Fiat factory. And
if Momi who was now by his side was no longer selling
umbrellas on the Piazza di Spagna, Clark felt as if he was.

"My films no longer have a political statement," he one
day said to Momi.

"*Che cazzo vuoi con un* political statement?" the other
replied. "Unless you like the police rummaging through
your underwear, it's best to keep it simple. . . . And, anyhow, *Delitto a cactus* had a little message in it I think."

"What was the message?"

"*Vaffanculo!*"

61

Buonaventura was excited. He was wearing a suit that showed some wear, but his shoes were well shined. It seemed he had been managing to put together a little business.

"I have someone who wants to meet you," he said, lighting a cigarette with a scratched-up gold cigarette lighter. "A Swiss French producer. His name is Alfred Périgord."

"I've never heard of him."

"He does good work. His system is to be on the cutting edge."

Clark shrugged his shoulders. Everyone had their projects. They all seemed the same to him. An hour later they were at a trattoria on the Via del Vaccaro opposite a small, sharp, obsequious man who drank his wine with water. Clark ordered a plate of spaghetti alla Bolognese and Buonaventura followed suit. He gazed at the quarter litre of wine the Frenchman had on the table with a certain pity and told the waiter to bring them a full litre. When it arrived, he drank three glasses very quickly and began attacking his spaghetti, sinking his fork deep into the noodles and pushing the noodles deep down his throat.

Périgord gently manipulated some farfalle around on his plate. He gazed at Clark shyly.

"We want to do a series of films, you see. This is not a single project, but a working relationship that I am talking about. You remind me of my brother, Frédéric. He's a dentist in Limoges. I like that you have a sense of humour, though everything I do is serious. No one will be laughing at you. I am looking for the dramatic. My goal is to make people cry."

"And who is going to be in the film?"

"Contracts have not been finalised, but there is some talk of Barbara Bouchet. Alain Delon. Christopher Plummer. Maybe Martin Brandt."

"A good actor," Buonaventura commented, momentarily looking up from his plate. His mouth was red with sauce.

"Yes, it is imperative that we have someone expert in playing Nazis. For an adventure without Nazis could hardly be called an adventure, because Clark will need someone to thwart. The film will be about how the enemies of peace must be defeated even as identities are confused and reflection grows deeper. It is about expanding, seeing things with a hungry lens. Nothing should be cheated."

The man rattled on about the project, in broad though rather uncertain terms delineating a film that would be grand in scope, a big-budget affair done with artistic pretence, a star vehicle specially moulded for Clark himself. Filming would begin in Egypt. Some location shots would need to be done in Portugal and Norway. He was already in discussions with Studio Canal about worldwide distribution and the director (an unnamed Englishman) had already drawn up fifty pages of storyboard.

Clark was mopping up the sauce on his plate with a piece of bread and nodding his head slowly. He looked at his watch.

"You need to be going?"

"Maybe."

The Frenchman signalled the waiter, and the latter brought the bill.

"*On partage?*"

"Eh?"

"Shall we split the cheque?" the other said in English.

It took a moment for the actor to understand what was being said and when he did it was as if he had been observing a vast Greek temple only to realise it was a pasteboard model and that the glories of this life are always of a comedic nature since in the swirl of existence humour was the only thing to keep a functioning lunatic from going insane.

"Unfortunately I forgot my wallet," Clark said, running his tongue over his teeth to dislodge a fragment of meat. "*Stronzo*," he murmured under his breath and got up to leave.

Périgord gave him an evil look and flared his nostrils slightly.

"I'll see you soon," Buonaventura said hopefully, as he poured the last of the wine into his glass. "We can talk about the contract."

Clark did not reply and strode outside and down the road. It was beginning to rain.

He bought a newspaper, *Il Messaggero*. The headlines read:

LICIO GELLI[1]
ARRESTED!

---

1. Venerable Master of the P2 (Propoganda Due) right-wing secret society. His arrest occurred after he attempted to withdraw a large sum of money from his bank in Geneva.

When, a quarter of an hour later, he ran into Bob Antony at the Bar UFO, the other looked at him rather sternly.

"You've been drinking and smoking a lot of grass," he said to him.

"I had spaghetti alla Bolognese."

"I mean in general."

"And?"

"Well, how can you act like that?"

"Look, I can play any part. Without thinking. It doesn't matter if they film me half drunk or on coke or asleep. My part will still be good."

"Well—the company you keep?"

"Well?"

"You could do better, that's all."

Clark looked at his friend as if he had been speaking Zulu.

"Eh?"

"You know a lot of good people. You still have a lot of admirers. There's no need to throw it all away."

"Well, enough about me. How is work going for you?"

"Just like with everyone else. The roles get worse, the pay less. And I'm not a kid this year. Remington Studio is doing rotten. I'm going to have to think of something before the cash flow dries up."

62

The people were milling around, looking at the paintings of Ernst Säflund.[1]

Clark, drink in hand, gazed at one, seeing in that nothingness a huge wad of universal anger such as had killed Sal Mineo six years before and had been the cause of those long beaks jutting out of men's faces with which they dug into the flesh and grated at the heart some sad foolishness being the foolishness at which one cannot laugh.

Jacopo Nobile, forty-seven, a restorer of old bibles, stepped up and offered this opinion: "It's beautiful."

Clark said that he also thought so, recalling that even a butcher's shop is filled with beauty and that lying is a legitimate form of social interaction.

"Are you Spanish?"

"No. I am from Paraguay."

"Ah. My cousin's wife is from Uruguay."

---

1. Represents the high-water mark of proto-post-apocalyptic monochromatic painting; his pieces created with impersonal, patient. impersonal. impersonal, patient, painstaking technique, involving up to three hundred layers of synthetic colouring matter suspended in liquid medium applied to vertical rectangles of birch plywood; the rigidity of the wooden supports offsets the velvety mass of the colour to create an elastically taut, implicatory environment, a peripeteia of pale buff.

Clark nodded his head.

"They are similar, I suppose," Signor Nobile continued. "Like Austria and Germany?"

"Like Malaysia and China. In Uruguay they sold their last four Indians to the French—to the Natural History Museum in Paris. In Paraguay they served the last four Indians at a banquet at the Palacio de los López."

The man opened his eyes wide and Clark walked away, thinking it probably would have been more entertaining to have spent the evening with Momi and some streetwalker.

"Do you remember me?" another man said in a strong French accent, extending his hand.

"Of course I remember you. How could I forget those long arguments we had over breakfast?"

"Arguments? No, they were discussions."

"I certainly hope so."

It was Henri Tardaux. His hair, now completely white, was brushed back with great care over his small head. An elegant moustache rested benevolently between his nose and lips, and this rose and fell as he spoke, asked questions, made declarations of admiration, random observations, mentioned that he had someone he wanted Clark to meet; the latter replying that he knew too many people already, was tired, uncomfortable, without much inspiration, not quite drunk enough.

"This is about art, though," Tardaux replied. "It might mean a part in a film—which I know means nothing to you now, as you are no longer a young man searching for his destiny."

"No, a middle-aged one."

"The best way not to find something is to look for it."

The Frenchman led the actor toward a couple. A gentleman in his 60's and a younger woman with long blonde hair.

"Let me introduce you. This beautiful lady is Sylvia Grath. And Count Mulino di San Lorenzo."[1]

---

1. The collector, a connoisseur of other men's emotions. [The rich are infinitely flat.] need buy the emotions. [even those of the equally flat] style built on regurgitated banter. a collector of sensations. man without religion/God. to be pitied. wanted desperately to live. It had seemed to him that America was where people lived. In Europe everyone was dead. Or, if not dead, broken—splintered into a thousand bits. So in New York (this is all many years before) he attended the clubs, listened to Howard McGhee high on heroin play the trumpet, the notes fragmenting against the glass of whisky he held in his own translucent agate-nailed hand; and art openings where drunken abstract expressionist painters would get into fist fights with bulbous-tummied critics who were as nearsighted as they were profound, nose-bleeds dripping their magico-symbological shade onto the wild paint-splattered wilderness of untreated canvasses while poets with thick Assyrian-style beards chaunted geometrical pantoums in tones vibrant with vodka and blooming bi-sexuality. And of course from all this Arnolfo (di San Lorenzo) felt that he was learning much— about life, about the 'new' art. Because it did seem to him that he had found a place where the creative spirit burned hot. In Europe the movements were all inbred, feeble like the offspring produced from generations of intermarriage rot of mildewing conceit broken chair legs upside-down marigolds Americans—the Pollocks, the de Koonings—had struck him as infinitely vigorous, bold, experimenting with the expulsion of objects altogether, with the revelation contained in the act of painting. And he bought some of their canvasses—for quite cheap: *Rhythm of Lavender,* by Pollock; *Number 10 B* by Rothko; a Franz Kline not unlike some piece of fine Chinese calligraphy, the brushstrokes of Li Bai or Zhang Ruitu or even certain characters in the upper left-hand corner of Wang Xun's famous letter to Bo Yuan. He acquired several works by an artist named Richard Bowling; and these items he gazed at for hours on end, lost in their rotundity, so that, when he turned away his eyes, when he left the apartment and entered the streets, all he saw was shaped like spheres. Women shaped like spheres, dogs, trees and hats shaped likes spheres, symmetrical,

"Arnolfo, call me Arnolfo," the count said generously.

He was short. In a double-breasted suit. Small feet which were undoubtedly connected to small legs.

Her face was heavily powdered. Her nostrils were lined with red pencil. A powder-blue foulard was wrapped around her neck.

Clark shook hands, immediately sceptical—sceptical not only of the rich, but of those who clearly felt the need to defy social conventions so blatantly, for it was often those with the most outrageous manners who were at heart the most conventional—carrying with them capitalistic leanings, anti-Semitic opinions, conservative values that propped up unjust infrastructures and devalued the lives of workers, of common men, finding spirituality in solitary and selfish visions that ignored rivers and lakes, the banks of green reeds and graceful water birds.

"Sylvia is an artist,"[1] Tardaux proceeded.

"That's clear," Clark said, looking at her.

"I like to challenge social taboos," she said dryly.

---

perfect in form. Spheral autos and spheral books. His head was a sphere; his pockets full of spherules. O . . . O . . . O . . . O . . . And when he read it was so many rolling, spherical spheres, rounded bodies, globular masses. O. The sounds that came from his mouth were spheres. O. o. o. rolling spheres. smoke blowing. he gazed at her spheres, paid to enter the sphere, screaming spheres, drank spheres, in the middle of the night he pissed spheres.

1. Mystical / metaphysical / psychological. She had a retroussé nose. When she smiled she showed two rows of sharp little teeth, like those of a cat. She drew childish, vaguely anatomical pictures resembling livers, lungs, and made sculptures out of paper that resembled deboned, dried-up people. Her work was a continual investigation of bodily fluids and hair. She photocopied her breasts and printed them lithographically onto Nepalese paper in odd-numbered editions that were purchased by fragile men and neurotically-tinted women who had never eaten cold rice.

"Bravo. To hell with social taboos, I say, eh?"

"She wants to make a film."

"Well, she is an artist, so we need to do all in our power to make sure she can fulfil her dreams, which are more important than those of a regular person—that waiter, for instance, whose only aspiration is probably to use the toilet when he has the chance."

"Yes, I agree completely," Arnolfo said with warmth, looking at a man with heavy thighs and a sad mouth who was carrying around a tray on which sat glasses of red and white wine.

"I think Mr. Clark was being sarcastic."

"Sarcastic? Not at all, I only . . ."

"You don't need to explain. I am very attracted to your candour. And I have seen a few of your films, Mr. Clark. You are just the sort of trash actor I feel that I need."

Clark smiled. Not with contempt, or even sadly. It was the same smile as one of those prostitutes he had dragged off the street must have given after a night's work—a smile of resignation, acceptance of a situation that he could already see would be a replay of that of his ex-wife—a woman using the camera to emasculate him in one way or another and he would accept it, not because he was desperate, but simply because it had become his pattern to accept any role offered, no matter what—an addiction not so much to making money as to having himself appear on screen, before others, to have his talent exploited, and to keep working, a distraction from the change of seasons, the strange martyrdom of being encased in a human skin.

63

electric red
mortal
bodies piled one atop the next. Smoke-filled ruins. the
hunt of the storm trooper and the smell of broken bricks.
axes. touch of dogs. colour of grenades. mechanical pul-
verization. screaming crimson. an essence which could be
tasted. felt. from the invasion of France. Kristallnacht. to
Hiroshima. so many melted, evaporated, shadows cast on
walls
born of an art-loving breed

———

muddy hair rolling around in eerie blue monosyllables

———

While partisans were stalking forests with missile-
shooting metal tubes, while others were being gassed for
race, belief, rebellion, Arnolfo had been in Switzerland, in a
comfortable Anglo-Svizzera-Chinese-style villa along Lago
di Lugano looking up at a brilliantly charming Caravaggio,
a Daumier, a van Dyck—outside the serene water, the
dramatically rising mountains. his somewhat translucent,
agate-nailed hands, were passive non-participants. his
limbs and muscles flowed into each other without sharp
division, surface parts irregularly curved, blended into

each other like waves, no firm place or lines for the eye to fix upon.

There was his father who brooded.

There was his mother whose eyes began to disappear into the depths of her skull, introversion becoming for her a veritable religion.

————

barmen are fat and unshaven in front of a firing squad

————

Germany surrendered unconditionally. Prime Minister Churchill proclaimed the historic conquest from 10 Downing St., President Truman from Washington and Premier Stalin from Moscow. Germany's official capitulation came at 2:41 a.m. (French time) in the big red Reims schoolhouse, headquarters of Gen. Eisenhower, Supreme Commander of the Allied Forces in the West. Five years, eight months and seven days after Hitler had invaded Poland.

————

the loneliest role of all.

————

"You should not feel compelled," Tardaux said, as they ate lunch together at one of the better restaurants on the Via Vittorio Veneto.

"Why shoud I not feel compelled? If someone slaps you in the face, you fight a duel."

"This is the twentieth century, Eric. Nothing matters any more. When I was at the train station in Paris last week, they found forty-five sticks of dynamite in a luggage locker. A bomb had gone off the day before, near the Champs-Élysées. Was anyone killed? Yes! A pregnant woman. Not even one swallow of air. So, nothing matters any more. The beautiful children—they are all gone. Your body has a certain mass, a certain energy content, but as I grow old I have a difficult time determining where the centre of gravity is. All this energy around me seems very inert. I love to see things, bright colours and small butterflies, but try to do so without a great deal of drama."

He poured some water into a glass.

"The drama is all that matters," Clark commented. "Without it, I am left with only memories. I don't fully understand physics. My skill is in changing who I am—but it is impossible to change back to what I was. There's no alchemy that can do that and I don't know that I would use it if there were."

"You were a very beautiful young man."

"Was?"

"You are certainly not ugly—but you are just as certainly not young."

64

Filming began on June 19th, 1982 and lasted fourteen days. Clark had no idea what the film was about and simply obeyed Sylvia's commands. He was the only actor, the only presence on the set.

In one scene he meticulously covers his body with pink pigment. In another, dressed in a blue jumpsuit, he walks back and forth in front of the camera for a full ten minutes, managing to stay absolutely natural, despite the artificiality of the situation.

He:

1) laughed maniacally

2) with back to the camera repetitively struck the strings of a violin with his open palm

3) rolled around a tree, lying on his side

4) played three people, identical in every way, who spoke with each other in monosyllables

5) sang while eating an egg (only mouth seen)

In a sense it seemed like she was purposefully humiliating him. But he was being paid 25,000 U.S. dollars for his time, so he did what he was told and when the shooting was done was invited to Arnolfo's villa on the outskirts of Rome for an aperitivo and brought Momi along, even though the latter had not been invited, was not even

242

known, but for some reason Sylvia was not there and the count cautiously shook the umbrella seller's hand and, somewhat embarrassed, showed them around the place to destroy time while waiting for the woman.

"My family used to have a fine collection of Renaissance paintings here. Many of them were decent, a few were masterpieces—an excellent *quadro* by Jacopo Bassano; a work by Francesco Mazzola, known as Parmigianino—a Madonna with an especially long, serpentine neck."

He did not mention that she also had the potbelly of a fledgling drunkard.

"What happened to them?" Clark asked without much interest, looking around at the slabs of monotonal colour that adhered to the walls.

"I sold them and used the money to purchase what you see. Back in Milan I retained a few things—some Japanese miniatures in gilded bamboo frames that were my mother's. Some paintings my father purchased—artists associated with the Futurist movement, such as Carlo Carrà, who used the plastic syllables of Giotto and Masaccio updated in the language of airplanes."

"*Mannaggia*," Momi commented. "So sophisticated."

And then they sat outside and drank and ate stuzzichini and watched a gardener wandering around a lawn down below and the actor suddenly felt as if he could understand the woman, a reincarnation of an annelid or some creature from hell simply looking for nourishment.

The count lit a cigarette.

"She doesn't treat you very well," Clark said.

"She doesn't treat either of us very well."

"Yes, but I'm getting paid to be humiliated."

"You might have a point. You are being paid, and I am paying. Still . . ." He leaned forward. "You see, it is what is inside her that I am in love with. Her concepts. Her abstract heart. The aesthetic quality of her soul. A man must train himself to trust himself if he wishes to reach the sphere of Saturn. It is not enough to live vicariously."

And then he opened up, became expansive, spoke about when he had first met her, at an exhibition in Milan. A brightly lit art gallery. Murmuring of cultivated voices. Occasional fizz of laughter. Walls hung with what looked eerily like human skins. Humans deboned, defleshed. And while sipping at a glass of prosecco he had become emotional, thinking he was witnessing the anti-commodification of art (he had not yet seen the price tags), getting a hit off pressing his thought processes against what was before him just as someone of more straightened finances might get a hit off a paint-soaked rag while sitting beneath a bridge and around him the women all had short hair, the men long, while he, Arnolfo, stood there immaculately dressed, his small person at ease behind the fortifications of a somewhat loosely fitting suit and then he saw her actual person, was introduced to her, talked with her, was amazed and for once completely forgot about his wife, who was lovely in her own way, but lacked————

"And where is she?" Momi interrupted. He was already working on his second drink.

"What was that?"

The collector seemed as if he had been awoken from a dream. He looked around with myopic eyes.

"Your wife. What did you do with her?"

"As you know, divorces in Italy are difficult to arrange."

"So?"

"And so the good woman shot off her ear."

"*Mannaggia.* Italian women usually just shoot off their tongues."

"Sylvia was there at the time. You can imagine the situation. The heartbreak, the overwhelming flood of emotions. There was blood and screams. Inspired by the sight, she later did some large, violently red drawings with crayon. Admittedly they were in bad taste, but if one understands the woman's past . . ."

It was then that the arist walked in. She was wearing a WilliWear jumpsuit and sunglasses and a frown on her face.

Arnolfo looked at his watch. It was half past six. She offered no explanation or apologies for her lateness. Sitting down, she told the butler to bring her a vodka martini.

"She's not ugly," Momi said to Clark under his breath.

Clark shrugged his shoulders with indifference.

"Who's this?" Sylvia asked, nodding toward Momi.

"He is an actor," Arnolfo said.

"Who would have known?"

Momi's lips stretched themselves out into a large smile. "The count was just mentioning your past."

"My past?"

"I did not say anything, Sylvia," Arnolfo assured her.

Sylvia lit an Alfa. "He must be talking about my father who is in prison in Michigan City, Indiana."

"What for?"

"Embezzling, murder. What does it matter? Arnolfo can't get over it though. The art he collects is on the edge, but he's not. He likes to think himself a father figure towards me, but fathers don't usually sleep with their daughters."

"She likes to be dramatic," the count commented in an even tone.

"All women need drama in their lives," the artist rejoined, taking the olive from her drink and putting it in her mouth.

"Fortunately for me," Momi remarked. "If not, I'd still be a virgin, Madonna Santa."

"Sylvia is an extreme intellectual," said the count. "She likes to be provocative, seductive. Her work is a kind of family of tendons, an orgiastic collapse of dissonant lines. To be with her is at once exhilarating and instructing. It is like being initiated into the rites of the pow-wow of the Plains Indians—doing a sort of corn dance of vapour and blue rain."

"*Mannaggia!*"

"She is an artist. A fine artist."

"And, coincidentally, I'm a lover of art," Momi said opening his eyes wide. "Raffael. Michelangelo. You have to have an open mind for this kind of thing, right? When I see a nice statue, robust, round—I feel a certain something. A strange sensation. Something rising up inside of me . . ."

The count's lips twisted at the edges.

"Show him your work. It would be curious to see this comedian's reaction."

"Maybe he doesn't want to see it. I know I wouldn't."

"I want to see. I want to see. Oh God, how I want to see! I'm ignorant, but I'm human." He suddenly looked as if he was about to cry. "I sat for so many years at the base of the Scalinata. The fountain there was built by the grand Bernini. I could put my feet in on a hot day and watch the water change colour. Dream of swimming with Anita Ekberg. Though in truth I did once take a bath with a woman named Tina Franzberg."

Sylvia got up and led Momi into the house, each carrying with them their drinks.

"Your friend is a bit of an imbecile," the count said when they had left.

"He might be more clever than you give him credit for."

"Shakespeare."

"Which would make me King Lear."

"I sense a certain tragedy."

The actor was silent and the count, nervously smoking another cigarette, began to talk at will, about fish eggs, Tony Smith, Indian mysticism, respiration, the plays of Ibsen, desserts made with almonds, Chinese business practices and strict obligations.

It was beginning to be twilight.

The count suddenly fell silent. He stood up and looked over his grounds.

The butler stepped out and began to clear away the glasses.

"Where have they gone to?" Arnolfo asked.

"Signora Grath left with the, um, gentleman about half an hour ago."

"Where to?"

"That I would not know, sir," the man said, averting his gaze.

Arnolfo looked at Clark questioningly.

"They are both artists," Clark responded. "I am sure they have a lot to talk about. Momi is an interesting character."

"So it seems." The count had become thoughtful.

"Listen," Clark said, changing the subject, "about the film. I haven't even seen the rushes. Is it going to get distribution or what?"

"Undoubtedly it will do very well," Arnolfo said, stiffening up. "Sylvia is a very famous artist."

The film was titled *Citizen Locomotion* and was given a special screening at the Museum of Modern Art in New York, which was attended by ninety-four people [to great acclaim].

65

Absurd violence. Desert. Mushroom cloud. Sound of motors.

In *Caduti del mondo anno 2029*, he played the leader of a post-nuclear biker gang who drive from town to town terrorising the survivors. Marred by an absurd, almost non-existent plot,[1] the most banal of Euro-disco soundtracks and childish sensibilities, the film was completely devoid of any opportunity for Clark to shine. Amazingly enough, however, it garnered two million dollars on its opening day at the U.S. box office—more than his previous three films combined during their entire runs.

It was turned in a sandpit outside of Rome during the hot summer months of July and August, subsequent to Italy's World Cup win against West Germany (3-1). The costumes were worthy of derision. The haircuts were all punk. Some had purple Mohawks, others absurd pink braids which stretched down their backs. Women wore leather short-shorts and carried crossbows, which they held up against their large breasts. Clark was shown with long hair that was patched white and a closely trimmed beard that made him look extremely cruel.

---

1. The apple tree in the yard. Out of pity for the world. Without trying, without action.

Due to the heat, the wine they drank at midday and the twenty grams of South African marijuana Clark had brought with him on the set, the actors went about their tasks lazily, half asleep, stumbling over their lines and their own feet as director Edoardo Gianbologni enthusiastically waved his index finger around and gave mystical instructions which sounded like extracts from the *I Ching*.

We see:

- Men with mud in hair
- Shotguns
- A woman in a steel girdle
- A fellow crawling around on an engine
- A big silly-looking knife

"The Australians had put out *Road Warrior* in March of 1981. By June of 1982 it had become a huge hit in the U.S. By August of the same year we had started production on *Caduti del mondo*. The script was written in three days. The film was shot over the course of nineteen days. Post-production took less than a month. By September '82 our film was showing in theatres all across Europe. In France, Germany and Italy, it opened just two weeks after Road Warrior. In Sweden, Finland and Norway, it opened before. A significant number of Europeans actually thought Road Warrior was an imitation of *Caduti del mondo*, instead of the other way round! And we Italians were trying to make something that could compete," Gianbologni said. "We really were the first ones to capitalise on the *Road Warrior* fad. There were a lot of films that followed ours, such as *Stryker*, *Gli Sterminatori dell'anno 3000* and Tonino Ricci's *Blood Rush*, but ours was really the one that set off the trend."

In Germany it instantly became a cult classic. In Hamburg it ran for ten months at the Kino theatre, garnering the attention of the punk community. The band Tollwut released an EP dedicated to it which featured a distorted, blood-splattered photo of Clark on the cover. The film was finally taken off the marquee when a nineteen-year-old boy was shot in the chest during a viewing.

Then chancellor and CDU[1] president Helmut Kohl condemned the film.

"Pictures of this type lead to the fragmentisation of our country," he said. "Violence should be done away with in all its forms, even in the cinema."[2]

---

1. Christlich Demokratische Union Deutschlands.
2. A dictum he later forgot while funds were being deposited into a CDU shadow account in Geneva for the sale of thirty-six German tanks to Saudi Arabia.

66

The early 80's were made up of long bouts of distraction interspersed with brief spasms of intense concentration. He would sleepwalk through a week's worth of scenes and then perform brilliantly for a few hours. Many of these films were bad; but none were without a bright spot—some flash of genius that set them apart.

From comedy, he turned back to violence; between 1981 and 1985 appearing in over twenty productions, for the most part set pieces of cruelty and bloodshed. The directors he worked with tried to outdo each other, pushed the limits of what they could get away with displaying on screen, made up for their abysmal budgets with gut-wrenching brutality; women displaying their naked bodies, undressing at every opportunity; men slobbering blood; fear and hatred become manifest through loud noises and quick movements; massacre of thrills and lurid turbulence with some abysmal waves of pleasure. Clark had no need of strategising a career that was on a downward spiral and offered himself to the highest bidder, often without even bothering to look at the scripts beforehand.

There was *Guerra Cobra 3*[1] and *Follia di paura*.[2] Audiences pummelled with radiant stupidity, shattered on the cheap in the stench of second-run theatres.

He became a specialist in the role of sadistic killers and psychopaths. The believability of some of these roles was astounding.

CUT TO:

INT. KITCHEN – MORNING (LATER)
C.U. – MAURO
Mauro is lying in the blood-touched kitchen. He is breathing deeply. His eyes open.

MAURO'S POV: KITCHEN RAFTERS FROM WHICH THE CHAIN STILL HANGS

CLOSE ANGLE – MAURO

MAURO
I've got to deal with this. Bastards . . . just don't understand. All those years no one wrote to me. I tried to be nice.

---

1. It should be noted that there was a *Guerra Cobra 4*, also starring Eric Clark, but this film was in fact shot at the same time as its predecessor and was made up mainly of out-takes of the first film supplemented by stock footage of the Indonesia-Malaysia confrontation.
2.   ***BEST FILMS IN TOWN***
CINEMA 1 Tonight 2 shows: 7:30 & 9:30
FEAR HUNTER
ERIC CLARK
"A man with a mission"
CINEMA 2 Tonight 2 shows: 7:45 & 9:45
GRANDMASTER OF SHAOLIN KUNG-FU
PHILIP CHEUNG
KING KONG

Mauro picks up a huge knife with his viscid hand and hurls himself out of the room, staggering.

He is wearing only a pair of jeans, no shirt or shoes. He sees Angela running in the distance.

MAURO

Angela! Angela. Don't be a baby! It's going to be alright. You just have to trust me. Alberto treated you badly. I'm not going to hurt you. I'm not going to hurt you. Just be decent.[1]

In *Il sangue, le droghe, la morte* he played Mark, a PCP addict who rampages through the city, throwing himself before cars, hurling himself through glass windows, madly dicing people up with a switchblade, lunging at their calves, teeth chattering, eyebrows flying. Technically, the film was of a very low quality. But Clark became so involved in the role, that it seemed almost a living document, a dramatisation of angel dust to the sound of klaxons and shaken steel manes. In West Germany it received some attention and it managed to penetrate other Northern European markets. Unfortunately, the only review the film received in the United States was from the *Philadelphia Enquirer*, where, on their 1-5 star system, it received a ½ and was, rather sophomorically, called, "An insult to the intelligence of your average eight-year-old," proving, if nothing else,

1. From *Sangue ripido*. It was said that in order to study for the role, he had spent days watching footage of snakes—pythons, rattlers, and most especially Lebetine vipers and cobras. Imitating their gestures, the way they moved. And, in fact, in the film itself he seems to be slithering from place to place, showing his fangs, discreetly slipping along from one recipient of injurious action to the next.

that the residents of the City of Brotherly Love were blind to the essence of good acting, to an art that was able to be crude, like an abandoned tangle of wires and damaged plastic—a strange beauty offered by certain pieces of weathered trash.

Salt is not white, coal is not black.

In *Turgo, guerriero sanguinoso,*[1] a Conan imitation, he played an evil wizard with long moustaches who fed off the hearts of his victims and was married to a giant snake which he kept in a pit. The film was full of fur, women with baskets on their heads and cannibals. In the brief periods when the actors where not beating each other with swords or clubs, walking through forests of young trees or over well-grazed meadows, or magically disappearing in clouds of smoke, they were eating meat or rolling about with women in caves. An adolescent fantasy without any creative aspirations, because these seemed to have been forgotten or lying dormant, the most pressing matter not to make a good film, but simply to make a film, some half-cooked stew to be carted through the marketplace by a man without a tongue.

The director was once again David Slonisko Sr., though for this film he used the pseudonym David S. Martin.

Before filming began, he talked with Clark about the enterprise at his apartment, over tumblers of J&B.

"Basically, I am trying to make a blockbuster here."

"So you have a pretty big budget then?"

The director paused before commenting, lighting an Alfa and blowing a narrow jet of smoke toward a bright orange lampshade.

---

1.   Playing at the Mustang Twin Drive-Ins
Directed by David S. Martin. Starring Eric Clark. Screenplay credit not available.

"No, not at all. But I have you, and I have a great lead man."

"Yes, tell me about that."

"Well, he has never been in a film before, but he's perfect. He's like a Greek statue. More beautiful than Lou Ferrigno. I met him in Capri last summer. He is very sweet. I bought him a *fritto misto* while he quoted Dorothy Parker to me."

"His name?"

"Enrico Oslo, but we're thinking of billing him as Benjamin Woodman."

Clark's lips twitched. Sixth sense. Flinching tide of blinding purple in a forest strutting before Indians. He could see he had aligned himself with another failure, a thing that would be done without money or skill, a collaboration which would send him further into a frightening obscurity from which he could see no possibility of detaching himself, but then he nodded his head, swallowed his drink, accepted the situation because at the very least it would keep him busy, and so it was that four or six days later he was there on the set, approaching Slonisko.

"Hey, listen."

"Yes."

"This lead you've got."

"Benji?"

"Yes."

"You don't like him?"

"No, it's not that."

"He's a nice boy. Very thoughtful."

"I know he is, but . . ."

"Well?"

"He's playing Turgo, right?"

"Obviously."

"And what kind of a character is Turgo?"

"A real man. A tough guy. The sort men admire and women fall in love with."

"Macho maybe?"

"Of course he's macho. Macho as hell. He can eat a whole bull and can drink a barrel of wine without taking his lips off the rim."

"Well, that's my point. You have an Albin Mougeotte."

The director stared into space for a moment, trying to decipher certain mysteries which seemed to be written there in invisible hieroglyphics as in the near distance a half-nude Benjamin Woodman crowned with Bon Jovi hair some mermaid wig swung around a cheap-looking sword and flies yawned as they made their way toward a table set with lunch meat and pickled onions.

1) Fighting invisible warriors
2) Hang-gliding into a castle
3) Throwing explosive bombs wrapped in leaves[1]

The film opened at the Cinema Metropolitana in Rome. Though neither the director nor any member of the cast were there, Clark slipped in to see it. There were only four people in the audience. The reel began to roll, characters swallowed up by huge plot holes which seemed to descend straight to Hades. After the first thirty minutes two of the

---

1. Miraculously enough, the Turgo series continued after this with three more installments: *Turgo il spadatore* (1984), *Falco rosso* (1985), and *Ultimo storia di Turgo* (1988). Each of these starred Benjamin Woodman, though Clark was absent in all three.

people in the audience got up and left, snickering as they strolled leisurely out of the theatre. After another fifteen minutes Clark was alone, staring up at the giant image of himself parading across the screen. The film only stayed in the theatre for two days and then disappeared. In Italy, it had come and gone without arousing the slightest interest, like a poem written on water.

But tastes change from place to place, and food that is not fit for a dog might be relished by maggots.

Though most of Clark's better films were ignored in North America, a few of his truly bad ones, such as *Turgo, guerriero sanguinoso*, did seem to get a foothold. On its opening weekend in the U.S., it grossed over three million dollars, due to an advertising scheme propagated by the distributor, Comworld Pictures, that made it seem like a big budget Conan-style film.[1]

---

1. [. . .] Looking like it was filmed in someone's backyard, *Turgo the Bloody Warrior* will only be outdumbed by those who actually pay to see it. [. . .] —Chris Sampson, *Chicago Defender*, July 12th, 1981

67

chilled snail horns
neon hearts
anempathetic sound

A fat man. He sleeps all day. When he wakes he drinks
J&B (forty-two different whiskies passing his lips). As the
song says:

> *There stands the glass, fill it up to the brim,*
> *Till my troubles grow dim*

In the mirror he sees his balding head. He makes faces
at himself, stretching out his lips, showing his teeth, lights
a joint of Panama red, puts on an LP of Barry White.
Like the sound of a gong. Sound shaped like a wheel rim.
He should have been a singer. He likes to sing—about
love, sadness, anger and mercy and habitual delusion.
Should have been a soldier, a farmer, deaf musician or
blind weaver—anything but what he is. Because an actor
is a nobody. A chimpanzee. A badly trained seal. Identity
sold. No one knows him, as he does not even know himself. And when they grow fat, bald. A lot of good actors
do. And then he is called out, to smile and jeer, frown
or shout—to become someone else—maniac or clown—
tortoise or jackal, jaws dripping with stage blood.

His mind floated off across the ocean—became lost in dense jungles, saw the sun and the moon weeping as he did China white, mother-of-pearl, ivory flake; rain of jewels; sat staring at the paintings on his walls, cold slabs of colour, at his feet, was no longer even much interested in politics and watched without emotion as the Right continued to strengthen its hand—as Russia and the United States continued to heat up their rhetoric and anarchists and communists were driven from the streets of Italy, his only concern being to gain enough courage to continue— to snort enough benzoylmethylecgonine and gulp down enough whisky to feel sociable, without shame.

This was no longer Jim, but it was Jett Rink—Jett Rink in the final stages of *Giant*—reeling from drunkenness— far from his unassuming beginnings—a man inflated by egoism and carrying with him a certain amount of destructiveness or self-destructiveness, the political advocate of the use of violence tossing a bomb into his own heart to try and distort the fact that he had come from some far-off planet or nation to appear in films that sidestepped first-run theatres, scratched up reels then tossed on curbs to be picked up by flea-bitten garbagemen, collectors of *monnezza*.[1]

Someone told him that Tina Treville was back in Italy and, thinking about her, he suddenly became tender.

She had an apartment on the Via Virgilio. He went there, late in the afternoon.

She opened the door and stood there hesitatingly for a moment before inviting him in. Her apartment was comfortable and clean. Well-tended house plants sat in

---

1. The only known reel of Clark's film *Contaminazione PCP* was in fact found on a curb in Naples, sitting next to a pile of trash.

the windows. There was a large and colourful photo of a giraffe on the wall. Another, in black and white, of a pregnant woman. She served him a cup of herbal tea.

"Tina . . ." he began, as he awkwardly stirred a spoonful of acacia honey into his drink.

"Yes?"

"I feel alone. There is nothing around. I have a lot of friends, yes, but somehow sense that these connections are superficial. Being an artist is difficult work. So much is expected of me. People want me to entertain them, give them emotions. But sometimes I feel stunted. Sometimes I feel that I have stopped growing. I'm tired of smiling when I'm not happy. It is difficult to explain. But we have always liked each other and I thought . . ."

"No," she said, "I won't."

He looked at her questioningly.

"No."

"But I'm not asking for anything!"

"Eric," she said, "I care for you too much to be with you. At one point I might have allowed something to happen. But it's too late for that. My feelings have grown too strong. I want beauty in my life. I don't want to see everything covered in blood and cocktails. It might surprise you, but I am a woman. I need sunshine and nourishing water. There is a need for infinity and trust." Her eyes became sad and he awkwardly averted his own. "I think you should leave. Just finish your tea and go."

68

From an interview with Giuseppe Lontano, barber,
Via Gaetana 21[1]

Q: So you cut his hair?

GL: Yes, I cut it. This street used to be all barbers. Now there is just myself, and another fellow whose hands tremble. Times have changed. Now everyone wants to go to what they call a 'hair stylist'. A simple haircut is no longer good enough for the young men. Papus predicted this would happen.

Q: What can you tell us about him?

GL: Papus?

Q: No, Eric Clark.

GL: Yes. He was an actor. A lot of actors used to come in here back then. Ennio Balbo. Ciccio Ingrassia. Fernando Sancho, who was a great connoisseur of women. Mario Carotenuto, who spent some time in the reformatory with my cousin Francesco before he became a big star.

Q: And Eric Clark?

GL: Right. He used to come in here with another fellow,

---

1. Not far from the train station, not far from the sight of the Baths of Diocletian; at night you can hear the ghosts of men diving into the frigidarium.

Momi, who still lives around the corner. They were always together those two. Signor Clark always tipped me. That is how you knew he was not Italian. The Italian clients never tip, but Clark always did. At first he did not like to have his hair cut too short. He was very vain about it. He had a fine head of hair, with dark brown, almost black follicles amassed thickly along his scalp, which was very firm and had just the right amount of moisture. Then, later, when he started to lose it, he was very depressed. He had me start to cut it very short and he would go about in a wig. I cried for him, because, you know, he really did have such wonderful hair. Sincerely I cried for him.

Q: Why do you think he lost it?

GL: He drank. He went with women. Maybe he even took drugs, because many actors did then. That was the lifestyle. But for a man to maintain his hair, he needs to be as celibate as a monk and abstain from alcohol completely. It is also a good idea to massage the scalp with olive oil. The hair is closely related to the nervous system. If you want to keep your hair, do not think too much. And pray to God, because in the end only He can keep you from going bald.

69

In 1983 he was asked to do a film with Mario Constantino.[1] The filming would take place in the Philippines, where Coppola had left a considerable amount of equipment and trained personnel from his *Apocalypse Now* adventure. The cameraman was Bianchi and the second unit director Walter Massini.

The story was about a group of commandos dressed in Adidas sportswear that go into the jungle in an unnamed South East Asian country in order to rescue the deposed president who is locked up in a gigantic bamboo compound in a remote valley guarded by hundreds of men with automatic weapons. The co-stars were Peter Herschell Lawrence[2] and Dave Swade.[3] Essentially it was

---

1. Constantino was convicted of illegal weapons possession when he assaulted three paparazzi (eight bullets fired) as they photographed his girlfriend (Maria Costello) on a beach near Torrevieja, Spain. He was sentenced to two years in jail.

2. His career took a sharp downturn in the 70's when he began to appear in a number of low-budget Spanish voodoo films (*Vudú y mi infierno* 1973, *Vudú negro* 1973, *Gusanos a todo ritmo* 1975). He currently resides in Boca Raton, Florida, where he works for a suicide assistance hotline. He is said to be writing his memoirs.

3. His real name was Josip Pijade. Born in Yugoslavia, he made a career for himself in Italy and Germany, starring in numerous westerns, gialli and war films. Recognizable by his signature moustache and large

a trio of actors who had seen better days, whose hair was only kept black with strong dyes (or in Clark's case, by means of a wig) and who wore loose jackets to hide their rather too-large bellies. Caucasian extras abounded: strange people who had come to the Philippines for various dubious reasons—brain-damaged Vietnam vets, drug addicts, ex-cons and perverts who would get paid five U.S. dollars a day to stumble around in the jungle with guns and sweat as much as possible.

The cast and crew were driven about one hundred miles north of Manila, deep into the jungle.

Peter Herschell Lawrence was in terrible shape, was constantly out of breath, moved with great effort and smiled the smile of an already defeated man. He delivered his lines with a boredom that almost lent them depth. He looked tired, vaguely angry, like a man who had lost both hope and courage. Whenever the cameras were not rolling he could be seen with a Cerveza Negra in his hand or opening a bottle of Manila rum. By three in the afternoon he was so drunk he could not see straight.

Swade had not worked on a film in almost five years, and was delighted to have been called in. He took his role seriously, but had trouble remembering his lines, was lost, sometimes wandered around the set aimlessly, lent cadences of Hamlet to his role, convinced as he was that his part in this rather ridiculous film would resuscitate his career, dust it off and move the cobwebs from his reputation, which was like a jar that had been forgotten in a field and had been passed over by the seasons.

He had been handsome, but those features, with age and hard living, had become almost like a caricature. A large

cleft chin, he gained a reputation as the archetypical American.

flap of fat hung beneath his cleft chin. A huge belly sat beneath his chest and though the smile beneath his moustache was still playful, one could see that he struggled—old age whispering in his ear the sad refrains of failure.

And so it was that this action film had three well beyond their peak; men who were unfit, had drinking problems, whose tired eyes belied the vigorous roles they had been selected for.

"I'm not sure I'm cut out for this anymore," Swade told Clark.

The latter lit a joint. "No one is cut out for it. You have to use it."

"Use it?"

"Yes, use it."

Rubber trees and palm trees. Dragonflies and jumping spiders. Animals cried out in the jungle. Snakes slithered down tree trunks. Strange, brightly-coloured birds opened their large cutlass-like beaks, shrieked and then, flapping their wings, ascended into the sky. Suffocating in the hot, humid temperatures which were in excess of 100 degrees Fahrenheit daily, with his clothes saturated with sweat, mosquitoes swarming about his ears, intoxicated by the spirits of trees, Clark went adrift in the role, something pressing down on him, pushing him out; he truly imagined he was there being hunted in the jungle and his wild eyes expressed terror, violence, because in fact there was something of a metaphor in this scene, primordial fear made manifest—the fear not of the unknown, but of the actual self—to find out that not only it does it not exist, but, worse yet, it is nothing more than a series of masks—tigers, apes, bats which belied the plastic façade of the civilised man, him now running through heavy growth, pushing away large leaves, shoving aside lemon-shaded shrubs. Into a clearing.

"Why are you all watching me?" he said in paranoia.

"Because we're filming you!" the director cried.

Clark shrugged his shoulders. He had forgotten. Peter Herschell Lawrence came lumbering up beside him, carrying an M-16.

"We should. Reach. The compound by dawn. Tomorrow. Rescue President Farvallo and get the hell outa here."

And then Swade, waving his right arm about dramatically, pronouncing his words with an uptown British accent: "Complete the mission we will, but it is the pay that I am after."

The cameraman zoomed in eagerly.

- Filming was done in a haphazard way
- The scenes were hectic / unorganised / savage
- There were no stuntmen and the cast, being made up for the most part of consummate un-professionals, caused numerous broken bones, first-degree burns, etc.

Constantino insisted on using live ammunition for much of the shooting, so as to make it authentic. This got mixed with the blanks used for close-in scenes and one of the Filipino extras ended up getting shot in the leg. Someone, drunk or high on drugs, pulled the pin on a phosphorus grenade and tossed it into a tent, but miraculously no one ended up being seriously injured.

The sound of the explosion startled Clark back into himself.

"Hey, I am here to shoot a film, not get killed," he said, suddenly feeling an inexplicable attachment to his physical form.

"Don't be a primadonna," Constantino replied.

Clark cursed at the other in very graphic Italian. In anger, he abandoned the set, jumping into a jeep and driving off. Constantino continued with what shooting he could, but two days later sent Walter Massini after him.

"Get him back. He's impossible, but he's the only actor we have."

After a bit of investigating, the assistant director found him in a Manila hotel room, waist-high in prostitutes. The naked arm of one spilled out from beneath a sheet. The naked legs of another could be seen hanging over the arm of a chair as she slept—some woman without a past or with a past Clark had never thought or enquired about, not out of selfishness (though he was selfish) but simply to avoid whatever lurid or depressing story lay behind that being who when awake giggled mechanically and whose existence seemed no more real than a mirage.

He lay on a bed, shirt off, in a pair of blue jeans, gazing at the television, at *I Dream of Genii* dubbed into Tagalog—at that far away adolescent fantasy which gave him neither comfort nor intellectual stimulation, which was nothing more than the movement of bodies; colours; unpleasant chattering which, for all its absurdity, in no way made him laugh but rather gave him a sense of unease like that derived from ventriloquist acts or bad vaudeville.

His beard and moustache were tinged with white powder. He somehow had acquired a jar of hash oil and was so stoned that he thought he heard his mother talking to him.

"Be good."

"I am."

"So famous."

"No."

"I asked that you be protected."

"Should ring the front desk."

The dubious luxury of a four-star Manila hotel in 1983. A window draped with yellow white curtains overlooking the bay. A vague smell of old oysters. A bed whose springs could be heard and felt and a bell-hop who would appear at the door every now and again with an ingratiating smile, a bottle of liquor, an offer of dope, an outstretched hand.

A depressing scene, not only for the fake luxury, which is of course far sadder than true poverty, the latter at least having dignity, but for the characters that were positioned there on stage. Two unhappy prostitutes and a stoned actor.

Door. A knock.

Clark looked over. Did not say anything. And it opened.

"Are you crazy?" Massini said. "Do you know what the cops do to you in this country if you get caught?"

REPLAY

Outside the yellow-curtained window was the bay and the room had a vague smell of old oysters. A bell-hop who seemed about 36 and whose mother was drying rice on the side of the road 40 kilometres away appearing at the door every now and again carrying with him an ingratiating smile, a bottle of liquor, an offer of dope, an outstretched hand.

Fake luxury. Two prostitutes and a stoned actor.

Door. A knock.

Clark looked over. Did not say anything. And it opened. Massini came in.

"Are you crazy?" he said. "Do you know what the fuzz do to you in this country if they catch you?"

"Who do you think sold me the stuff?"

The younger man lit a cigarette. Paced around the room and began talking about his childhood, when he would go out fishing for eels with his grandfather in Veneto.

"Those were simpler times. When it thundered he said it was the devil playing *bocce*. And maybe it was true. There is another aspect to life that we don't see. He told me he had purchased three hectares of property in heaven from a travelling salesman."

"My grandfather was fed to caimans."

"Caimans?"

"Crocodiles."

"There are worse things that can happen. A friend of mine was fed to pigs when he was on vacation in Brazil."

"He probably deserved it."

"Maybe, but what I don't understand is why you won't finish the film with us, since your grandfather was eaten by a crocodile."

Clark was silent. The symbolic logic of the other's statement made sense to him and, in the end, he was coaxed back to the set.

Constantino came and kissed him on both cheeks. There were tears in the director's eyes. He said something in a very soft voice and pointed toward the sun, which was just beginning to go down. The camp cook prepared three stuffed chickens that had been beaten to death with a large stick and the director told Clark that he was the best actor he had ever worked with.

"We are both geniuses, that is the problem," he said.

"Yes," Clark replied before biting into a drumstick, "when two hungry dogs are together, there is a danger that they might eat each other's tails off."

In any case, filming went somewhat more smoothly from that point forward. The director allowed Clark some of his eccentricities, realising that the important thing was to get back to Italy with a completed film, and a few stories to tell around the dinner table to make women with large mouths laugh.

During one scene Eric Clark was supposed to eat a snake, but instead they gave him pulled pork which had been sewn to a rope.

"Hey, if I am supposed to eat a snake, let me at least eat one." He was interested in realism.

"If you want to eat one, do it!"

Shirtless trotting through the jungle with a sharp stick quiet eyes sharp observant splinters toward olive-green tree snake with dorsal stripe speared and grilled on the end of a stick hot eaten on haunches the truth is also true.

On the last day of shooting, Clark was approached by Mikey Lim, of Golden Moon, one of the bigger Filipino production companies.[1] They offered him $5,200 U.S. plus expenses for five weeks worth of shooting on their own films.

"A Filipino film?" Clark asked.

"No, it's an American film. With mostly Filipino actors and a local production team, but the film is American."

---

1. Though Golden Moon productions were filmed in the Philippines, they generally had English titles, used Caucasian leads, and were dubbed into English—for the most part were marketed to Third World countries as American action films—licensed to Turkey or Malta for four or five thousand dollars and in the U.S. bypassing theatrical release for direct-to-video circulation.

"Without Americans actually being involved?"

"You have U.S. passport?"

"Yes, but I'm from Paraguay."

"U.S. passport lead man means American film," Lim said gravely.

As he had no work pending back in Italy, Clark dug his hands into his pockets and accepted.

The result was the bizarre *Jungle Nightmare*.

A large, curly wig, a bandana and sunglasses, body dripping with perspiration like some candle set alight. Depicting a Vietnam POW (Tom Brancy) who, after being tortured by the Vietcong (sleeping in a pit, toenails pulled out, made to dine on worms, kicked in groin, hung by ankle from tall tree), believes himself to be Christ, escapes and leads a band of Vietnamese hoodlums which he delves up from the suburbs of Saigon and refers to as his apostles against a secret U.S. military base where they are manufacturing a deadly chemical agent to use against the Vietnamese. The U.S. soldiers, when not chewing on cigars and abusing the local women, wear chemical suits and are armed with flamethrowers. Clark is armed with a bazooka. An M72 LAW. There were the usual scenes of macheteing through thick jungles, pulling leeches off legs, shinnying up palm trees, an astounding amount of pyrotechnics: helicopters blowing up, jeeps blowing up, cars blowing up, motorcycles and bicycles blowing up, bodies and body parts rushing through the air, jungles smoking and crackling to the continuous rattle of machine-gun fire. As in many Filipino movies, dwarves were made use of, and Weng Weng[1] even had an uncredited appearance. In

---

1. Paratrooper and star of the Eddie Nicart film *For Y'ur Height Only* (1981).

the final scene, after having his disciples crucify him in the middle of the burnt-out military base, Brancy blows himself up with a timed explosion credits rolling to the sound of a Casio keyboard playing the theme to *Crawlspace*.

The director was Mike Ronny, a short, fat Filipino from Parañaque City whose real name was Miguel Santiago. His artistic merits were certainly slim, but he was able to keep to schedule and produce films on the smallest of budgets and was therefore highly valued by Golden Moon, who in the heyday of the Filipino movie boom were entrusting him with no less than eighteen films a year, including a much-celebrated series of martial arts films starring Tom Kynhart.[1]

---

1. Most notable of these was *Bamboo Demons Kill Imperiously*, which received a FAMAS (Filipino Academy of Movie Arts and Sciences Award) nomination for best production design. Kynhart died in 1989 after letting a rabid puppy lick a cut he had received during the filming of *Manila Homicide Squad*.

Manila. Bar at the Pan Pacific Hotel. Overhead fans. Sweating beer bottles. Flies whispering against walls and resting on windowsills.

"Yeah, yeah, yeah. We pay you five thousand dollar."

"Right, I understand this. But what's the film?"

"Action film." The man gazed at Clark through the huge lenses of his glasses. "We make big action film and you star."

Clark was silent for a moment and took a sip of his Long Island iced tea; looked at the smiling face across from him; the plump hands which rested on the table; a gaudy gold ring wrapped around a finger that twitched about before reaching for a glass of beer—a finger that had probably pulled a trigger more than once as during this time there were many triad members in Manila. They would use the Philippines as a base to run drugs, guns and stolen goods through. There was the Tiger Group and the 14kts. The Philippine National Police (PNP), Philippine Drug Enforcement Agency (PDEA) and the Presidential Anti-Graft Commission (PAGC) were all in their pockets, bribes and gifts being handed out in abundance. Clark was unsure exactly what the current gentleman's background was, but felt that a background he had.

"Can I see the script?"

"Script being written. When you get to Hong Kong you see script and then we do big action film. Hong Kong full of action film right now and we give you good work. Build your reputation international. The Asian film market going crazy. You do work and we pay you five thousand American dollar for short footage."

"And travel expenses?"

"Travel no problem buddy." The man grinned. His gold-capped teeth glistened dully. "We got boat here in harbour. Right here in Manila we got thirty-footer. We take you to Hong-Kong no problem."

"I don't know."

"Thousand dollar U.S. up front buddy," the man said, tossing a somewhat greasy envelope toward the actor.

And so, a few days later, he found himself pulling out of Manila Bay on a yacht with a number of Chinese who spent the voyage playing cards and mah-jong, drinking beer and cleaning their guns. Clark had no idea what the boat was carrying, but felt rather sure that its cargo was less than legal. He had blow, though, and thought it just as well to travel this way than by airplane—staring at the waves, at some far-off corner of the sea, and breathing in the salt air through his numb nostrils while letting his mind soar and plummet as his career had.

He caught sight of a school of flying fish. One of the men on board, excited, began to shoot at them, nicking a wing off one, sending another to the realm of the dragons.

"John Wayne," he told Clark with a grin.

"Your heroes have always been cowboys."

"Almost on 1978 Hong Kong Olympic team in Seoul. Twenty-five metre rapid-fire pistol. Personal record 578."

Clark offered him some coke and the man, in a sudden burst of momentum, confided in him.

"My younger brother is boy prostitute living with a rich man in Oregon with six dogs in yard. Presa Canario. I do this work to get him out of bondage. Got to raise 50,000 U.S. He studied at Lingnan University. Degree in Cultural Studies. Wrote a ninety-pages book about *Hundred Crab Scroll* and did short poems in the style of Ou-yang Hsiu. String beans coil and so do rat tails. Once wanted to live in Sky Clear Monastery. It's not like life is carved in stone. Big dishonour to family now, but no one talks about slave trade."

"He's good looking?"

"So-so. But real well-mannered."

In Hong Kong he was put up at a cheap hotel. There was a slot next to the bed. When a coin was inserted it would vibrate.

The director, Steven Chong, an extremely young-looking man with glasses, who spoke good English with a faint British accent, came to meet him. His eagerness was almost embarrassing.

"Ah, great, Mr. Clark. You're going to do some fine acting for me, aren't you?"

"Can I see the script?"

He was handed a few sheets of paper with cursory staging instructions, a few lines of vapid dialogue, no appreciable plot. It had been written by a teacher of English who worked at the Kiangsu and Chekiang Primary School—a man in his late thirties who had small literary pretensions and had been hired for two hundred dollars U.S. and was later listed in the credits as the PAP Creative Unit.

"I'm not sure I . . ." Clark murmured.

Chong smiled ingratiatingly.

"No, don't worry. We are filming silent. Afterwards we will put in your voice or the voice of another. You can say what you like, it doesn't matter. The dialogue might change. We don't need to commit to anything!"

Clark was familiar with this way of doing things.

"And what's the name of the film?"

"Strike Force. Mission Wild Dog. We're not sure yet, but we have some working titles. Everyone's very busy with this thing. Big production! A lot of excitement! It is magnificent to be able to work with you, an international star!"

Clark shrugged his shoulders. The fellow seemed nice enough. Naïve maybe, but nice enough, and so they shook hands and the director left and the actor collapsed on his bed and was shaken to sleep and the next day, after having a beer and a bowl of congee for breakfast, he was picked up by two suited gentlemen in sunglasses who did not speak a word of English and driven through the busy streets to the studio—which in fact was nothing more than a warehouse in Wan Chai, wedged between a rug dealer and a tenement that smelled of fried foods.

"Co-stume," one of the men said, handing Clark a bag.

The latter went into the changing room and came out wearing:

1) A blue silk blouse
2) A bright yellow sash
3) A bandana with the word "Ninja" in Asian-looking script tied around his forehead

"What part exactly am I playing?" he asked Chong.

"Um, you're sort of like a boxer. A really powerful boxer with some special skills. Eight-trigram style. It was invented by a eunuch named Dong Haichuan who understood both the earth and the heavenly bodies. We are doing location shots today, so everyone needs to hop in the van."

They drove to Victoria Park, where young men were playing soccer and Indonesian baby-sitters strolling with perambulators.

"Now you run over and you hit that man," Chong told Clark.

"And then?"

"That's it. You hit him and then we'll film the next shot."

"Dialogue?"

"None."

For lunch he was fed noodles and diced pork in a styrofoam container. The technicians had sallow cheeks, looked like opium addicts, constantly scratching themselves, eyes darting about nervously, often fidgeting with their shirt collars. The cast members were all unfriendly. Most of them only spoke Cantonese and it was clear that the majority were not actors, but out-of-work thugs. They glared at him and said things under their breath that he could not understand but felt were surely unpleasant— those insults typically mumbled against rich foreigners and hairy dogs.

There was one other westerner on the set. His name was Tom Dover. He was an Irishman, a black belt in tae kwon do who was being paid U.S. 150 to lend the thing a bit more of an international patina. The Chinese would abuse him terribly and he would sustain injuries on an almost daily basis.

"I'll show you some moves," he told Clark. "See, this is the knife-hand block. . . . And here we have the crescent kick, which is pretty heavy on the yang. If you're standing there in command position and I come at you like this . . ."

In slow motion he swung his foot around so it hovered around Clark's ear.

"Hey," the latter said, "do you know where to get any coke around this place?"

"Well, if you have the fever for the flavour . . ."

Afterwards they all loaded in the van and drove to the outskirts of town, to Diamond Hill, where they had a set of sorts, consisting of a few hovels placed in the trees. Clark was once again asked to run around and hit people and the day's shooting ended with him driving a hypodermic needle into a very ugly woman's neck and Steven Chong clapping and shouting some interjection of praise.

Then the Chinese crew all went off to drink beer and eat noodles and Tom Dover took Clark to Lan Kwai Fong to show him around.

"How did you end up in Hong Kong?" Clark asked.

"Well, I was living in Dublin and studying martial arts with a fellow called Barry McGrady. I'd always go to the Theatre De Luxe where they showed kung-fu triple-feature matinees. I figured it would be good for my yin to get into the real thing so I came here and have been doing a little Flexible Power Boxing over at the Bamboo River Martial Arts Centre and doing my acting. Just trying to stay centred."

"You don't mind being pushed around?"

"Are you kidding man, I love it!"[1]

The next day the routine was repeated, minus the hypodermic needle. They all climbed into a van, drove to some unremarkable spot and ran around while being filmed. Walking. Moving his mouth. Punching. Pretending to kick. Some elemental episode of inanity joke without laugh skit clusters of physical and mental existence. At one point Kang Chin[2] came in for a cameo and was treated with great respect by all present.

Clark continued to try and discover what the film was about, but without success.

They seemed to want to provide him with as little information as possible. When he asked questions they would act like they didn't understand him or become evasive.

"Maybe this is just the Chinese custom," Clark thought, "their idea of being polite."

But it was not even completely clear who was bankrolling the production or who it was who was actually paying him, as his money was delivered in four or five modest parcels of cash, each time by a different hand.

The bizarre frenetic role he played seems to have been a result of Chong insisting that he "act a lot."

The director's ideal of high art was what he had seen in Taiwanese opera, wusheng fantasies, where the actors would stamp their feet before walking and fling their hair about to express sadness—long voyages expressed by a few pompous strides; a big battle by a sword being swung about—the acting done on an almost primeval level for

---

1. This was truly a case of, "When the moon is up in the west, punishment and reward are meted out in the east."
2. Cult Taiwanese actor who often appeared under the pseudonyms of Kong Kam, Gang Jin, King Kong, and Kum Kong.

those with expansive minds or inhibited intellects or for those who were in innate communication with heroes and gods.

"Please, could you act more?" Chong would say, and Clark would obediently, possibly even maliciously, exaggerate his role even more, making wild expressions, broad sweeping gestures, almost miming—raising his eyebrows, thrusting forward his chest, walking in a highly affected manner as if he were in a silent film, knees lifting high in the air, toes pointing outward.

"Great!" Chong shouted with enthusiasm. "This is what it's like working with a star."

In the evenings, Clark stayed in his hotel room, doing coke which Dover managed to score him and working on his own script, *La Vida di Tiburcio Vasquez*, with a certain amount of energy—sending his thoughts to old California—to the ringing of pistol shots and the robbing of banks, images occurring like memories, whether real or invoked by the powder or some kind of elemental inspiration.

This was the film he wanted to make. To both star in and direct.

71

"More acting please!"

DOUBLE KARATE FEATURES!
CHINESE KUNG-FU!
CHEN SEN'S
"A GATHERING OF HEROES"
(English subtitles)
PLUS
ERIC CLARK IN
"NINJA DEATH GAME"
2nd SMASH WEEK!

The movie used ample Filipino footage[1] and also used the Pink Floyd album *The Dark Side of the Moon* in its unauthorised soundtrack.

From a review of *Cobra Powerforce*

[...] The story offers reason of interest actualised by a plot where homicide and savage violences are provided.

---

1. While it seems that at least five films were spliced into *Full Metal Raider*, three of these have been identified: 1) *Kapitan Eddie Set: Mad Killer of Cavite* (dir. José Yandoc); 2) *Batang Quiricada* (dir. ?); 3) *Dirty Hari* (dir. Jun Gallardo).

Director Wallace Chong, other than the part of a certain specification whose other things are deep in all possible resources of barbarity and during sufficiently agile impression, has made the narration clear. A film of skilful appreciation. Actor Clark, as moustached leading part, appears pliable. Especially in the scene at the bathroom between George and Rosemarie. George the "black belt" has known karate one way. Under psychological profile, the design which makes heavy from dark ones the mark false Orient of cliché. But this is the bond in the life and Rosy is beautiful. Unfortunately, Clark is no Lee Fan Cleef.[1] [...]

—Ma Ching-Kuo, *The People's Liveliness Newspaper*,
March 8, 1983

---

1. Translation provided by Yi Shin Translation Service, Room 901, Building No. 3, Pudong South Rd. 1645, Pudong, Shanghai, China, 200120 (incorporated under approval of the concerned authorities of Shanghai).

72

He arrived back in Italy in a strange state of mind—paranoid, proud, his eyes eternally shielded by a pair of oversized sunglasses, his nose constantly on the lookout for powder. Momi was there for him, with his large, grotesque smile, like a demon. Tina Treville rang his doorbell but he did not answer, finding himself strangely repulsed by her kindness, that nature which he could not understand. Then there was Buonaventura, who did not bother ringing the doorbell, but simply walked into his apartment.

The agent of talent was wearing a new and fashionable suit and carrying a brand new leather briefcase and seemed to have climbed out of the gutter he had been in when Clark had last seen him.

"Eric, you're back," he said, grasping the actor by the hand with a firm grip.

"You smell of cologne."

"Pino Silvestre. The fresh smell of the forest. It has become my habit to smell as nice as possible."

"Are things going well?"

"They are picking up. I managed to land some young talent with television spots. I have felt the need to change my system somewhat. Films might soon be a thing of the past. Television, television, television. You might consider *Cinquant'anni di amore.*"

Clark gave an inquisitive look.

"Television!"

"I'm a film actor."

"So it seems," the agent said with a hint of sarcasm. "I see you have been doing some work in the bowels of Hong Kong."

"Yes, I did a film there."

"A film? More like fifty."

"I am not sure I understand you."

"Look at these . . ."

He opened his briefcase and emptied six or eight VHS boxes on the table: *Blood Mission*, *Thunderbolt Force*, *Ninja Death Game*, *Phantom Peer Roses War*, *Dirty Ninja*, etc.

Clark picked up two. One showed him on the cover holding a samurai sword, another with the ninja headband. His name was written in large red letters and the box designs evoked a cheapness that was anything but charming.

"All these movies . . ."

"This is not all. There are many more titles that I know of. These things are being pushed all over the place. Particularly in Turkey and Greece. The market is being flooded with this trash. If this is your new system . . ."

"They ripped me off."

"*Ti hanno preso per il culo*, my friend. That is what comes from going freelance. You shouldn't be such a cowboy. I'm telling you, television . . ."

"No," Clark said decisively; because television was the ultimate representation of capitalism, an electric tombstone people set in their houses in order to move further away from the great sky, to be distracted from the dirt and poverty outside their windows and the wounded crawling along gasping for help since man was becoming a creature who got its pleasure from living as vicariously as possible off the inane actions of others; and then seeing those miserable video tapes there made him feel clouded, shabby—something was in his throat that he wanted to let out but could not and when he drank it would not go away either.

73

He was going through a crisis, mental, spiritual, where he could no longer relate to the people around him, could no longer relate even to himself or understand who he was or what his purpose was in living, how much less so in acting. He was empty—intellectually, artistically, morally. What stock he had had, had been greatly depreciated by his Hong Kong adventure. He no longer read books or even newspapers. Sometimes he would turn on the radio for five minutes. The happy songs made him sad and the sad songs filled him with disgust. His tomorrows were uncertain, existed merely due to the impetus of his yesterdays, which were fading into the past, disappearing, decaying and the world around him seemed like a thin and colourful veil that hid an infinite darkness.

"Why am I not more like Clark?" he asked himself.

The thing held up a mirror, and he saw his own reflection—as he was: overweight, balding. A slight double chin lay about his neck. His eyes looked tired, vaguely degenerate, full of a somewhat hollow depth. And he saw within those features that, despite his great skill, his great ability, he was in fact no more than any other actor, than any other leper, and whatever secret treasure he might have received, he had misused, spent on worthless causes, insignificant films—and even in this prognosis there was falsity, because his adventure was a great one, but one not always easy to endure—defining one's life in a few thoughts or words or feelings an impossibility, like describing the flavour of water or catching wind in a fishing net or trying to remember what you never knew.

He was disoriented. Sometimes he thought of suicide, of jumping off some old bridge or killing himself in a latrine—something horrible that would be a fitting end for his sadness, because his personality was as fragmented as his ideals, both lost somewhere—in some hotel on the French Riviera or some subsidiary universe in which the flight of birds, the speed of automobiles and the shape of clouds were all signs, a form of cosmic speech.

"I need to find myself," he thought—not as some strategist might closely think of the future, or as he had once desultorily thought about physics, but rather primordially, instinctively, as a matter of survival and then when he saw the flyer, fluttering along the ground on the Via del Gesù, near an ancient marble foot, it seemed like providence.

Radiance Fellowship in Vrindavan, India
Self-Discovery
Come and harmonise your mind!
Immerse yourself in the Spiritual Life!
Creating your Inner Glow
Harmonising with the Rhythms of Nature
Take a Quiet Walk Inside Your SELF
come

to

the Birthplace of Lord Krishna
and hear the discourses of Sri Sri Sri Babolmzloe
Vrindavan, India (50 m from the Imli Tala tree)

74

He boarded a plane at the Leonardo da Vinci-Fiumicino Airport. It rose into the air, travelled over islands and deserts, over mountains and then jungles, and deposited him in New Delhi.

He got off the plane. Dizzy, he was swallowed up by a taxi.

"What do you want?" his driver asked him.

"Nothing."

"Hey, do not tell me that. Everyone wants something. I can get it for you. A woman. The marijuana. Hashish. Opium. A good time."

"I'm trying to find myself."

The man frowned. "Ah, another spiritual tourist. No wonder India is so poor."

Clark looked out the window as the taxi carried him on, through the city, toward the Hilton Hotel. The people vaguely reminded him of those of his own country, of Paraguay, for this was another land of poverty, another place of permanent decline where ghosts and phantoms lived alongside men of meagre flesh—men who did not so much struggle to survive as simply survived, as if by no will of their own. Some cooked vegetables in little pots right there on the sidewalk. Knots of young men in white, short-sleeve shirts hung about on street corners. People went about performing obscure activities—carrying donkey-loads of brass pots, cobbling shoes, shaving heads, selling snakes and then he was ushered into the exaggerated, sterile luxury of the hotel where he fell asleep on a very broad bed and then woke early the next morning and was served coffee and Danishes in an almost empty dining room before taking a taxi to Vrindavan, flying past women urinating by the side of the road, a man with a trained bear, and boys riding old orange bicycles.

As soon as they entered the town the vehicle stopped moving.

"It is the time of the pilgrimage," the driver said and then Clark paid him, took his small bag and walked.

The place was full of pilgrims, the air rich with stench. Music, the sound of widows singing bhajan hymns, came seeping from doorways and lepers loping, crawling after him, their palms outstretched, seeming to ask for more than just alms, seeming to want to grab and take away his very soul and though he did not hurry his steps, choosing to go deliberately slower instead, it might well have been that he felt like running, because if New Delhi vaguely reminded him of Paraguay, this place did not, with its carved sandstone temples, spiral columns and water tanks. A thick yellow slime oozed along the gutters. The streets were constricted, ancient and seedy. As no one spoke English, Spanish or Italian, he found his way with difficulty. A minute doorway which he had to stoop through to enter.

Sri Babolmzloe was seated in a small room with a number of devotees around him. He had a short beard, large impressive eyes, and a gourd-shaped belly. One man played the sitar. Another sang, somewhat off-key. When

Eric entered, all looked up. The sitar twanged. The singer stopped. Silence. And then the guru spoke, fixing on Clark a gaze tranquil as a pond, affectionate as a mother, and full of authority, like a magistrate:

"You have come."

The actor quivered. He wanted to fall to his knees, but could not bring himself to. There were tears in his eyes and he began to say something, a few disjointed words, when someone tapped him on the shoulder.

"Your shoes."

"What?"

"Take off your shoes, friend."

He looked down. He was wearing leather boots under his blue jeans. He took them off and put them down next to a long row of sandals, where they stood like two towers.

"What an egomaniac I am," he thought.

The guru was now talking:

". . . ineffable bliss. The kundalini surmounts the chakras, winding up the skein of the human nervous system, moving from the seats of defecation, procreation and regeneration up to the region of the heart, then it mounts to the throat, punches through to the third eye, and finally the culmination, the thousand-petal lotus at the crown of the head, the seat of consciousness. As in the music you heard, which fixed its attention on Sri Krishna, and you in turn turned your organs of sense to that sound, so should you turn your attention to your next birth and tame your fickle mind."

"What about human love?" a woman with long oily hair asked.

"Passion by nature comes from thirst and attachment. It is the cause of births in future bodies. The soul needs to be protected by restraining the senses. Otherwise it endlessly travels from birth to death, is like a prisoner transported from one cell to another. In this degenerate age one must refrain from unwholesome actions."

And later, instead of talking to the guru, he watched as the latter went out of the room. Clark once again held back by his ego, or at least so he interpreted his inability to go and speak, attach himself to that sage, and then in the middle of thinking, wondering, one of the disciples approached him.

"Are you from Canada?"

It was the woman with long oily hair. She had very sincere eyes and a somewhat dull face.

"No. Paraguay. My name is Eric."

"Eric. It means 'ruler.' My name is Sadhya, which means 'twilight.'"

"My real name is José. So maybe I am not a ruler."

"My non-spiritual name is Keren. I came from Milwaukee to be with Sri Babo."

"You are alone?"

"Yes. I am trying to learn how to exist."

And then came an evening of long philosophical discussions over tea and lovemaking at her guesthouse room and the next day he was asked for a donation and handed over a purse full of money and received a 'spiritual name' which meant 'from whose body clouds emerge.' It was only a few days later that he realised that this guru who spoke so eloquently about restraining the senses was himself one who liked to touch the vellum lips of his disciples, their earth-bound bodies, always managing to glance

292

against them as they passed and have the prettier ones crawl through his door after dark to learn about the path travelled by those who seek the truth and the mysteries of the milk and water embrace.

Clark noted this to Sadhya.

"He will teach you how to live," she said. "You will have to be alone tonight. But it will give you time to think. Remember that you have to give up attachment. You will never make progress if you are attached."

"Well, if you need me . . ."

"Your guesthouse?"

"The Floating Lotus."

"How much are you paying for your room?"

"Paying? Eighty rupees[1] a night I think, why?"

Sadhya opened her eyes wide.

"So much," she said. "They really are taking advantage of you."

Clark smiled pleasantly. But her comment made him think about his ideals. Of socialism. Anarchism. The ideals he had left behind, but which suddenly appeared very relevant to him since the spiritual path it seemed required a certain amount of bargaining and none of the guru's disciples, by Indian standards at least, were by any means poor and why was it that even enlightenment was not free?

Cut to the actor wandering around the place disconsolately, like a man wandering around the streets of some lost civilisation that he felt unable to connect with, a place where monkeys scrambled everywhere and sad widows planted their tears which, nurtured on the proteins of time, grew into mythologies like boxes in boxes.

---

1. Approximately three dollars U.S., based on the 1984 exchange rate.

He stopped in his path.

A deformed creature sat on the side of the lane and Clark was at least glad that his position was better, because even if he was lost spiritually, was losing his hair, possibly even losing his mind, at least he could be grateful that he was in a better situation than that, whose limbs were like ropes and out of whose wound-like mouth a swollen tongue protruded.

He threw a few rupees into its hand. Its tongue wagged. It spoke.

"You look upset."

"You speak English."

"Yes. Both scoundrels and beggars speak English. Before I was struck by this horrible disease I taught forensic science and criminology at Punjab University in Chandigarth. I had many friends and women looked at me fondly. But no one respects an unfortunate man. You are following Sri Babo?"

"I don't know."

Camera cuts quickly to some drool sliding out of the beggar's orifice, off that hanging tongue which looked like a raw cow's liver.

"India is full of people who claim spirituality and your goods and chattels as well. Religion was born in this country, but so were thievery and greed. Some of the richest men in the universe live here, but so do lepers and blind children. Go to the Pink City, tall man. There you will discover round and bright stability. Leave your sadness behind like you would a broken sandal. If you set to work with sincerity, you are bound to succeed."

Clark shrugged his shoulders and moved on; returned to his room and packed his little bag. When leaving, making his way through town past the tala tree, he met Sadhya.

"Where are you going?" she asked. "Sri Babolmzloe is waiting for you. He is going to teach us about the Sixth Way of Clean Living."[1]

Fade to Jaipur. Designed like an ancient zodiac. A city of commerce and someone exhibiting a fascinating display of old weaponry. The sights: the Hawa Majal, or Hall of Winds (with 953 windows); the Amber Fort; the Jal Mahal, a palace sitting in the middle of a lake (below the water's surface, fish and tiny dragons salute each other gracefully). A city of activity, crowded lanes and a figure riding by on a camel.

In a café.

Sipping tea.

A tall, extremely thin man stood staring at him with a heated gaze. Clark nodded and the other came and collapsed in a chair opposite.

"Hey."

"Hello," Clark said.

"I am an actor."

He spoke with a strong German accent. He looked hungry. A small insect could be seen crawling around in his moustache.

"Oh," Clark replied, measuring the other's restless eyes.

"You have probably heard of me."

And the man waited for the question that Clark never asked and then answered it, though it had never been spoken and maybe never even been thought.

---

1. Do not eat food or dainties burnt by fire and do not drink anything made with liquid jaggery or pineapple. Do not climb stairs or scaffolding. Do not kill dews, flowers or ants and do not step on fresh moss, but do offer adequate donations to the guru who is like your mother, brother and spouse coiled together in one.

"I am James Dean," he said, looking at Clark with a strange mixture of pride and fear.

"You look thin."

"I have not eaten for two days. Only tea. I came from Hamburg a few years ago and have been getting by."

Clark ordered him a plate of shahi paneer, paid for it and left, walked down the road, past rug dealers and dealers of textiles, perfume vendors and young men selling diamonds at discount prices, thinking, reminding himself that he had that great spirit within and should be guided by it and then he was walking through a pair of gates into a tranquil courtyard and then through a door and he was talking with a very rigid Indian gentleman who sat behind an enormous desk.

". . . because, you see, we cannot just let anyone into his presence," the other was saying. "It's a twelve hour bus ride and then an hour on foot but I have one ticket left if you want to purchase it."

The room began to spin somewhat and he heard Alec Guinness tell him something and then the beginningless series of creation self-surrender tears wailing crimes waves tossing him this way and that while the hands of titans churned up above.

75

Mist clung to mountains. Tall trees stretched out. Water cascaded down rocks.

He was introduced to Sri Brahmavishnu on July 7th, 1984.

The guru was a short, somewhat round individual who smiled a great deal. A necklace of red beads hung below his throat and he spoke with a slight lisp. When he spoke, he would pause significantly between every few words, so that it took him a great deal of time to express even the simplest of ideas—his words taking on great significance due to the prolonged nature of his oratory.

"You must sit quietly with your legs crossed," he said.

"And?"

"When you rub two sticks together you create fire. Just as the kuravaka tree will only bloom when embraced by a beautiful woman, your inner lotus will only open its petals when embraced by truth. Penetrating earth and water is not enough. Not enough is it to penetrate fire and air and even sky. It is the mind that must be penetrated and this is done through the diagrammatic symbol of worship. Who could imagine, seeing a sprout come out of the ground, that one day it will turn into a giant banyan tree?"

Clark scratched his chin, listening intently to Sri Brahmavishnu's words, and then, later, after dining on saffron-coloured rice and curried lady's fingers, he walked into the night. The moon sat like camphor in the sky. The forest around radiated its nocturnal sounds—insects chirping, branches rustling faintly. A figure walked by him rapidly and he thought he recognised it—but was unsure if it was not simply his own fear, his own paranoia that he had carried with him from Italy or maybe had been carrying with him since before he could remember.

The next day he took up residency in a cave, watched his mind carefully, maintaining awareness of thoughts without following them, allowing the impulses to drift away and disappear into space without either cutting them off or repressing them. He tried, without trying to try, to maintain a position of meditational equipoise, letting his mental apparatus sit, neither too tight, nor too loose, and letting the footage run by without really looking at the images, of crocodiles, jazz musicians, automobiles, cogitations opening their wings, circling through the air, and then disappearing in the mist, vague memories, thoughts of mother and ex-wife, which in turn gave way to visions of flowers, waves of milk gently lapping over his mind. Without question the state was peaceful and the ensuing bliss pleasant. His body felt indescribably light. An ecstatic trembling now and again coursed through it. His forehead tingled as if someone had set a piece of ice on it or maybe blown cocaine onto his frontal lobe.

He went to Sri Brahmavishnu and described his state of mind.

"If you change a few rupees into paise, you get a great deal, but in fact the value is not so much," the guru said.

"You need discrimination. You need to separate the rice kernel from the husk."

"How can I do this?"

"By striking it with a pestle," the Indian replied, making a strong motion with his fist.

Clark returned to his cave. He crossed his legs in lotus fashion, channelled his energy, worshipped internally; saw once again that bird with its long black beak, that pecking raven, which began to rip at his flesh, draw his mind back toward his body which seemed as if it were chained to a rock; some Prometheus having his liver torn out. He tried to ignore it, to let his mind rest in tranquillity, but found it impossible—an incessant itching trembling numbness pain.

He described the experience to the guru.

"It is some sort of demon," the other said. "It is your bad karma."

"And how do I get rid of it?"

"Ah!"

Clark waited expectantly for more information, but Sri Brahmavishnu was silent, as if he had already given explicit instructions.

<h1 style="text-align:center">76</h1>

Devoid of attributes / emptiness / isolation.

The actor underwent many trials. He stayed alone in that cave for a week, meditating on the milk of the goddess's breast (a milk-ocean flowing from her heart), and then on a hilltop sat and meditated on the hair above the navel. He slept without cushions and did not sit on stools, benches or chairs. He did not drink liquor or eat meat. When he walked he avoided stepping on insects and when mosquitoes sucked his blood, he watched without crushing them.

In meditation he saw, or at least thought he saw, his past lives—long before, when he had been a goat nibbling on grass, then a basket maker in Beth-Horon, and then when he had been Tiburcio Vasquez the bandit, and it was with a certain amount of satisfaction that he would recount these things to Sri Brahmavishnu, almost seeming to take on the various characters as he spoke, almost seeming to bleat like a goat or move his hands about like a basket maker or smile like a wanted man.

"You have had reincarnations," the guru said. "What you are now experiencing is their residual karma in the form of your present state and also in the form of memories which are arising. You were once a giraffe."

"I did not see that. But the bandit, yes."

"Maybe by stealing . . ."

"Yes?"

The guru abruptly changed the trajectory of his discourse:

"In the ten-thousand world system, there is an infinite variety of living beings. There are very small animals which eat a great deal and also tall monsters with very small mouths which make it difficult for them to even swallow a grain of rice and there are people who have large ears like elephants and others who can live without water. A man falls asleep and sees trees, lakes, cities and palaces. He enters one and sees beautiful women and piles of gold and many fine things. But it is only a dream. One must determine the difference between the illusory and the real." And then, with a sudden widening of the eyes and pointing to a man who was just entering: "Ah, but here is a very wealthy devotee who came from your Europe to see me."

Clark turned his head and noticed a gentleman around sixty or sixty-five years of age with a cultured nose and soft, pompous eyes. It was the Count Mulino di San Lorenzo. He was dressed in his normal way except that he wore sandals. With hands clasped together he bowed a little to the guru.

"You?" Clark said.

Arnolfo did not seem surprised to see him.

"Yes."

"Why?"

"Sylvia."

"She left you?"

"No. She ingested an extract of Nerium oleander mixed in with a cocktail. She was raving. I listened in amazement as she called me a worm and said that we would meet in the afterlife, where she could torment me more. She told me that she would take my subtle body, chop it up and build furniture with it, running over it with an adze, nailing the pieces back together like some ugly sculpture."

"I see."

"Not a very nice experience," the guru noted.

"Since going off with Momi that evening, she had not been herself. Always washing her face. Singing 'Volare' in an off-key voice and making subdued references to his higher aesthetics. I had a tomb built for her. A sixty-metre high column made of bricks, granite and glass with a spiral staircase surrounding it. The architect was a young Swiss-Italian by the name of Mario Botta. The ecclesiastical authorities lodged formal complaints, saying that since it was higher than the local cathedrals it was a desecration. I had my old school master, Padre Peone, set things right though. When it was completed, I laid her ashes in there myself. I did not even cry. I couldn't. . . . Some emotional monochrome."

There was a moment of silence.

"All things in this world are transient," the actor said, thinking of his boots.

"I know all this."

Clark looked in the eyes of the other, could see the one who had behaved with cruelty, great coldness, who had made Arnolfo devoted to her somewhat rancid charms—him having offered the quivering passion of his aged lips to her breasts, dragging the silky tenderness of his aristocratic heart through the mud of her spiteful lovemaking.[1]

The actor returned to his cave. He was irritated. It seemed that he could not escape his past no matter what he tried. Why had Arnolfo, that smog-breather who only knew about proto-post-apocalyptic single toned painting and pictures that vanished into coloured vibrations come to invade his little corner of India? The actor could indeed see the workings of karma as he sat rigid and stared into space before him, stared into some past life where Arnolfo was a hunter of birds and he, Clark, was a bird with his long legs dipped deep in the water and the hunter, sitting on the bank fixing an arrow in his bow lets it fly through the wing of the water bird and Clark, wounded and bleeding, sinks beneath the lotuses while demons beat on large drums. **Pum! Pum! Pum!**

Meanwhile Arnolfo was not far away, sitting in his own little cave on a small rug and concentrating on the root of his nostrils.

- Prosperity = yellow
- Peace = white

---

1. orange
   dawn
   vapour
   blue
   rain
   gorge
   pink
   fats
   gorge
   flinching
   heat
   blinding purple

- Killing = black
- Attraction = red

In the morning, after being served some tea by a fourteen-year-old boy named Biplab, the collector would exit his cave and do some feeble stretches in the soft light. Looking over the forest, he pressed his thin lips together. He felt that a sort of magic was becoming his, some form of consolation for the horrors of his pampered life.

Clark wrote Arnolfo's name on an arka leaf, using an ink made from rye seeds, ginger and citraka fruit and then threw it onto his fire-pit in which a fire of khadira wood was burning, reciting ten thousand times the secret mantra. Arnolfo very quickly came down with a high fever and felt as if his insides were being clawed at by demons with long arms.

"You have received a curse," young Biplab told him, and quickly went and purchased about five gallons of milk and, returning to the cave, began pouring the liquid over Arnolfo until his fever had subsided, having been quenched by the cold vibrations.

"It's Clark," the Italian count muttered to himself. "Some old and incomprehensible grudge."

"You must defend yourself," Biplap said. "Take charcoal from the cremation grounds and draw a picture of a snake here on the floor. Then, while eating jack fruit, recite the mantra 'nagan karsay karsay' again and again. Surely that man will be bitten by a viper."

Arnolfo did as had been suggested, and with his mouth stuffed full of jack fruit, mumbled the invocation.

Clark, the next morning, woke up with a Naja naja wrapped around his foot. It raised itself up, showed its hood and hissed. Clark recited the mantra 'ili mili phuh phuh' and the snake became docile and slithered away.

About two weeks later, he came across the Italian eating a mango under a tree.

"I am meditating many hours a day," Arnolfo said.

"I'm not sure it will be enough for you," the actor commented. "You have a lot of negative karma built up. Suppression of the poor. Capitalist money."

"I come from a family of aristocrats."

Clark shrugged his shoulders.

- Grass, weeds and small bushes all come from one's own nature
- Arnolfo concentrated on the seed syllable, Clark on the solar mandala
- The secret inner chamber is located out there

77

One day the actor wandered out of his cave. He felt tired, hungry, yet extra-ordinarily clear; could hear a bird flying high above, insects eating grass, all this a result of his concentration on various realms of existence, on sound vibrations, those conceptual imprints of the psyche. Making his way over the hill, through a thicket of trees, he caught sight of something flying through the branches—a being of great beauty seated on a tiger skin and moving at a reasonable clip about three metres off the ground. Clark dashed after him. His body was white, smeared with ashes, a blue throat, and four arms. In one hand he held a trident, in another an hourglass-shaped drum. On his head was balanced a crescent moon.

Clark ran forward, cast himself at the feet of the deity (for a moment feeling that he had finally arrived, was finally seeing something real).

"O giver of bliss! O blue-throated one!" Clark cried out. "Are you revealing yourself to me?"

The grave face of that being broke into a smile. A silly, infantile laugh and pointing finger bouncing of body.

"CUT!"

A number of men in trousers and white shirts came forward. The director, a stylishly dressed individual, approached Clark, shouting at him in Hindi punctuated by swift, unmistakable hand gestures.

"I'm sorry, but I don't understand."

"Then let me say this in English, you damned hippy: Get off of my set! You are spoiling my film!"

"Ramesh? Ramesh Raj?"

"Of course I am Ramesh Raj. And who are you?"

"From New York. Clark. Eri——José. 1955. You had an apartment on West 78th Street. We used to drink Champale and sing the theme song from *Shane* together."

The man looked at him for a moment in consternation.

"José?"

"Yes, José."

"José! My South American actor!" (Embracing him tenderly.) "And didn't you go on to do some wonderful things in Italy?"

"Yes, I changed my name. Eric Clark."

"Of course you did. I must have seen *Namak Haraam Tonino*[1] a half dozen times at the Eros Theatre on Maharshi Karva Road in Bombay. What wonderful suspense and moving drama!"

Mr. Raj immediately swept Clark away, into a jeep, and then a five-minute drive to a near-by residence where over tea he tried to explain the plot of the film. It involved an ISS (India Secret Service) agent who marries the disabled daughter of a criminal in a black turban and is soon on the tracks of a maniac who plans to poison all of India. The agent (played by Narendra Datt)[2] must seek out three

---

1. *Si puo' essere piu carogna di Tonino?*

2. Legendary 1.89 m Indian actor who started out selling imitation jewellery on the streets of Calcutta. He was discovered by director Vijay Kapur and cast in *Amrita Svarupa Ca*, which catapulted this handsome leading man to stardom.

supernatural treasures in order to stop him and in the process has his foot bitten by a tiger.

"The problem is this bastard who is playing Siva. He only needs to be on film for five minutes, but it is impossible for me to get him to behave properly. He is unable to channel the vibe, though we do take after take. Now you—with your wild look and unkempt beard. . . ."

"Me?"

"A born actor, my friend. Of legendary skill. We just add a wig and blue-up your face."

"I'm on retreat."

"Retreat? A man cannot retreat from his karmic duty. Just as Krishna said to Arjuna in the third chapter of the *Bhagavad Gita*, freedom from action can never be accomplished by desisting from action."

In the end Clark was convinced to play Siva—taking part in one day's shooting before returning to his cave to meditate on a full moon—which he sat staring at, mind wandering—to films, to the bandit Tiburcio Vasquez and to that destiny which cannot be escaped or outwitted.

———

Clark packed up his few belongings. He had already said farewell to Sri Brahmavishnu and now made his way out of the cave. There was a bus that morning for New Delhi and all he had to do was tramp down the hill.

A figure came walking rapidly up to him. It was Arnolfo.

"What are you doing?"

"Leaving. Back to Italy."

"Already? But I have not been here for very long."

"I have. I'm hungry. I want to eat something besides rice. I want to eat beef and clams."

Arnolfo looked confused.

"Do you consider me a friend?"

"Of course not. You're rich. The money your family left you came from repressing the working classes. You have profited off of men and women working for very little, being maimed by machines and leaving their blood on rivets and then by buying paintings you don't quite understand think yourself redeemed."

"But I too can go to paradise."

"Paradise? You're in the wrong country for that. This is where you contract lupus and dengue fever, not where you go to paradise."

78

He returned from India spiritually renewed, somewhat thinner, though still lacking much of the hair on his head, a fact which he concealed by wearing a black beret. He was very calm. Though he would still drink an occasional beer, though he still smoked, he no longer did hard drugs. He had energy and was eager to work. But he was sceptical Italy was the place to do it. He was afraid he would get trapped in the same situation. Start doing illicit substances again. Once more find himself in roles he did not wish to interpret and have his waking hours be dark dreams scattered with unhappy smiles.

And in recent years the Italian film industry had truly passed into the world beyond. The only things left were ghosts. The price of production had skyrocketed, possibly due in part to the Milan-Genoa-Turin industrial economic boom of the 60's,[1] the after-effects of the collapse of the Bretton Woods system in 1971, and the incredible inflation that had followed,[2] making many foreign producers prefer to make the films in their own countries where, even though the cost was still often higher, the differential

---

1. In the 60's, Italy was the second fastest growing economy in the world, only being outpaced by Japan.
2. In 1980, consumer prices had given a peak increase of 20.4%.

was far less than it had been in the Italian movie boom of the 60's. It was true that by the time Clark had returned inflation had got under control: but despite still having a Third World bureaucracy, Italy was no longer a Third World economy.

By the mid-80's the Italian film industry was in a state of complete asphyxiation and churning out little more than sleaze, exploitation films and soft porn. Great actors were found working in cafés, going off to live in the country, committing suicide, growing long beards, smuggling opium. Many of the foreign actors returned to their countries of origin, married women significantly younger than themselves and had four children (the youngest of which is currently studying economics at MIT). Some disappeared from the face of the earth, vanished like things that never were. A few, the more industrious, adapted to circumstances, started small businesses or made quick fortunes by taking their theatrical abilities into the world of commerce. And two or four even went in for politics. Marco Nizzica, due to the influence of his godson, became mayor of Pietracatella. Branko Goric, who had been naturalised, turned vice-secretary of the far-right LFP (Lega del Fronte Padano) party.

Owners of movie theatres scratched their bellies as flies buzzed around premises which were all but empty. The only people that came were young men who needed a place to shoot up heroin and zonk out in peace or old perverts looking to infiltrate any dark corner. Cinemas began closing their doors, boarding up their windows. Some were converted into perfume vendors, clandestine meeting places for hitmen, bingo halls, plumbing factories, nurseries or auto showrooms. Others were simply demolished, replaced by cement housing complexes and glass office buildings. Many, like the Ambasciatori in Rome and the Ritz in Bergamo, became adult, painted their walls and ceilings black, and catered to a strictly male audience—shy husbands who needed a place to express their sexuality away from home and lonely gay bachelors who sighed between cigarettes and felt repressed by a society whose pseudo-machismo often manifested itself in ugly ways.

Only those professionals who could whore themselves out to television stations were able to work.

Private television networks had devoured the market by broadcasting between four and five films a day. Movie -going had declined by eighty percent since the 60's and 70's.

"Why should we pay to see films when we can see them for free at home?" people asked themselves, opening their eyes wide in naïve fluency as spots for Algida ice-cream cones and Paraflu oil pranced before them.

And so, having already renounced their artistic liberty, they now renounced their liberty of thought as well.

"On the one hand there was television, on the other the Americans," Luigi del Marco recalled. "They were crushing the life out of Italian cinema with their large budgets. It was true that Italians could perform miracles with limited means, but only up to a certain point. In the 60's the Italians were making films for 1/10th the budget of your average American picture. In the 70's it became 1/20th. But in the 80's it became unmanageable as the budgets for American films were often 40 or 50 times greater than for Italian films. They were making special effects with computers, while we were still using clay and wood."

In one sense, it was true that the big-budget American

pictures and television had killed the Italian movie industry. In another sense, the blame could be clearly put at the doorstep of the Italians themselves. The reasons that their films had been popular had never been due to them competing with Hollywood, but rather that they offered an alternative to Hollywood—a sort of substitute universe of the imagination in which anything could happen—in which six men in sandals might be an entire Persian army or a dusty field the entire state of Texas. When they had taken up westerns, they had shown a harder, more bizarre west, where morals did not exist. When they had taken up cop films, they had shown an Italy in many ways far grittier than the United States. Their car chases had been more splendid, their police more brutal, their criminals more sadistic. In the mid-70's they had started to see that they could get away with less—with scripts that were highly derivative or nonexistent. Story began to lose its importance, and films were often nothing more than a number of loosely connected set pieces.

79

It was 1987. Napoli, captained by Maradona, who had just come off a World Cup win for Argentina in Mexico, won the *Scudetto*. A month later they won the Coppa Italia.

In the three months Clark spent in Rome, only one part was offered to him, that of Clifford in *La Storia di Lady Chatterley*, but he did something he had seldom done before—turned it down,[1] seeing that not only would he not gain much money, but he would also be put in yet another demoralising situation and he did not want to be around to see rats nesting in the trees of Italian film-making.[2]

Momi appeared at his door. He smiled his big sloppy dog smile.

"My friend, you have returned to Italy."

Clark invited him in hesitantly.

"We all went crazy when you left," Momi said. "I was tangling with Sylvia, but she killed herself and then I shacked up with an older woman from Norway who couldn't stop holding my hand. And I wished I had a good person who would listen to me. Someone who understood

---

1. The role ended up being interpreted by Bruce Williams.
2. In November of 1988, rats were in fact noticed nesting in the trees at the Villa Ada. Chang Fang, in his *Commentary on the Changes*, says that rats nesting in trees are a bad omen.

my fragility. Because when I talked to myself, I knew I was talking to an idiot. Look, I brought you some fun."

He pulled out a little bag of white powder.

"No thanks," Clark said apologetically.

The ex-seller of umbrellas shrugged his shoulders.

"Did you become a Hare Krishna over there in India?"

"I understood some things."

"*Vaffanculo!* If you can't swing a little with your friends . . ."

80

His primary concern now was to make his film, his *Life of Tiburcio Vasquez*.

"I'll film the picture on location in California," he told Gino Baj.

"That could be expensive."

"It's not as if Spain is as cheap as it used to be. And I want my picture to be authentic. This means a great deal to me. I am filming my own biography, so to speak."

"You're dreaming."

"I don't deny this. But none of us are really awake."

He left Italy with more regret than hope. He had spent more than twenty-five years there, gained fame, and it might even be said lost it, and he was leaving behind not only friends, but an entire culture which, though it was, like a huge piece of gorgonzola, beginning to rot, still had some fascination, with its old buildings and piazza culture. There was the tomb of Julius Caesar and the frescoes of Michelangelo. Pickpockets rubbed against spectres and virtuous prostitutes were swept aside by the skirts of ambitious seminarians. It was a place of ridiculousness and mystery, of ten thousand shattered Pompeiian pillars encircled by the war dances of sharp-voiced Vespas as the sun bloomed huge and vibrant in the sky.

316

When he arrived in California, what surprised him most was not the measure of the streets or the grandeur of the reception, but how unknown he was. In Italy, anywhere he went he had been recognised. In Los Angeles, even when he told people who he was, people in 'the industry' for that matter, they simply stared at him with vacant expressions on their faces as if they were looking at a wall or a man who wasn't there and Clark wondered if his life had not been some kind of hallucination or if now he were in a purgatory of ugly shirts and pot-bellied men with waxed legs.

A few palm trees stood wearily beneath the lead-tinted sky. Citizens in shorts and sandals walked lazily down the streets and long Oldsmobiles with tinted windows and Pontiac Firebirds which might have hidden the faces of Genghis Khan or Psammetichus II, though more likely those of pimps and hustlers, slid slowly around corners.

He stood behind his sunglasses and watched. The country had changed since the 50's. The heroes had fallen, been ignored, or gone off to live in the mountains, where they ate pine nuts and observed the seasons follow one after another. A new generation of actors had taken over. Young men and women with ugly voices who looked like mannequins, their beauty superficial and talent trivial—a set who gloried in their perverse youth and were praised falsely, since truth had become something that only caused embarrassment and hard times.

A person sees myriad things, but is even one real?

He spent a week in Hollywood: knocking on doors, meeting with producers in cafés and strip clubs where, though these individuals would disappear into bathrooms every quarter hour to fill their noses, he managed to stay sober. Very young men and very old women would flirt with him and barflies shake his hand and start up shoe-string metaphysical discussions. He recognised no one, and no one recognised him.

About ten years earlier, while he had been enjoying the success of *Milano sotto fuoco*, one Hollywood agent, Bernard Brower, had tried to convince him to come to California, had tried to seduce him away from Buonaventura and the Skout agency.

"I can do big things for you in the USA," Brower had said.

Now Clark was there.

"You told me to look you up," he informed the agent as they sat at an outdoor table at a café on Vine Street.

"Did I? When was that? Back in '78? You sure took your time."

"I was busy."

"But you're not busy anymore I imagine."

Brower looked at him and smiled, his dentures glisten-ing in the hospitable California sun. He had had a hair transplant and the follicles stood in neat rows, upright and alert. His bronze-toned skin appeared to have been rubbed with some kind of tropical oil. This was a man who looked at the outside of things. A man who cultivated his shell, not his heart, and sat comfortably in a shallowness that was almost enviable.

Clark set out his idea, tossed his script down in front of the other man.

"There are some problems," the agent said as he turned over a few leaves of the manuscript abstractedly. "First off, no one is really interested in westerns now. Hollywood has grown up. It's pretty much impossible to have a box-office success with a western. But your script doesn't look all that bad. I see you have some action scenes. A little gunfighting. So maybe we could find someone who would be willing to entertain it, maybe make a modern version. Something along the lines of *Smokey and the Bandit*. Throw in a few jokes. I'm a friend of Dom DeLuise. He comes over for barbecue sometimes. It's even possible you could be in the film. But as the lead . . ."

"Of course as the lead."

"You might be a little too old, don't you think?"

"I can be any age I want to be. I'm an actor."

The lips of the other man curled as he reached for his Zinfandel. Then, after taking a sip:

"Look, Eric, if you leave the script with me, I'll see what I can do. But I'll tell you right off the bat that I probably won't be able to do a whole lot. The script probably won't fly unless we bring it up to date, cut out most of the dialogue and get a few guys who have graduated from the UCLA school of film to work it into something. Keep the verbs but not the verbosity. And I don't think I could get you a lead part in anything right now. Most people here in California don't know who you are. And those who do know who you are associate your name with the Godfrey Ho films."

"But I've worked with Bandini, Mario Brodo, Enrico Fabbri."

"Right, sure, you're a big deal. I realise that, but the guys around here don't. They don't know what's going on. At best they would call you a has-been. Which isn't such a bad thing, but you have to know how to play your cards."

"And your advice?"

"Well, I know you're facing hard times. I have some good connections. I could probably get you a spot on an episode of *Matlock* if you're interested."

"*Matlock?*"

"TV, brother. Television. That's where the action is."

"But television is too lonely of a medium for me. It's thin. People stay at home and watch it."

"Home is where the heart is, baby. The industry is going that way."

Naturally Clark considered television to be against his principles and turned down any offer for assistance in that direction, but looking elsewhere quickly realised that what Brower had said was true. Due to his experience in Hong Kong, no American film director would have anything to do with him, even though he was acknowledged as a great talent by certain individuals—producers with villas in Tuscany, collectors of spaghetti western memorabilia, voyeurs who got a strange, sadistic thrill out of watching the decay of actors—men who drank in the last pathetic films of Errol Flynn like fine wine and enjoyed greatly the nasally voice of John Gilbert in his last Poverty Row pictures.

Clark had become somewhat of a video store legend, a hero of adolescents with low attention spans and teenagers who spent their days lost in hazy weed patches while their husbandless mothers worked at secretarial jobs; or simply men who wore thick glasses and prided themselves on their encyclopedic knowledge of Eurotrash and whose romantic lives were confined to observing women trying on pumps in the shoe departments of large clothing stores. But even his acting style was not subtle enough for most American directors, or, for that matter, American audiences. He was far too baroque—an actor who made great use of gesture and facial expression while ignoring those subtle inflections of voice and the ability to look bored in front of the camera which the Americans and their European facilitators had decided was acting. Furthermore, since the Americans did not dub their films, Clark's South American accent would have made him fit only for certain stereotypical roles—as a dictator, a drug lord, one of those exuberant Latins who spend their time touring farmers' markets and seducing younger women.

In any case, he himself could not pretend that he was a box-office draw, that his name would do anything but cause curiosity when stuck to a marquee in San Francisco or Little Rock.

81

José Fernando del Torres, better known as Eric Clark, found himself in a shabby motel on Hollywood Boulevard. He looked out the window, saw a neon sign coldly staring over a street along which sad-looking prostitutes marched. He turned on the television, watched publicity open its nasty mouth and, after sitting for five or seven minutes in grim fascination, extinguished the device. A device that both destroyed the careers of many actors and cheapened the human condition, flattening people's awareness and drowning out the sound of the wind with its screams and making great things, pyramids and vast lakes, appear small and seedy.

"If I could just . . ." he thought.

But he was unable to finish the reflection, words and images falling away useless, dropping into oblivion.

He got up, stepped outside, and went for a walk.

The streets seemed lonely. They were very broad and lined with ugly buildings and the only places that were open were diners and a few unpleasant-looking bars and Clark thought of the days when he himself, embodied as the bandit Tiburcio Vasquez, had wandered these places at night, wanted and feared, a dream-figure who stood a stark icon against the coming blob of manufactured existence with its dumb strength, a seeming omnipotence quite horrible.

"Hey cowboy, want a ride?"

A long car with its window rolled down was pulled up next to him.

The actor turned down the charitable offer; approached a payphone, from his pocket took a small black address book and made a call. After a great many rings:

"Bob? This is Eric Clark. . . . No, I'm in Los Angeles. . . ."

———

Out of darkness something people generously call the sun rises; and the next afternoon Clark went to meet his friend.

In the mid-80's Bob Antony had tried to cash in on a scheme for a series of 3-D westerns, but the scheme had failed[1] and he had been forced to sell Remington Studio. Unable to make a living in Italy any longer, he had moved back to California, after a more than twenty-year hiatus, where he had developed a very small cult following among the bodybuilder crowd who admired him for the work he had done in sword and sandal epics. He was managing a Gold's Gym on Sunset Blvd. and had a Mexican wife thirty years his junior.

Clark arrived and looked around.

The place was full of muscle-bound Californians, macho fellows who would stare at each other romantically as they pumped iron and flexed their legs. A large man with a moustache winked at Clark who had just then caught sight of his friend.

Antony walked up and hugged him.

———

1. The only 3-D film he actually ended up completing was the entirely self-financed *Angry Guns*, which, in an attempt to be different, included such absurdities as Russian bandits, a man eating a bull entire and a hero (played by Antony himself) who was in the habit of throwing anything that came in his way (horseshoes, rocks, women) at the camera.

"Hey buddy . . ."

His jowl was somewhat heavier. His wrinkled biceps were greased with coconut oil.

"Life isn't bad here in Cali," he said. "Do I miss Italy? Of course I do. But I couldn't make a living back there anymore and things were starting to get dirty. You know that better than anyone. We're not kids anymore. We have to look out for ourselves."

"I've been trying to sell my script around town."

"That western thing you were always working on?"

"Yes. *La Vida di Tiburcio Vasquez.*"

"No luck?"

Clark shrugged his shoulders, which signified not only that he had not had the good fortune to interest a producer in the script, but that he in fact had never truly expected to interest anyone in it and had been acting not so much out of hope or confidence, but simply fulfilling the stages of his karmic obligations.

"If I can't get a backer, I'll make it on my own."

"Go independent, eh?"

"Right. But listen . . ."

Antony smiled uneasily.

"Listen—there might be a place in the film for you," Clark said. "There's Sheriff Roland. It's an important role. But I think you could manage to interpret it. If you could just grow a moustache and frown a little."

The bodybuilder looked embarrassed.

"What's the problem?" Clark asked. "Does my picture seem too small for you?"

"It's not that."

"Well?"

"It's Maria. My girlfriend."

"You're married, aren't you?"

"Right. My wife. I promised her I wouldn't do any more films. Somehow she found out about that *Django Porno* thing.[1] She doesn't understand that if you kiss a woman on camera it doesn't mean anything."

"You won't be kissing anyone in my film."

"I would love to help you, brother, but I just can't. My movie-making days are over. Unlike you, I never really considered myself an actor. I just did it for good times. I've found myself a nice woman. She's going to have my baby."

"Congratulations."

"Yeah."

Bob Antony hung his head. And then after a pause:

"I'm sorry. I just don't want to blow what I've got going here. I was so proud of Remington Studio and it pulled my heart out, and then the 3-D thing fell flat. I would produce your film myself if I still had the studio. But I got bruised, man. I got put out of it. You can find someone better than me anyhow."

That evening Clark walked along the beach, along a soft carcass of sand. Endless water. A lonely dog. An overweight man jogging. And children. Poking at a crippled bird.

The waves licked at his feet as if asking for his attention and he kneeled down and touched them, cool and somewhat oily and he realised that the only person he could trust with his vision was himself and thought he heard Dean's voice telling him it was so.

---

1. In 1969 Bob Antony, under the pseudonym of Bobby Bigund, starred in *Django liebt es, seine Waffe zeigen*, an adult western filmed in West Germany under the direction of Rolf Thiele. In 1982 a somewhat edited version was released on VHS in the United States under the title *Django Porno*.

82

He hired a cameraman, a thin twenty-six-year-old with red hair and a space between his front teeth, and started setting up locations around Los Angeles, where Vasquez had roamed, but found it difficult.

"The area is too developed," he said. "Man has completely changed the landscape."

And it was true. Where there had once been prairie, there were strip malls. Automobiles slithered over countless roads and highways. Hilltops were covered with radio antennae and modernist mansions and the skyline was a bleak grey. Everywhere he looked there were ugly buildings, power lines, hillsides eaten away at by bulldozers, sky criss-crossed by jet trails. Golf courses, tennis courts, parking lots.

He visited the old site of Kingston, the village Vasquez had robbed, tying up thirty-five men, but not a single building still stood; and then San Quentin, hoping to get some vibes from the place, but all he saw was a giant rambling compound jutting out into the San Francisco Bay.

The only footage he actually ended up shooting in California was that done at the Vasquez rocks near Agua Dolce, a twenty-five-second scene in which we see him walking swiftly by the camera, a pistol in his hand.

And then there was the problem of finding actors. At first he tried to negotiate the other primary roles with various stars: with Edmond Purdom and Ray Lovelock and then finally with the famous Mexican actor Jorge Luke, but all of them were either too expensive or engaged in other projects. Or, just as likely, had no faith in Clark's film or his ability to pay them, as he carried with him a reputation as an eccentric, sometimes difficult actor, not an organizer or one whose every effort was marked with financial success. Even those who he tried to sign on for tertiary roles, people virtually unknown, asked for an amount of money that in Italy would have seemed outrageous.

"They are unionized, so there are certain minimums that you have to pay," Bob Antony advised him.

"Yes, this is the American version of socialism where even the trees must grow to a certain height before you can climb them."

He briefly considered using actors from pornographic films, but decided against this, not for any moral reason, but simply because none of them looked like bandits, none of them could he picture in the Old West, in Old California, and, furthermore, he knew well enough that such actors were often drug users and that was something he desperately wanted to avoid because he still at night had dreams or nightmares about being devoured by cocaine, injected with truth serum by giant women who wore leather boots.

"No matter," he finally said. "I'll play the lead and all the other parts will be done by non-actors, by out-of-work construction workers or undocumented immigrants. In the end, they'll be less problematic and the film will have more truth. Actors, after all, only act."

But, looking around, the faces he saw were not those that afflicted his dreams and the sky was not blue for him and the place was one of sadness where the shirts men wore seemed limp, like those hanging on a clothes line, and birds built their nests with reluctance above the grind of traffic and there was a certain falsehood even in the chins of the people he saw. It was apparent that California was no longer California and that he would have to look for his template elsewhere.

He met Bob Antony for a protein shake and said goodbye.

"It can be hard to make it here. We aren't young anymore."

"No. I don't want to be young."

"Well, you have spirit."

"Yes."

He bought a Pontiac Firebird and drove through Arizona, and then down into Mexico, with a .35mm camera, ecstatically taking location shots—of run-down buildings, dry hillsides, old missions. In the villages, he would talk to the locals, stand them drinks of mescal, listen to the old-timers as they told him lies or truths, spoke their mythology, of who shot who twenty years previously. Of houses burned down and strange romances involving young women with thin moustaches who knew how to love like the wind and midnight bloodshed or even farther back some revolution that had failed or gone underground or a man who had once turned a ghost into a pig and sold it at market or stories of prophetic dreams and stuffed ballot boxes.

He finally found himself in real places talking to real people.

He stopped in the village of La Lagartija, a place of dust and poverty where graffiti struggled to stay attached to crumbling walls and the benches in the plaza supported the pulque-soaked frames of out-of-work labourers.

"My father rode with Pancho Villa," an old man told him. "When I was young everyone around here respected me just for that. Maybe they even feared me. But my father was never violent. . . . Not like the bandits these days, who care nothing for the revolution, who only care for their coca and marijuana. Yes, *La Revolución* . . . lies buried over there by that long row of crosses."

Clark turned and looked at the weed-grown graveyard in the distance, surrounded by a low and cracked white wall, filled with the bodies of heroin addicts and young men killed with knife and gun and the bones of women who had given birth to heroes one hundred and fifty years before who now lay near them and had been forgotten by all but Buddha and Yamantaka and Jesus of the underworld. The same types as Vasquez probably was; the same, in some ways, as Dean; the same, he liked to think, that he himself was at heart. A creature who could never quite be domesticated. Some solitary tree or isolated mountain—a distant object that disappears before it can be discerned or understood.

He turned back to the old man.

"I'm going to be filming here. I need a place to stay."

The other looked sad, somewhat lost. His eyes glistened from the mescal he had just drunk and memories invoked.

Someone nearby spoke up:

"The Ramírez house over there is empty. You can buy it or rent it."

"Why is it empty?"

"Suicide."

"Everyone who lives there gets robbed."

"Life is empty, isn't it?"

And so the village of La Lagartija became his home base, its streets used to represent old Los Angeles, its precincts old California.

He had some money of his own, around eighty thousand dollars, and raised another seventy thousand by mortgaging his apartment back in Rome, and with this he decided to begin production in Mexico, and find more money as he went.

From Italy he flew in cameraman Ottavio Bianchi, who he had worked with on many films, including *Paura a Torino* and *Cannibali del Borneo*. Bianchi, receiving a salary of two thousand dollars a week, also ended up working as second unit director; in an ambiance of penury and frustration.

"His excitement far outweighed his resources," he later said, referring to Clark and the filming of *La Vida di Tiburcio Vasquez*. "He didn't allow me anything. Not a focus puller or gaffer or anything. Yet he seemed to imagine he was working on a major epic. He talked about the huge sets that would be built but there was hardly enough money to buy film let alone build expensive sets. I was probably the only person involved who was getting paid more than a few pesos a day. I felt bad when he would give me my money, but I am a professional and have my rates. And the truth is, that for the last three weeks of shooting he didn't give me a penny and I never sued him because I am a big-hearted guy. He claimed he was making the most historically accurate movie ever, but at the same time had a complete disregard for many historical facts. In Tres Pinos

Clark had Vasquez kill six men rather than three. When I mentioned this discrepancy to him, he became upset and asked me why I was telling him about accuracy when he had actually been there and not I. I thought he was crazy. He said that he was following the memories of his past life, but I question if he wasn't just remembering those old radio plays of his childhood, in which everything was exaggerated, fabricated, turned into cheap melodrama. The real Vasquez was a bandit, a murderer. But Clark wanted to make a film about a hero—a sort of revolutionary. . . . A communist? Eric was a communist who wasn't a communist. He loved to talk about the liberty of the people. Fraternity. But he was an introvert. He would pass by a beggar without giving him a coin. But not because he didn't want to. He wanted to give them a coin more than anything. But he was too shy. He was unable to make that human connection. I did the film with him because at that time there was very little work in Italy. And also because I saw that he had some kind of vision which I thought I could help him realize. It is of course too bad I was never paid in full for my work, but in this life you cannot dwell on such things."

Clark stayed up late at night working on the script, rewriting, revising. He discarded almost everything he had done before, stripping away superfluous scenes and adding monologues—making the dialogue less colloquial, more emblematic, words as if they were uttered by apostles or desert hermits—phrases profound, religious, overtly political, which chastised rich men, big landowners, those who lived off the hides of the poor. His script was rambling, symbolic, depicting Vasquez as a Jesus-like figure, a messiah, putting long ponderous speeches into his lips—snatches of Descartes and bits of Plato. Sometimes the bandit would talk like St. Augustine, at others like a Roman senator. In the end, it seemed Tiburcio Vasquez had very little to do with the historical figure, with the man from Monterey, but was rather a mouthpiece for all the dispossessed of the earth—for the coffee farmer in El Salvador and the leper in India—for the left-leaning sympathies which had lain dormant in Clark and now bloomed under the Mexican sun. It was a scream against injustice—not any injustice he personally felt, but the in-justice of modernity, the injustice of the paved roads that rip through deserts and the injustice done to the ancestors, their cultures long since cast on bonfires and sent to far away spheres on the backs of rockets.

Vasquez was both noble and merciless, a poet and truly bad hombre, ready to kill at all times and harbouring a great anger against the gringos who represented the death of the spirit and a future of nuclear power plants and sanitized torture, who represented the vast prisons which would be the fruit of capitalism and the ultimate death of both the small land owner and hopes of a functioning communal property—since film, Clark reasoned, should not be an imitation of nature, but do what nature cannot—give voice to certain sentiments a sunflower, grasshopper or dead man might feel, but were unable to express.

In the mornings the actor/director would sit cross-legged and watch the sun-rise, spill its soft light over the desert, before going about his work, concentrated or at least considering himself to be so.

He made long, contemplative shots of people stand-ing speechless against a background of cactus and baked rock, women working, old men riding on donkeys.

"Beautiful," he would say in a soft voice.

The 'actors' had no idea what to do or when to say their lines. Clark would tie strings to their toes and pull them when he wanted them to speak.

"But what do I say? I can't remember the lines."

"Just say *uno, dos, tres*, and we'll dub in your voice later."

To play Clovidio Chavez, he hired an out-of-work pecan picker from Santa Rosalía de Camargo, a man who was completely illiterate, but who had a wonderful face—expressive as a canyon. His name was Jesús Valdés and he was known to carry a knife in one of his boots. For Romualdo Pacheco he hired the waiter at the local bar—a bulb-shaped man with a moustache and a very sensual lower lip—a fellow by the name of Ernesto de Peralta who was renowned throughout Sonora for his ability to dance the polka and for being able to pick up a woman, any woman, in less than a quarter of an hour, despite being far from handsome himself. A one-armed man, an ex-member of the Liga Comunista 23 de Septiembre, he hired as Abdon Leiva and the daughter of the local mescal vendor as Rosaria, Leiva's wife and Vasquez' lover.

"These people are real human beings. They are authentic. You could never get these faces if you looked around Hollywood and Cinecittà for years."

And it was true. These were men with calloused hands and faces burned by the sun and made rough by the wind—men who drank cheap liquor and who would most likely die only ten metres from where they were born. Not that they lacked aspiration so much as that their aspirations were limited by their surroundings, their economic situation, and a certain disdain for the riches across the border.

"You could make a lot of money if you went to California," Bianchi told Valdés.

"Doing what?"

"If nothing else, picking pecans."

"No. I would rather be a poor man in a poor country than a poor man in a rich one. Though, to tell the truth, if I ever went abroad, it would be to Japan. It has the longest life expectancy in the world, the people eat ceviche and soy beans and there are islands everywhere. The way of emptiness."

"You like the ocean?"

"The ocean of my mind."

83

The sun beat down on the Mexican desert. Rattlesnakes lay basking in the heat and scorpions scurried about rocks. The men stood around in the shade of their hats, while Clark in a short white Panjabi embroidered with a blue floral pattern around the collar gave instructions, approaching the men quietly. Laying a hand on the shoulder of one, murmuring a word into the ear of another. He was preparing to film the slaying of Constable William Hardmount.

A man with a huge belly and sunglasses approached him. "You're Eric Clark?"

"Yes, I am."

"Someone wants to meet you."

"I'm busy, my friend."

"Art can wait. Señor Hernández can't."

De Peralta, who was standing nearby, nodded his head and by this Masonic signal Clark understood that the Hernández in question was the local heavy and so he and the other man climbed into a dusty Pontiac and drove off—wound along the deserted road at high speed, the radio blaring the sound of Cornelio Reyna (Botellitas de Jerez) and the man next to him without voice, not even so much as tapping his fingers on the dashboard to the frantically joyful music which was playing, either to deny himself the embarrassment of having to speak or to cover up the voice of his passenger if he were to try and ask questions that would have been unacceptable to answer.

They drove up a seemingly endless driveway, then to a large house which sat stranded in a vast expanse of sun-dried dirt. There was an empty swimming pool. A lazy gardener, his sad moustache drooping in the heat, was tending to a yellowing patch of grass that might have been called a lawn or might have been called a piece of fenced-in desert that was inhospitable to all things green except for cactus and yucca.

A large man came out. He wore shorts and sunglasses and his moustache appeared to be dyed black.

He shook Clark's hand.

"My name is Max Hernández," he said. "I like your work. *El Pistolero famoso de Albuquerque*[1] is one of my favourite films. I show it to my grandchildren on VHS."

"Thanks, Señor Hernández."

"Don't be so formal! Call me Max."

"Max."

"You want a drink?"

"Something soft."

"Amanda, get us some lemonade."

A short, unhappy-looking woman silently did as she had been requested.

They sat down on the porch. A dog stretched itself out and yawned. Señor Hernández' face glistened with perspiration.

"Look, I do all kinds of business. Around here and all over Mexico."

---

1. *50 carogne per una colt.*

"That's good."

"You're damned right it's good! Only a fool starves in the middle of a meat forest. When you see cream, you drink it. So, I have a production company.[1] Well, we do distribution and production. I never get involved in the artistic aspect. My interest is happiness and money. I heard you were over in La Lagartija filming and got interested. From here I learn about everything. My ears are like flying saucers. All the news. You've been having trouble paying your crew."

"A little, yes."

"Well, look, I'm interested."

"Interested?"

"You're looking for a backer, right? Well, we can talk a little business. I'm crazy for the westerns. I need to support this thing. Lend my assistance. How much do you need?"

"A million at least."

"Pesos?"

"No, a million dollars."

Hernández laughed. "You're in Mexico, amigo. To see a million dollars you would need some real good eyesight. You would need to see straight into the land of dreams."

"Well, what can you provide?"

The Mexican leaned forward.

"Look, I like you," he said in a confidential voice.

"So do I."

---

1. This company, Producciónes Mars, dealt almost exclusively in sexicomedias and extremely violent vigilante/revenge films, such as *Muerte y Tragedia*, *Narco Sangre*, and *.357 Hombres*. It was a subsidiary of the Monterrey-based Grupo Hernandez y Alfa S.A. de C.V. which derived the bulk of its capital from the production of adulterated fruit juice under the XuperJugos label.

"We're talking about a million. It's a good number. So I'll give you a million. Pesos."

The actor agreed without hesitation—without contract, terms or conditions—as one might who felt they were guided by destiny rather than cleverness, who knew that it was not riches that made exceptional films but men and that even plain rice tasted good if prepared with love.

The two men shook hands and then Clark drained off his lemonade.

When he got back to La Lagartija, he celebrated by having a few sheep killed and roasted, treating the whole cast and crew to meat and cold beer. A group of musicians were there to play a fandango. Ernesto de Peralta seduced two women and Jesús Valdés, somewhat tipsy, stabbed another man in the ankle.

Though the amount of money was certainly not great, it was enough for Clark to proceed with filming in a reasonable fashion. He had worked on so many low-budget films that financial constraints were the norm rather than the exception.

Despite Bianchi's objections, he insisted on using natural lighting so those scenes which were filmed indoors or at night were often so obscure that the actors' faces could barely be made out and a few long sequences were nothing but voices in the dark, spiced with an occasional streak of yellow as moonlight shone on a forehead or was reflected in a man's eyes.

He felt as if he were fulfilling some sort of mystical function—interpreting himself and evaluating human consciousness, especially relating to capitalism, where one man is allowed to earn one hundred or one thousand times more than another and he who does so is infinitely respected while he who earns but little is looked upon not only with a sort of pity but often even fear, all this perfectly manifested in Vasquez, who rose up out of his humble origins by means of a pistol and a fast horse, through murder and robbery. And old California might as well have been Mt. Sinai, Vulture Peak or Galilee; because Clark was far less concerned with labouring his production with the traditional historical trappings than he was in creating a raw staging ground on which to display what he at least thought was the higher truth of not just his own existence, but that of the entire working class, which ironically enough he was not part of—or maybe there was nothing strange in this, since most of those who have struggled with the causes of the poor are themselves far from poor, though at least in Clark's case it could be said that he had been raised in a situation that was at best middle-class in a country where an American or European of modest means would have been considered a person of great wealth.

84

From Clark's original outline for
La Vida di Tiburcio Vasquez

(x) indicates an indecipherable word.

1858 San Quentin Prison and the inmates are wandering around the yard dressed in the outfits of those times striped I suppose.

He is released and the first thing he does is acquire a gun and steal a horse and it is clear that he has no intention of obeying the laws which men made already broken. He sees that his people are oppressed living in poverty surviving on tortillas beans pimentos a sad way to live.

—it is Pacheco who is the real traitor

—poster offering $1,000 reward

—posse dust

—is justice a synonym for revenge?

characters

—Clovidio Chavez (should be handsome with a weasel's face)

—Romualdo Pacheco ugly governor with billy goat beard and (x) around / half goat half pig

—Red-Handed Dick
—Judge David Belden use a fat gringo off the street or
professional butcher because (x) (x) they always said that
—Abdon Leiva (like my father)
—some woman attractive but not pretty (use anyone off
the street without discretion I don't care who I kiss even
a chicken)
—Sheriff Roland (get Bob Antony if you can otherwise
try to (x) anyone else because anyone without talent will
do so long as they are in the right place)

<u>locations</u>
—Sydney's Store, Tres Pinos
—Greek George's ranch (camels) tie some rocks on the
back of a horse and cover it with a dirty sheet
—Littlerock Creek, some scene of a man wading across
pistol pointed at heaven

When completed, the film was over four hours long, for the most part made up of clumsy footage of men riding horses from one place to another, of women crying in an exaggerated manner, and of poor folks going about their daily lives—all this punctuated by the occasional gunfire and decorated with occasional speech or long speeches. The great majority of the lines were those spoken by Clark, and this it must be admitted was admirably done— now taking on tints of Sir Lawrence Olivier in *Richard the Third*, now Gian Maria Volonté in *Sacco e Vanzetti*. Through much of the film he wore an extremely large black sombrero. His presence was powerful and the very crudity of the other actors and the setting lent the film an almost painful credibility.

Bianchi suggested that they cut it down to ninety minutes. Clark would not hear of it.

"But you might be trying people's patience," the cameraman said.

"Great films take great viewers. To cut it down would be like cutting off my own hands."

86

On July, 17, 1988, Clark, together with Bianchi, arrived at Hernández's with the reels in the back of his Firebird. Hernández was in high spirits and slapped Clark on the back in a friendly manner. A projector was set up in the hobby room. A very fine quality Tequila was poured and the film began to run. Credits. The sound of a guitar. The first ten minutes rolled by and not a great deal happened on screen. Señor Hernández moved about uncomfortably in his seat. Bianchi coughed. A fly could be heard buzzing about the room. Clark became somewhat self-conscious. But then he noticed that, through a door which led onto the patio, the gardener had entered. He was standing, looking thoughtful, interested.

"At least it shows that the proletariat understand my film," Clark thought. "Poor people always have better taste than rich."

The scene that was playing was of Vasquez galloping across the desert, alone.

The gardener leaned over to Clark.

"That's a nice horse," he whispered "Where did you find it?"

"Eh?"

343

"That's a nice horse he's riding. That pinto. One just like it was stolen from my cousin Joaquín about a year ago. Right from the corral. During the night of a full moon. Which is not to imply . . ."

Hernández, on the other hand, had no interest in horses. He was furious.

"What the hell is this?" he cried after the first reel had run its course. "I gave you money for an action film. But I'm still waiting for the action! If I want to stare at a cactus I just need to look out my window, I don't need to pay one million pesos for the privilege. Where the hell is the ketchup? The naked girls? The shooting, for God's sake!"

"I made a film about real people."

"I'm talking about real people. Real people like fornication and blood. If you had told me you were a poet . . ."

"I believe in it."

"Bueno. But it's hard to convert beliefs into money. I'll send this to my technicians in Monterrey and see if they can do anything with it."

Clark tried to protest but Hernández was already on his feet walking out the door and his assistant was packing up the reels.

"He's not happy," the gardener commented.

"He has no taste."

"Perhaps. But about Joaquín's horse . . ."

Whatever the true value of the film, Max Hernández was correct about its financial possibilities—or, if not correct, was unable to exploit it in a way that would prove profitable.

Something called a world premier was staged at El Cines Teatro Orfeon in Mexico City. It consisted of some refreshments, a few second-tier journalists and about ninety unknowns who had received free tickets—women whose only friends were their cats, one or two hysterical homosexuals, a few lonely bachelors eager to socialize and who carried condoms in their wallets behind forged library cards. The theatre's seating capacity was 3,165, but the place was almost entirely empty as most of those invited—celebrities, politicians, photogenic women—never arrived. Hernández tried to get people to sit close together so that when photographed they would seem like a crowd. Clark spoke a few words before the film began to roll and a few flashes went off. The Producciónes Mars technicians had cut the film in half, added music by Los Cadetes de Linares and, in order to draw out the gunfight scenes, spliced in footage from Alberto Mariscal's *El sabor de la vengenza*, so the result was something completely incoherent, that was neither art nor entertainment, a hybrid of dullness and incompetence.

Thirty minutes into the showing Clark and Bianchi rose from their seats and left the theatre. Walking through the lobby, a young man looked at them with the eyes of a frightened chihuahua and a woman wearing lots of make-up grinned. Outside, cars were rushing by and the unhealthy air gave everything a grey tint. Someone tried to sell them cucumbers, but Clark was not in the mood for such things.

There was a restaurant down the street and they went there. They ordered beers and tacos.

"Someone, I can't remember who, had their life saved by eating a cucumber," Clark said.

"Vivekananda."

Clark nodded his head and took a bite of a taco filled with chopped cow tongue.

"I'm going back to Rome tomorrow," Bianchi said. "And you?"

"There's no more Rome for me. The film is good, I believe, despite the fact that they cut off its arms and legs. People just need to see it. And if somehow I could recut it and let it be shown as it was meant to be . . ."

"Distribution?"

"I will try."

"And what else?"

"What else do you want? An actor likes an audience. I'll find other roles. And even without them, I've had a good run."

Bianchi was on his second beer.

"You're the best actor I have ever worked with," he said. "A thing happens when you get in front of my camera. A kind of Eden. Some scenes in this last film were really affecting."

"I know."

"Do you have money?"

"Well, I won't be sleeping on the street just yet."

"Good, good. So my back pay . . ."

———

Despite Clark's best efforts, no distribution could be found in the U.S. and, in fact, the film never was released to an English-speaking audience.[1] After a limited run in some rural theatres in Tamaulipas and Tabasco, it quickly galloped onto Spanish-language VHS and was sold for cut-rate prices in Columbia and Chile. The only language it was ever dubbed into was Portuguese, a severely cropped and cut (70 minutes) VHS being released by Carlota Produções Artísticas in Brazil.

———

1. Bob Elroy, of Libra Distribution Company, refused to distribute it, calling it "a piece of existential horse dung."

Though the film was a failure on almost every level, the final scene might very well be the finest of Clark's career, if not one of the finest ever filmed. Clark gave the performance with such pathos and truth that the scene actually had to be shot twice. The first time the cameraman (Ottavio Bianchi) lost his concentration because he was crying. Clark scolded him and did a retake:

March 19, 1875.

He had a large moustache. A slightly unkempt goatee.

Many women stood watching. Quivering. With handkerchiefs to their mouths. As he was led up to the gallows—calm, heroic, not so much bandit as avatar, a concrete manifestation of the spirit of the Californiano, the timeless revolutionary.

The hangman kneaded his greasy hands. The rope had one big eye open. Tiburcio Vasquez gave a faint smile.

"Pronto," he said.

A moment later he was hanging by his neck.

87

James Dean had gone out of this world with sensation. Clark's case was not the same.

Some said he died by overdosing on weight-loss medicine. Others that he opened a bar in the Philippines. And, yet again, there were those who claimed that he lived in Texas, had settled down with a woman from Guatemala and had four children.

It is also said, by men who convene at badly lit bars at late hours in the cities of Rome, Milan and Turin, drinking espresso laced with peach grappa, that he is planning a comeback, and like the Messiah, will return, reprising those supreme roles of the 60's and early 70's.

But great art is like this. It sleeps until people remember it again. Until wise men see that not only the beautiful is beautiful and that sublime things are done in relative obscurity, simply because this is the will and play of the universe and people in all parts and occupations try all they can to be something other and distract themselves from nature but Clark had become himself.

Appendix

Filmography

La Vida di Tiburcio Vasquez (1988) . . . Tiburcio Vasquez
Chaakara Chamaram (1986) . . . Siva (uncredited)
Blood Mission (1985) . . . Phil
Thunderbolt Force (1985) . . . Rod
Godfather of Ninjitsu (1985) . . . Master Terry
Cobra Powerforce (1985) . . . Jim
Ninja Death Game (1985) . . . Master Terry
Full Metal Raider (1984) . . . Jim
Phantom Peer Roses War (1984) . . . Master Jim
Dirty Ninja (1984) . . . Master Terry
Jungle Nightmare (1984) . . . Capt. Rodriguez
Operation Python (1984) . . . Tom Finch
Kommandantin zum Manöver blasen (1983) . . . Col. von
Küppes
Follia di paura (1983) . . . Carlo
    Fear Hunter
Caduti del mondo anno 2029 (1983) . . . Shade
    End of the World 2029
Violenza senza pausa (1983) . . . Domenico
Citizen Locomotion (1982) . . . Man
Sangue ripido (1982) . . . Mauro
    Steep Blood . . . Mark
Contaminazione PCP (1982) . . . Robby

Agitato, agitatissimo . . . praticamente cretino (1982) . . . Dario Di Pietro

Guerra Cobra 4 (1981) . . . Tommaso

Turgo, guerriero sanguinoso (1981) . . . Afram
    Turgo the Bloody Warrior

Il sangue, le droghe, la morte (1981) . . . Mark

Guerra Cobra 3 (1981) . . . Tommaso

Un uomo senza salsa (1981) . . . Gian de la Brète

Sono polizzzzzzziotto (1980) . . . Al Siracusa
    Cop Time

Le calde notti di Faustina minore (1980) . . . Avidio
    Bed of an Empress . . . Avidius

Due ladri umili (1980) . . . Leopoldo
    The Little Rip-Off

Giuseppe Cotone, praticamente detective (1981) . . . Giuseppe Cotone

Soft Dogs (1980) . . . Matto Charlie
    Soft Dogs . . . Psycho Charlie

Un polizioto con scrupoli (1980) . . . Al Siracusa

Wanda (1980) . . . Gregor

La vedova affamata cerca un vero uomo e muore di fame (1980) . . . Filippuccio
    A Hungry Widow In Search of a Real Man Dies Without Eating . . . Albert

Una trappola per topi (1979) . . . Enrico Ricciolini

Cannibali del Borneo (1979) . . . Professor Jack Martin
    Borneo Cannibals . . . Professor Jack Martin

Violenza omega (1979) . . . Lalo

Delitto a cactus (1979) . . . Butch

Il guappo immaginario (1979) . . . Graziano Manalese

Claudio Claudine (1978) . . . Claudio Dagoberto

Dimentica la legge e fai la tua (1977) . . . Luciano Di Grazia

Le droghe di Napoli e la polizia è tutta morta (1977) . . .
Fabio
    Overdose
Marco, Giulia, 20-4 (1976) . . . Marco
Si puo' essere piu carogna di Tonino? (1975) . . . Tonino
Astarita
Un indiano a Dayton City (1975) . . . Babu
La stessa cosa (1975) . . . Nino Giuliani
Io bebé, tu bebé, lei bebé (1974) . . . Riccardo
    I Baby, You Baby, She Baby
Milano sotto fuoco (1974) . . . Renato
    The Dirty City
I due calibro .38 di Tony Romano (1974) . . . Tony
Romano
E' una lunga strada fino a Tombstone Malcóncio, rilassati,
(1973) . . . Malcóncio
    It's a Long Road to Tombstone Melancholy, Take it
    Easy . . . Melancholy
Il bastardo, l'ipocrita, il pazzo (1973) . . . Flavio
La polizia fa schifo (1972) . . . Commissario Malacarne
Maledizione Malcóncio, sei proprio un figlio di . . . (1972)
. . . Malcóncio
    Melancholy, You Son of a . . . . . . Melancholy
La luna uccise sette volte sul sette (1972) . . . Enzo
Paura a Torino (1971) . . . Lucciano Maggio
Farfalla, farfalla, fiore, fiore, ali sanguinose e profumo di
morte (1970) . . . Pietro Galli
    Butterfly with Bloody Wings
I dannati della guerra (1970) . . . Colonel James Vincent
    Bastards of War
Zamora (1969) . . . Pedro Zamora

Prego per te . . . ma prima ti uccido (1969) . . . Tucson/
Thomas Lawrence
    I'll pray for you, but first I'll kill you (literal English
    title)
    The Revenge of Thomas Lawrence (theatrical release)
40 pistole per Jiminez (1969) . . . Jesús Jiminez
    Revolution
50 carogne per una colt (1968) . . . Martinez
    Mean Outlaw
I cadaveri si moltiplicano, le taglie aumentano (1968) . . .
Reno
This Is Not A Film (1968) . . . Todd
T'ammazzo bastardo (1968) . . . Red
Un grilletto facile per quelli che vogliono il morto (1968)
. . . Lee Cardigan
Una colt per ogni carogna (1968) . . . Rizo
    A Colt for Every Scrounger
Tre buchi in fronte (1968) . . . Jonny Dixon
    Three Holes in the Head . . . Jon Dixon
Senti quei colpi di pistola? Significa che Django sta am-
mazzando tutti (1967) . . . Django
    Django Kills You (West Indies release)
Il winchester crudele di Yuma (1967) . . . Yuma
Una carogna, un gringo e un bounty killer (1967) . . .
Juarez
    Django Rides Again
    A Scum, a Gringo and a Bounty Killer (West Indies
    release)
Quando arriva Django non puoi contare i morti (1966)
. . . Django
Grand Prix (1966) . . . Uncredited
770 chiama Z-8 (1966) . . . Agent 770

770 sfida 668 (1966) . . . Agent 770

Agent 770 a Beirut (1966) . . . Agent 770

Operazione Maraketch (1965) . . . Agent Hale

Agent Interpol Daring (1965) . . . Agent Daring

Scotland Yard jagt Dr. Hipnoxi (1965) . . . Igor

Juke Box '66 (1965) . . . Gastone

Rocambole ruba ancora (1964) . . . Rocambole

L'Arciere rosso (1964) . . . Norbetto

Ercole sfida Golia (1963) . . . Xanpactos

Zorro contro Robin Hood (1963) . . . Zorro

Pirro dell'Epiro (1962) . . . Pirro

Qui êtes-vous, Madame Depreux? (1962) . . . Maxence

Golia alla conquista di Babilonia (1962) . . . Gionatan

La spada di Ursus (1962) . . . Mage

L'Amore di Benvenuto Cellini (1962) . . . Benvenuto
Cellini

Erloff, il vichingo sanguinoso (1961) . . . Gultreg
    aka Erloff, the Bloody Viking

Cronache di una villa (1961) . . . Aldo de Maria

Le avventure di Fiorenza (1961) . . . Piero

Ragazzi d'argento (1961) . . . Renato

Il tradimento di d'Artagnan (1960) . . . Enrique de
Montmorency

La congiura di Pisone (1960) . . . Rufrio Crispino

Maciste contro i Tartari (1960) . . . Subutai
    aka Hercules vs. Genghis Khan

Aladino nella citta' degli uomini formica (1960) . . . Mage
Omar

Les fils du lieutenant Brévannes (1959) . . . François

Bas les pattes (1959) . . . Émile Brissard

Beast from a Dark Hole (1958) . . . Jeff